"I DON'T UNDERSTAND YOU, BRIANA!"

Drake cupped her chin gently. "Every time we're alone together you put up a barrier."

Briana caught her breath as his fingers explored the warm recesses of her bare shoulder. "I…I feel unsure when I'm with you. I always wonder what you're thinking."

"I'm thinking about you," he whispered. "Trust me!" With a feather touch he ran his fingertips along the swell of one breast and then the other.

Briana closed her eyes, lost instantly to the hunger he aroused in her. His lips trailed liquid heat across her skin and she moaned, arching her body instinctively. She wanted Drake, wanted this, wanted— "No!" she gasped. "I can't!"

His husky voice was soothing, seductive. "I want you, Briana."

WELCOME TO...

SUPERROMANCES

A sensational series of modern love stories
from Worldwide Library.

Written by masters of the genre, these longer,
sensual and dramatic novels are truly in keeping
with today's changing life-styles. Full of intriguing
conflicts, the heartaches and delights of true love,
SUPERROMANCES are absorbing stories —
satisfying and sophisticated reading that lovers
of romance fiction have long been waiting for.

SUPERROMANCES
Contemporary love stories for the woman of today!

LEAH CRANE

DARK ECSTASY

A SUPERROMANCE FROM
WORLDWIDE

TORONTO · NEW YORK · LOS ANGELES · LONDON

For Amy Berkower

Published June 1983

First printing April 1983

ISBN 0-373-70066-0

Printed in Canada

CHAPTER ONE

Drake Rutledge pushed away from his desk, strode to the massive pane of glass and stared out at the harbor. Across the serene water from his office window two giant cruise ships inched their way to the docks. Beyond the bustling waterfront the red-roofed buildings of Charlotte Amalie spread out over the virescent slopes of Denmark Hill, their white walls glistening in the January sun. Drake had gazed upon the perfection of this verdant paradise for thirty-four years, and in spite of being frequently waylaid in the lobby of his plush hotel by guests who rhapsodized over the charm of St. Thomas, he was rarely immune to its loveliness. At the moment, though, the breathtaking beauty failed to ease his oddly dissatisfied mood.

He was viewing the world he loved from a vantage point toward which he had strived all his life. The legal paper he clutched in one hand represented the final, until now elusive, goal that had been the impetus behind his relentless driven rise to power and wealth.

Now, at last, his reach no longer exceeded his

grasp; and a ripple of disappointment ran through him. Surely there should be cymbals clashing, there should be shouting in the streets. At the very least, triumph ought to be swelling in his chest.

Five minutes ago Erik Ivensen, the embodiment of all that Drake had resented and despised for as long as he could remember, had left his office. Defeat and venom had warred for ascendancy in Erik's blue eyes as he had signed over the deed to the old Ivensen great house, the last remnant of the vast holdings once controlled by that ancient blue-blooded Danish family. Then he had thrown down the pen and with a look of undiluted contempt had turned his back on Drake. The gesture had spoken volumes. It was almost as if Drake Rutledge was once again that dirty tattered child whose mother had worked as a menial in the Ivensen house, instead of Erik's employer, a man who had the power to have him arrested and jailed. With his shoulders held rigid in his expensive hand-tailored jacket, the young man had left the office and the Grand Reef Hotel, probably for the last time.

The Ivensens, descendants of Danish royalty and early-day governors of St. Thomas, had made several fortunes in sea trade over the years. Erik, the last surviving male, had in the end been a weak and unworthy opponent. In truth, Erik had brought about his own downfall, and Drake's victory felt a little hollow.

Drake left the window and, tossing the deed on his desk, reached for his pipe. With automatic movements he tapped sweet-smelling tobacco into the bowl, tamped it down and thrust the stem between his teeth. Striking a match, he lighted the pipe, sucking absently to get it going. Then he refilled the soft leather pouch from the tin in his bottom desk drawer, grimacing as he realized he'd filled it only that morning, and it was now just after noon. A year ago he'd switched to a pipe in order to give up cigarettes, but he was smoking too much again. He had to cut down.

He left the office through an interior door, entering a small private apartment. This was where he stayed when the demands of his work made it necessary to overnight on St. Thomas instead of returning to his home on St. John.

Going into the beige-and-brown bathroom, he laid the pipe aside and washed his face and hands. He ran a thick brown towel over his face and looked at his reflection in the walnut-framed mirror, half expecting to detect a difference in himself, some sign that he had done what, as a boy of fourteen, he had vowed to do.

That long-ago day, with blood and tears streaming down his face, he'd cried, "You're gonna pay for this, Ivensen! I'll make your whole family sorry for what you did to us!" He could still feel the sobs that had been torn from his fourteen-year-old throat with the words. His impotent rage would surely have choked him if he hadn't passed out from loss of blood.

But nothing had changed with victory—not his dark brown hair nor prominent facial bones nor long straight nose. Not the deeply tanned skin slashed by a scar that marked his left cheek from near the corner of his wide mouth almost to his earlobe. Drake stared at the ragged scar tissue. In spite of daily exposure to the sun it never tanned. Usually he took little notice of the deformity, which had been a part of him for twenty years. But today he had finally broken an Ivensen, son of the man who had slashed his face. He wished Frederik Ivensen had lived to see it happen. . . .

She was still alive—Margaret von Scholten Ivensen, Frederik's mother. Drake's dark eyes narrowed as he wondered if Erik had told her yet that she must leave the house she had come to as a bride. The house where she had lived like a queen, lording it over servants and family alike—even over Frederik's frail wife, Ingrid, who was Erik's mother.

And what of Erik's sister, the blond Briana? She had been in the States for years, going to school, but Drake recently had heard that she was home again. His lips twisted wryly. Briana might have to put her expensive education to some use now and find gainful employment to support the family. Her brother had certainly made a mess of the attempt. Where would the three of them go, he wondered, when they moved out of the house, his house?

He picked up his pipe and went into the compact kitchen where he made himself a ham-and-cheese sandwich and some iced tea. He preferred preparing his own lunch from the apartment refrigerator to calling room service. Regardless of the fact that he had made more money in the past few years than any man had a right to expect, he still didn't like having people wait on him unnecessarily. He ate his lunch on the apartment's private balcony, his long, lean frame sprawled in a cedar lounge.

From where he sat, he could see a corner of the roof of the Ivensen house, to the east and higher up the hill than Government House, its flags flying. He looked at his watch. It was a few minutes past one. About now, unless he had stopped somewhere on the way, Erik should be entering the house to confront his grandmother and sister. Drake regretted that he couldn't be there to hear whatever cock-and-bull story Erik had invented to explain his loss of their home.

Margaret Ivensen might rant and rave at her grandson. She might even shed real human tears within the family circle. But Drake knew for certain that no one else would see any reaction from that arrogant old lady.

And Briana? What sort of woman had she become, that curled and ruffled little girl whose wide horrified blue eyes were the last thing Drake had seen before he lost consciousness on that fateful day twenty years ago? He'd heard that she had married a Spanish count four or five years back, but it hadn't lasted a year.

Drake's eyes clouded. It was always possible that her ex-husband was supporting the Ivensen family. But rumors that had circulated at the time of the divorce had it otherwise. Apparently Briana had been so eager to end her marriage that she had waived all rights to a financial settlement. Later he had seen her name—Briana Ivensen—in the paper in connection with some scholastic honor awarded by the New England university she attended. She had resumed her maiden name. Drake wondered ironically if there had been a defiant sort of pride in that, a declaration of her independence.

His lunch finished, he went back into the apartment to find his pipe. Hearing his secretary, back from her lunch break, moving about in his office, he returned to work, pushing thoughts of the Ivensens into a corner of his mind. He would give them twenty-four hours to adjust to their loss. Tomorrow he would call at the house and ask how much time they would need before vacating the premises. He could handle the whole thing through his lawyer, of course, but he wasn't going to. He had to go back to that house again while they were still there, perhaps to prove something to himself.

"YOU DRIVIN' MR. ERIK to the airport, Miss Briana?" A tiny black woman, her head cocked to one side, stood in the study doorway.

Briana looked up from the box of von Scholten family papers she had carried down from the attic that morning. She had been lost in the past, and for a moment her smoky blue eyes were glazed with incomprehension. She was sitting at an old oak rolltop desk that had been brought to the house by her grandfather. In the only memory she had of Daniel Ivensen, Margaret's husband, he had been seated at this very desk, his white head bent over his work. That had been a few short weeks before he died. The house was filled with the ghosts of her ancestors.

"I didn't know Erik was going anywhere, Nenie Ida," Briana finally replied. "Nen" and its more familiar form, "Nenie," was a title common among the black population of St. Thomas. It meant godmother. Several generations of black children had grown up calling Ida, "Nenie," and Briana and Erik had fallen into the habit when they were learning to talk.

The little woman shrugged. "He in his room, packin'. When I ask how come, he say he goin' New York."

Briana brushed errant waves of long blond hair away from her face. As usual a few locks had escaped the combs at her temples. "It must be a business trip," she said. "I wondered why he didn't go to the office this morning." She anchored two stacks of papers on the desk with a glass paperweight and a dictionary. Getting to her feet, she pulled the white cotton of her shirt away from her damp back. The air conditioning in the old house hadn't been working for weeks. "I'll go and see if he wants me to drive him."

"Me, I jes tryin' to find out how many be here for lunch," Ida said.

"I'll let you know as soon as I talk to Erik."

Ida nodded, then smiled suddenly. "It's good havin' you home again. I guess I gettin' old. I don't know how to handle 'em anymore. Mr. Erik's mad at the world. And poor Mistress Ivensen sometime acts like it's fifty years ago. The other day she tell me to send Jobie here and Nan-Sue there, like them other servants didn't leave here years ago. No one but me to do her biddin' now, but she forgets."

Ida had lived in the Ivensen house since she was sixteen. She had her own room in the servants' wing, back of the kitchen; it was the only home she knew.

"I know," Briana said sadly, "but don't worry, Ida. We'll manage."

She watched as Ida turned and ambled slowly toward the kitchen. The old woman was favoring her left hip, where her arthritis gave her the most pain. Briana suspected that before she herself had come home, Ida's wages hadn't been paid regularly. Now she tried to leave money for the black woman on the kitchen table every month—though, heaven knew, she couldn't really spare it. She thought longingly of the day when she would be able to start her career as a college teacher.

Going down the long second-floor hall, Briana noticed how much dust had accumulated on the brass light fixtures and the antique tables. She made a mental note to do some cleaning later that day. Climbing stairs was becoming too painful for Ida, and besides, she had enough to do with preparing the meals and cleaning the ground-floor rooms that were used by the family.

Before turning the corner that led to Erik's apartment, Briana stopped to look at a particularly valuable Sheraton side table that sat in a hall niche. It was in excellent condition and would, she knew, bring a handsome sum from an antique dealer. They might have to consider selling a few of the more valuable pieces of furniture soon, she thought with a frown. It was going to take at least a year for her to finish her research and write the dissertation required for her Ph.D. A year before she was qualified for a job in the History Department at the College of the Virgin Islands.

Erik seemed to spend a lot of money on himself. He was earning a decent salary as special assistant to the president of the Rutledge Corporation, but there was seldom much left over for household expenses. Briana decided to speak to her grandmother soon about selling one or two pieces of furniture. Legally the house and everything in it had come to Erik on his twenty-first birthday seven years ago, but Margaret von Scholten Ivensen was still a force to be reckoned with, in spite of her increasing vagueness of late. Briana wouldn't think of urging Erik to sell anything from the house without her consent.

The door to Erik's sitting room stood open, and her brother, dressed in brown slacks and a muted blue-and-brown plaid sport jacket of raw silk, entered the room from his bedroom. Briana's surprised regard took in the tall, slender young man whose coloring matched her own. "You must be planning to be in New York for several days." She indicated the two large suitcases that he set beside a smaller carry-on flight bag of the same supple tan leather.

She had hoped that the prospect of a trip would have put him in better spirits, but she could see from his impatient scowl that he was just as dour as he'd been ever since she'd come home. Briana had given up trying to find out what was bothering him, aside from the fact that he'd had to take a job that had severely curtailed his playboy life-style.

"I'll be staying indefinitely," he muttered,

going into the bathroom. He returned with a toothbrush and tube of toothpaste, which he dropped into a side pocket of the flight bag.

"I don't understand," Briana said. "Is Mr. Rutledge thinking of opening an office there?"

He straightened abruptly and turned to glare at her. "Rutledge be damned! I've taken my last order from Drake Rutledge!"

She had known that Erik disliked his employer, that he chafed at taking orders from him. Nevertheless, Briana was stunned by the naked hatred she saw in his blue eyes now. "Erik, what happened? Did he fire you?"

"I resigned," he snapped. "I should have done it months ago."

"But I thought it was such a good job with so many fringe benefits."

His eyes narrowed suspiciously as he looked at her. "What do you mean by that?"

She stared back at him, nonplussed. "I'm just repeating what you told me when you took the job."

"Oh." He walked about the room, checking to see if he'd forgotten anything. "Well, it didn't work out. Low-class scum like Rutledge don't know how to deal with people like us. My background and education intimidated him, and he came to resent me for it. So I'm going where there are more opportunities."

He stopped his nervous pacing and gave her an ingratiating smile. She had seen that smile too many times not to be suspicious. Erik wanted something. "You'll explain to grandmother, won't you?"

So he wanted to avoid Margaret's questions. "No," she replied firmly. "You tell her, Erik."

"I went to her room earlier, but she was resting. I don't have time now. My plane leaves in an hour. Tell her I'll call when I get settled."

"Erik, why the rush? You haven't even mentioned to grandmother or me that you were considering leaving your job. And now you're off to New York. Just like that?"

"It was a sudden decision," he responded.

Briana sighed helplessly, trying to assimilate the fact that he was actually going. Why hadn't he at least informed them of the possibility? It was clear that she would have the task of breaking the news to their grandmother, whether she wanted it or not. "Do you want me to drive you to the airport?"

"Jane's picking me up. In fact, I think I hear her honking out front now."

Jane Fitzcannon was a girl they'd grown up with. She was twenty-six, a year older than Briana, and already she'd been married and divorced twice. Jane was nice enough, but like Erik, she had a strong streak of irresponsibility in her. She had inherited money from her grandparents, and Briana was afraid that Erik might be considering becoming husband number three. But if he was moving to New York, he apparently wasn't considering it. That was the one good thing Briana could see in this otherwise troublesome turn of events.

Erik slipped the flight bag's wide strap over his shoulder and picked up the suitcases. He kissed her cheek. "Hold the fort."

"Call soon," she said as she followed him down the hall, wishing she could do something to delay him, at least until he had faced their grandmother.

But he had started down the stairs. "Sure," he called back. "Tell grandmother not to worry. I'm a big boy now." Then he was gone, kicking the front door shut behind him with one alligator-shod foot.

Briana stared at the door, wondering what he would do in New York. Her brother was intelligent enough to perform well in any number of jobs. The problem was he didn't really want a job at all. He felt that work was beneath him, that it was degrading for an Ivensen to have to go to an office every day like other people. When their father had died ten years ago, their grandmother had transferred the adoration she'd felt for her only son to her grandson. Even before that she'd spoiled the boy dreadfully, instilling in him her own certainty of blood superiority.

Briana's family had lived well on money left by Daniel Ivensen until the last few years. But at last the funds that Margaret, in spite of repeated warnings from her financial manager, had obviously thought were limitless had run out.

During recent years they had lived on the small income Margaret received from a few modest investments in her own name. There had been enough for Erik's education at Yale, but Briana had had to finish her last two degrees on scholarships and grants. The experience had been good for her, she now realized. It had taught her she could manage on very little, and it had given her a feeling of accomplishment and self-worth—one that she had needed very badly after her disastrous marriage to Ricardo.

She turned away from the door and walked slowly toward the kitchen, planning to see if she could help Ida by preparing her grandmother's luncheon tray. Blast Erik for walking out so blithely and leaving her to deal with Margaret! And now there wouldn't even be the small sums Erik had contributed to the household. It did seem their only recourse was to sell some of the furniture. She should have mentioned the idea to Erik before he left, but she'd been too disconcerted by his abrupt departure to think of it. She would have to ask him about it when he called. In the meantime, perhaps she could find the right moment to bring up the subject with her grandmother.

THIRTY MINUTES LATER, Briana entered her grandmother's apartment, carrying the luncheon tray. Margaret von Scholten Ivensen spent most of her time in these once elegant rooms on the ground floor. Her suite was crammed with French and English antiques, mementos of her world travels. Photographs of several generations of von Scholtens and Ivensens gazed from gold and silver frames on every shelf and table. A small electric fan stirred the warm air.

Margaret was at her cherry-wood secretary, her journal open before her. Most of her ancestors had kept daily journals, and she continued to uphold the family tradition.

At Briana's entrance she laid aside her pen and stood up, a tall, slender figure in lavender silk. Her white hair was arranged in close waves about her fine-boned face, and her stance— shoulders back, chin up—still exuded an aura of command. She smiled at her granddaughter.

"Why didn't you let Ida do that? I know you wanted to work on your project today. Did you find the von Scholten papers?"

Briana set the tray on a marble-topped table in front of a faded Victorian settee. "Yes. I've spent the morning going through them. Oh, grandmother, there's so much I can use in my dissertation! I've even found some information I don't think other researchers had access to. It's quite possible I might end up with a publishable book. That would add a nice touch to my résumé." Briana's deep interest in her work was evident in her face and gestures as she spoke.

Margaret's "that's nice, dear" was clearly automatic. It was acceptable to her that her granddaughter wanted to know more about her ancestors. But she had never approved of Briana's plan to teach. No von Scholten or Ivensen woman had ever worked for a salary, and Margaret couldn't understand her granddaughter's insistence upon being the first.

Her position was totally illogical, of course. Briana had pointed out to her several times that the family was impoverished, and that times had changed. The world of superior class and privilege that Margaret had grown up in no longer existed. But the old woman stubbornly refused to accept the fact, and Briana no longer tried to reason with her on the subject. She was old and proud, and she suffered not only from a heart condition but from hardening of the arteries, as well. She was beginning to be forgetful at times, and Briana felt she should be allowed to live out her last years with as few disruptions as possible.

Margaret sat down on the settee and picked disinterestedly at the crab salad on her tray. Briana took one of the fragile-looking Queen Anne chairs. "I have to tell you something, grandmother—about Erik."

Margaret added a lump of sugar to her tea and stirred slowly. She looked at Briana expectantly.

"He's gone to New York. He came by your

apartment to say goodbye, but you were resting.''

Margaret made a moue of distaste. ''I suppose Drake Rutledge sent him. I can't understand how Erik can kowtow to that man. He
shouldn't have to do it.''

Briana couldn't hide a smile. As with many of
her grandmother's opinions, she had never
understood the deep-seated resentment the older
woman felt toward Drake Rutledge. Briana
didn't recall ever having seen the man herself,
although her grandmother had said his mother
once worked as a maid for the Ivensens. Obviously Drake was a self-made man; perhaps
Margaret merely disliked the idea that her
grandson was employed by someone from such
low beginnings. She suspected, though, there
was more to Margaret's resentment than that.

''Carrying out his employer's instructions
isn't exactly kowtowing, grandmother,'' Briana
chided gently. ''Anyway, Erik won't be doing
that any longer. He's left the Rutledge Corporation.''

Margaret set her teacup down decisively.
''Good. I never approved of his working there
in the first place.''

''Why do you dislike Drake Rutledge so
much?''

Margaret's blue eyes blazed for a brief moment. ''You wouldn't remember, I'm sure, but
he was a wild, unmanageable boy. Like his

mother, he never knew his place. When I had to let her go, he. . . .''

Her voice trailed away, and her lined face took on a blank expression. It was the look she always got when she had lost her train of thought.

It hurt Briana to see her grandmother so weak and vulnerable. For as long as she could remember, Margaret had been the stabilizing influence in the Ivensen house. Briana's mother had been a pale sickly woman. That was all she remembered of her. She had died giving birth to a stillborn child when Briana was four. Margaret had been the one who ran the house and directed her grandchildren's lives. Their father had been there, of course, but somehow always in the background, drinking his rum. There had been a deep sadness in her father that Briana had never understood. She could remember him holding her in his arms and muttering, ''Don't let anybody dictate to you, love. Follow your heart. Be happy.'' The husky regret in his tone had brought tears to her eyes, although she hadn't known the cause of his feelings.

''Now, what was I saying?''

''Never mind,'' Briana said. ''Erik told me he'd call us when he gets settled.''

''Settled? Where?'' Margaret looked suddenly lost.

''In New York,'' Briana replied patiently. ''He'll be looking for a position there. Some of father's friends are still active in Wall Street financial circles. Erik will have some good contacts. I'm sure he'll find something quickly.''

Margaret was shaking her head. ''I don't understand you young people nowadays. We have an adequate income from your grandfather's stock portfolio. There's no need for either of you to work. It just doesn't seem proper.''

The stocks had been sold years before, but the fact had evidently slipped Margaret's mind again. Briana didn't want to upset her further by reminding her. ''Erik and I need to put our educations to some useful purpose,'' she said, adding gently, ''It's the way of the modern world, grandmother.''

''I suppose,'' murmured Margaret. ''But it's time you thought of marrying again, Briana. We should have a party, invite all our friends so you can get back into the social whirl. Perhaps a dinner in the garden. We'll hire that little orchestra we always used....''

Margaret seemed to have also forgotten that the garden was overgrown, the flowers were gone. And they couldn't begin to afford the sort of party she was thinking of.

''I can't spare the time that would be required to get everything ready for a party,'' Briana said. ''You're sweet to think of it, but I really don't want to get back into the social whirl. I'm going to be too busy for that sort of thing.''

As for marrying again, Briana could only shudder inwardly. The painful emotional scars she carried from those months as Ricardo's wife were proof against her making that mistake a second time. She hadn't let a man get close to her since her divorce. The few men she had dated occasionally in Vermont had been told at the outset that they could expect nothing but friendship from her. One or two of them hadn't taken her seriously at first, but after several dates they'd realized she meant it. Eventually they had all lost interest. She was a puzzle, a young attractive divorcée who chose to live like a nun.

Margaret pushed her tray back and regarded her granddaughter with a fretful expression. "You work too hard. I don't understand why you must spend all your time on this history book of yours. How can a few months, more or less, matter?"

"It matters to me. I've been working toward my degree for so long! Now that the goal's in sight, I'm eager to reach it."

Margaret sat back against the faded upholstery of the settee. Her blue eyes softened wistfully. "You are very like my father, Briana. He was always a striver. When he finished a project, he couldn't rest until he'd found another improvement to make in his business operations, another company to buy out. I realize now that he was not a very contented man." She looked faintly troubled. "The world tends to overlook that in the male sex. But I don't like to see you becoming the sort of woman whose ambition overshadows her more feminine instincts. If only you had tried to work out your differences with Ricardo—"

"My differences with Ricardo were irreconcilable," Briana interrupted. "As for the other, I'll be quite satisfied to finish my dissertation and take up teaching. I have no ambition beyond being the best teacher I'm capable of being, for I love history and the stimulation of the classroom. Everyone must find contentment in his own way, grandmother. I wish you'd try to understand that."

"I understand more than you think. I suspect you're using this obsession with the past to escape the present. A failed marriage doesn't mean there can never be another one, a happier one for you."

Briana hesitated. Was Margaret right? Did she bury herself in history to avoid dealing with the emptiness of her personal life? Perhaps. But no one save Briana knew what she had been through with Ricardo. She'd been barely twenty when she married him and had known very little about men, certainly not men with a penchant for cruelty like her ex-husband. All her friends had envied her for snagging a wealthy titled older man, and during the courtship she'd lived in a dreamworld, flattered that such a man wanted to marry her. After the wedding Ricardo had smashed her romantic dreams in short order, however. Now she could hardly think of him without trembling. But these were not things she could speak about to her grandmother.

Instead she said, "You can't conceive of a woman alone having a full satisfying life, can you?" Sometimes she herself wondered if it were possible over the long run, but she brushed the thought aside, adding, "That may be the greatest change in attitude between your generation and mine."

Margaret's lavender silk shoulders lifted in a weary little shrug. "I sometimes think I've lived too long. Everything is changing."

Lately Briana had noticed a tendency toward self-pity in her grandmother, a trait that in the past had been foreign to her nature. She didn't know how to cope with it, except by trying to divert Margaret's attention. "Aren't you going to finish your lunch?"

"I don't want any more, except for another cup of tea—in a while."

"I'll tell Ida to bring you one in a half hour," Briana promised, picking up the tray. "In the meantime why don't you try to rest? Would you like me to put one of your records on the player?"

"No, thank you, dear. I'd rather have it quiet."

Briana took the tray back to the kitchen, her fine brows knitted in thought. Her grandmother did look particularly tired. She probably hadn't been sleeping well, and Briana decided to speak to the family doctor about prescribing something to help her rest.

She wondered if what she'd told her grandmother about Erik had really sunk in, or if she'd be asking where he was the following day.

CHAPTER TWO

AFTER DISPOSING OF THE TRAY, Briana returned to the study, eager to get back to sorting the voluminous von Scholten papers. Thank goodness for her ancestors' penchant for keeping journals, she thought—and for the self-importance that moved them to save all notes, letters and newspaper clippings concerning themselves.

She had planned to spend the whole afternoon on her work, but Ida interrupted her shortly after two.

"I know you don't want to be bothered, but there's a man in the parlor askin' for Mistress Ivensen. She just now got to sleep, but he say it very important."

Reluctantly Briana put aside a letter. It had been written by her great-grandfather in England on business to her great-grandmother at home. "Did he give his name?" she asked.

"He say Rutledge, same as Mr. Erik's boss."

"Drake Rutledge?"

"Yes'm. That's the name."

"It must be Erik he wants. Tell him he's already left for New York."

"No. He say plain, Mistress Margaret Ivensen."

"Oh, darn!" Briana muttered, getting to her feet. "I guess I'll have to see him, then."

Ida nodded and shuffled off down the hall toward the kitchen.

There being no mirror in the study, Briana made but a half-hearted attempt to smooth her hair and anchor the combs at her temples. The slightly dust-smudged white shirt and red shorts she wore would have to do, she thought with irritation, since Drake Rutledge had not felt it necessary to phone ahead for an appointment.

What business could he have with her grandmother, anyway? As she left the study, she still felt certain it must have something to do with Erik—maybe with some records that had been misplaced—and that she could take the message as well as Margaret. She only hoped the man's business wouldn't take long. She wanted to get back to work.

The rarely used parlor was dim and shadowed, for the blinds were always drawn to keep the room as cool as possible. A tall man wearing a white linen shirt and dark trousers stood beside the rosewood spinet piano. He was examining a porcelain figurine that rested on the keyboard cover.

Briana switched on one of the hand-painted

lamps to dispel some of the dimness. "Mr. Rutledge? I'm Briana Ivensen, Erik's sister."

He turned to face her, and she saw for the first time the angry scar that slashed diagonally across his left cheek. For a moment she stared at him, arrested by the almost diabolic look it gave his rugged tanned face, and at the same time she had an odd feeling of *déjà vu*. She didn't know Drake Rutledge—didn't remember even meeting him—but the scar touched a deep chord in her memory. Momentarily, she felt as if she had seen that scar, or something like it, at some point far in the past.

"Miss Ivensen." He was walking toward her, his hand extended. Pulling her gaze away from his scar, Briana placed her hand in his and felt sudden heat and strength.

"Won't you sit down?" She indicated the brocade sofa and took a chair that stood at right angles to it. "Evidently you don't know that Erik left for New York this morning?"

"Oh?" There was little surprise or interest in the response. "How long will he be away?"

"Indefinitely. He plans to live there. I expect you'll be asked to provide references for prospective employers."

Black lashes came down, but not before Briana had caught the irony in his dark eyes. "I hardly think so." The words sounded curiously sarcastic.

She blinked and tried not to stare at the scar.

Drake Rutledge wasn't anything like she had expected. She had imagined a conservatively dressed businessman whose rough edges had been smoothed away years ago. Not this somehow primitive, overpowering male who looked at her as if she were a slightly dim-witted schoolgirl.

"My grandmother is napping," Briana said, trying to get to the reason for his visit so that he would leave. "I don't want to disturb her. She needs the rest. Perhaps I can help you?"

"Can you tell me when you plan to move out of the house?"

She stared at him for a long moment before she said, "I see I didn't make myself clear before. Grandmother and I won't be moving to New York with Erik. We both prefer to live here."

He frowned, as if he didn't fully accept what she had said. Then a dawning realization widened his eyes and settled in grim lines about his mouth. "Your brother didn't tell you of our... agreement, did he?"

His intentness was making Briana feel uneasy. She moved restlessly in her chair. "He merely said that he had resigned from his position with you; that it hadn't worked out. Are you saying the decision to leave wasn't entirely his?"

She was aware of his hesitation and realized suddenly that Erik hadn't told her the full story. "Did you fire him?"

Drake Rutledge stood up abruply and, thrusting his hands into his trouser pockets, paced across the time-dimmed Persian rug. "Damned coward!"

Briana looked at him in perplexity. She assumed he was cursing Erik, but it was unclear to her what her brother had done to bring on such a reaction. "Something tells me you did fire him," she ventured. "I wish I could say I'm surprised, but I'm not. What did he do—phone in sick once too often? Was his work slipshod?" She paused, collecting her thoughts. "In any case you haven't come here just to tell us that, have you?"

Abruptly he pulled a folded paper from his shirt pocket, staring at it for a moment and then at her with an expression that sent an uneasy premonition through her. "What your brother did was much more serious than falling down on the job." He handed her the paper.

Confused, she took it, but she didn't immediately open it. She couldn't seem to pull her eyes away from the hard set of his face.

"Read it," he instructed tersely.

Her hands shook as she unfolded the paper and scanned it slowly. When she looked up again, her face was pale under its delicate golden tan, her expression stricken. "This... this is a deed assigning our house and everything in it to you." The words were low, barely more than a whisper. "I don't understand.

Erik can't do this!'' Her voice rose on the last words.

He sat down again on the sofa, watching her. ''You knew nothing about it?''

She shook her head once, white-faced.

''And your grandmother?''

''I'm sure Erik didn't tell her. He left in such a rush.'' She paused, the reason for Erik's great hurry coming clear to her at last. ''He...he took the money you paid him—'' she gestured helplessly ''—and left. The house belongs to him, of course, but to take it all....''

He ran a hand distractedly across his cheek, as if the old wound pained him. ''I didn't pay him anything, not directly.''

She swallowed, her throat suddenly dry. ''I don't understand then. Why did he sign this deed?''

''Maybe,'' he said guardedly, ''I'd better explain that to your grandmother.''

Briana pulled herself stiffly erect in the chair, her hands refolding the deed and dropping it on the table beside her. ''No. She isn't well. You...you have no idea what this house means to grandmother. I don't know what this will do to her.''

He could see that she was exerting a great effort of will to keep her composure, and he felt an unwanted flash of pity. He muttered under his breath, then said, ''Miss Ivensen, your brother embezzled almost a quarter of a million dollars from my corporation over the past eighteen months. When I confronted him with the evidence, he offered to transfer title of this property to me if I would agree not to press charges.''

The harsh unadorned revelation rocked Briana's rigidly held composure and set off a roar of blood in her ears. She felt hot, then cold, and then there was a panicky sensation in her chest, all in the space of seconds. Watching her, Drake thought she had the look of a wild deer cornered by a wolf pack.

The feeling that finally emerged strongest in Briana was anger. She had known that Erik was irresponsible, but she hadn't dreamed he would do anything so desperate. Yet it never occurred to her to doubt Drake Rutledge's word.

She closed her eyes for a moment. When she opened them again, he was frowning and leaning forward on the sofa, as if he thought she might be about to faint. Her eyes were drawn to the scar on his cheek again, and suddenly an image flashed across her mind. Unaccountably she saw her father struggling with a young boy. There was a silver flash of a knife blade, then blood poured from gaping flesh. . . .

Briana's hand flew up and pressed against her mouth. She heard the sound of her own breathing as she tried to remember more, but nothing else came. Just that evil flash of metal—and blood. The bizarre images must be due to the shock of learning what Erik had done. Her mind couldn't deal with the consequences of her brother's betrayal yet, and so it had gone off on a tangent. Dear Lord, what was she going to do?

Consternation gave Drake a stern look. "Are you all right?"

"Yes," she murmured. "For a moment I thought...." She shook her head. "It's nothing." Nothing that she could understand.

"So Erik left without telling you anything," Drake remarked in the silence. "Wonderful brother you have."

Briana tugged her thoughts away from the strange picture that still wavered at the edge of her consciousness. As she bowed her head, one comb lost its tentative hold in her hair and dropped into her lap. Distractedly she pushed the pale gold strands away from her face.

"Please...I must have some time to think, to figure out what we can do," she said, raising her eyes to his. Her voice sounded thready and insubstantial, as if it could hardly penetrate the warm, close air in the room. "The first thing is to speak to my grandmother's doctor. Maybe he'll prescribe something to cushion the shock. May I phone you tomorrow?"

Drake debated for a moment, raking her with eyes that appeared black in the subdued parlor light. The examination was keen and slightly calculating, and she thought for a moment that he would refuse even that short reprieve. Then he said, "All right. I'll be at the hotel all day tomorrow."

When he stood up, she remained seated. She felt too upset to worry about niceties. She looked up at him briefly. "Do you know the way out?"

"With my eyes closed." He retrieved the deed, and she watched him leave the parlor. His long loose strides made her think of a panther she had once watched pacing in its cage in a Vermont zoo.

Briana continued to sit alone in the parlor for long minutes, trying to take in the fact that she no longer had a home. Earlier she had been worried about approaching her grandmother about selling a few antiques. Now both the antiques and the house belonged to Drake Rutledge. Dear heaven, how was she going to tell Margaret that? And there was Ida to consider, too. Where would they go? They were three women without home or adequate income. The appropriate adjective was "destitute," a word never before applied to an Ivensen, Briana felt sure.

She looked about her at the worn brocade furniture and the dark mahogany tables. Everything was so familiar. She had always been comforted and reassured by that familiarity. And now....

She got to her feet, suddenly unable to endure the room, the house any longer. She went to her bedroom, which was on the ground floor, and snatched up her handbag. She left the house by a side door.

Her car, a four-year-old Japanese-made economy model, was parked at the back of the house in an old wooden barn that had been converted to a garage. She drove slowly along the steep road leading down Denmark Hill. Within a few minutes she arrived at the waterfront and parked in a lot next to the old fort.

Climbing out of the car, she began walking at a brisk pace along Veterans Drive, with the boat-dotted harbor on her left, shops and other business establishments on her right. Some of the tourists who had come for the Christmas holidays were still there, sunburned, milling from one shop to the next in their brief attire. Briana took no notice of them, except to step aside now and then to allow a group of them to pass. Once she had to make way for a particularly boisterous bunch, and she felt a stab of resentment for their carefree manner, for the money they could afford to throw away on souvenirs.

When she finally left the shopping district behind, she stopped to sit on the seawall and stare out over the harbor. The most important thing, she told herself as she strove for calmness, was to protect her grandmother from the knowledge of what Erik had done. But how? She couldn't just move her out of the house without a convincing explanation; she wasn't sure that Margaret would agree to leave even then. Briana pushed away the image of her proud grandmother being removed bodily from her home of more than fifty years. No, there had to be another way. She would have to find a job, of course, regardless of what other arrangements she made. There would be rent to pay now.

She had a sudden fierce wish for Erik to materialize beside her. She would wring his neck without a twinge of conscience. Now she understood how he had managed to afford the expensive clothes, the trips, the gambling. She wondered how much of the embezzled money her brother still had in his possession. Could he possibly have run through a quarter of a million dollars in eighteen months? She couldn't recall his ever offering to contribute to the household expenses; every penny she had got from him she had asked for. Now she wished she had pressed for much more.

Her blood boiled when she realized that, when faced with the consequences of his own criminal actions, he had signed away their home. He hadn't given a thought for what would become of her and Margaret. He knew perfectly well that Drake Rutledge would contact them. As a result, Erik probably wouldn't be calling home for a long while. Briana had frequently felt disappointed in her brother. Now she almost hated him.

To think that he had skipped out and left her to deal with Drake Rutledge! A small shiver of apprehension ran up her spine at that thought. She sensed that Drake was not a man who could be manipulated. With someone else she might have tried appealing to his sympathy; with Drake Rutledge the idea was ludicrous.

She admitted to herself that under other circumstances something in her might be drawn to him. He wasn't handsome in a conventional sense, but the scar on his cheek seemed to stamp him with an air of mystery. He certainly gave off sparks of vitality—like no other man she'd ever met. And she sensed he kept his own counsel. Only once or twice during their meeting had his angular face given her a hint about what he was thinking.

It seemed odd that such a busy man had come to the house at all. Why hadn't he sent a lawyer to handle what must be a small matter in comparison with his other interests?

He had asked to see her grandmother, obviously he had intended to speak to Margaret about moving out of the house. When she'd introduced herself in the parlor, Briana had got the feeling that he was disappointed, that he had hoped to see Margaret. Had he wanted to gauge her reaction to the loss of her home?

Briana knew that her grandmother disliked the man. Perhaps the feeling was mutual.... The thought caused a quivery sensation in the

pit of her stomach. Did Drake Rutledge hold
some grudge against her family? She wouldn't
like to have him for an enemy.

She wondered how he had come by the savage
scar on his face. And why had it made her imagine what she had—pictures so vivid they seemed
real? Had she actually witnessed such a scene as
a child? Was there truth in her dimly remembered nightmare?

Sighing over so many unanswered questions,
she tucked a few long blond strands behind her
ears, then lifted the heavy weight of her hair off
the back of her neck for a moment. For a long
time, she sat there going over and over the problem facing her and trying to come up with a
solution that would not destroy her grandmother.

WHEN DRAKE LEFT the Ivensen house, he didn't
drive back to the hotel immediately. Instead he
headed west out of Charlotte Amalie until he
reached a high point of land overlooking the
blue Caribbean. He pulled off the road, then
took his pipe and tobacco from the glove com-
partment. After lighting up, he got out and
stood on the cliff, where a lazy breeze was blowing. For long moments he gazed down at a
stretch of beach below where several swimmers
and sunbathers were enjoying the day.

Nothing about the confrontation at the Ivensen house had gone as he'd expected. In the first

place he hadn't planned to deal with Briana. He knew for a fact that she was somewhere in her mid-twenties, but in those red shorts, with her hair falling about her face, she hadn't looked much older than his seventeen-year-old niece, Patty.

Crazy as it now seemed, when the combs had fallen out of her hair, and she'd looked up at him with such stricken eyes, he'd had an irrational impulse to bury his fingers in those golden strands. To feel them slipping through his hands like fine silk.

The whole scene had disconcerted him badly. The worst shock, of course, had been learning that Erik had left St. Thomas without telling the women that the house was no longer theirs. So much for noble aristocrats!

Drake grunted angrily. He should have suspected that Erik wouldn't have enough backbone to face his grandmother with what he'd done. That tall commanding woman had been a detested figure of authority in Drake's own childhood. She had seemed then to have the power of life and death over the other people in her world, including Drake's family. He had always blamed her as much as Frederik for what had happened.

He took a deep drag on his pipe and shook his head. Briana had spoken of her grandmother as being ill and needing rest. Of course, Margaret Ivensen was much older now, but he could hardly imagine her as a figure capable of bringing out her granddaughter's protective instincts. He wondered suddenly if, should he see this old and ailing Margaret, he would be able to go through with the eviction.

Muttering a curse, he kicked at a stone near his foot, sending it bouncing down the cliff face. What was wrong with him, anyway? He could have had Erik thrown in jail, which would have blown Margaret's nice respectable life to smithereens. The house was his now, however. He would go ahead with his plans to have it restored and possibly opened to the public. It was a fine example of an early St. Thomas plantation great house. When the restoration was complete he might even turn it over to the government as a gesture of civic goodwill.

Stubbornly his thoughts returned to the Ivensens. Why should he make any more concessions to them? They had never made any to him. In fact, they had destroyed his family, had left him motherless at fourteen. It was true that Frederik had come to the hospital and offered them conscience money. Drake, still weak from loss of blood, had been outraged at the sight of the man he blamed for his mother's death. He'd tried to get up to attack him once again, but had fainted before he was able to. He hadn't learned until months later that Ruth, his older sister, had accepted the money, had paid his hospital bill with some of it. She had wanted to use more of it for plastic surgery, for an operation that would make his scar less noticeable. He'd refused angrily, saying he wanted no more favors from Frederik Ivensen.

Drake had been emotionally marked by the loss of their mother, but he'd been a tough kid. Although older, Ruth had had a more difficult time of it. She'd run a little wild for a year or two, then had married and promptly got pregnant. Her husband, Tom Heyward, proved to be a shiftless sort, so after Patty's birth, Ruth had gone to work to support them. Meanwhile her husband had jumped from one impractical "deal" to another, in the process losing every dime he could pry out of Ruth. Eventually he had disappeared—good riddance, as far as Drake was concerned.

Just a few years ago, Ruth and Patty had come to live with Drake on St. John. His sister fit in comfortably. She seemed to be quite content running the house, coming over to Charlotte Amalie occasionally for shopping. Now it was Patty he was worried about.

Drake knocked the ashes from the pipe by tapping it against the sole of his shoe. Straightening up, he ran long tanned fingers through his wind-tossed brown hair and started walking back to his car.

One problem at a time, he told himself firmly. He would wait for Briana to phone him tomorrow. It might be interesting to see how resourceful she was. Once the Ivensen house was taken care of, he'd decide what to do about Patty.

EVEN THOUGH SHE'D SPENT a sleepless night, Briana waited until ten the next morning to phone the Grand Reef Hotel. The switchboard operator connected her with a secretary, who put her employer on almost immediately when she heard who was calling.

Dispensing with formalities, Briana said, "Would it be possible for us to meet today?"

"At the house or here?" The deep voice sounded businesslike.

She wanted to keep him away from the house, at least until after this meeting; on the other hand, she knew that she'd feel at a disadvantage on his home ground. "I'd prefer meeting in town if that's not inconvenient for you."

There was a short pause and the sound of papers being shuffled. He was probably consulting his appointment calendar. "I can get away for lunch. How about Sebastian's at twelve-thirty?"

"Fine. I'll see you then." There was a click as he hung up.

Briana dressed carefully for the meeting. She chose a simple powder blue linen suit with a belted short-sleeved jacket and a slightly flared tailored skirt. Classic white pumps completed the outfit. She brushed her hair off her neck and away from her face, securing it in a loose coil at the back of her head.

After surveying her cool neat reflection in the mirror, she added pearl ear studs and a matching single-stranded necklace. Finally satisfied with her appearance, she left the house, wishing that she felt as calm and collected as she looked.

She arrived at the waterfront restaurant a few minutes early and was shown to the table reserved for Drake Rutledge. On the upper level, it had a magnificent view of the harbor. But Briana couldn't enjoy the colorful sight. Instead she watched the door and a few minutes later saw a tall broad-shouldered figure enter the room. For a moment the light was behind him, but there was no mistaking the big-boned frame and the loose swinging stride as he came toward her.

Halfway to the table, Drake was intercepted by one of the other diners and stopped to talk. Briana took the opportunity to study him. His pale gray silk shirt and trim charcoal trousers fitted like a glove. He was standing in profile, his right side toward her, and she took note of his firm jawline, the deep bronze tone his skin had got from the island sunshine. He seemed to radiate a tough energy even when he was relaxed and still.

Without warning, he left the other table and turned toward Briana. She didn't know that the sunlight streaming through the glass behind her touched her hair with white gold highlights. Or that against the bright background he couldn't see her expression clearly. For a moment their eyes met and held. An odd jarring awareness ran through Briana before she glanced away, castigating herself for staring at him—and being caught at it.

When she looked up again, he was seating himself in the chair facing hers across the small white-clothed table. "Hello, Briana," he said in his deep voice. "How are you?"

"I've been better, Mr. Rutledge, as you've undoubtedly guessed."

He smiled crookedly. "Call me Drake."

Again her blue eyes met his. She was trying to decide whether to broach the subject of their business immediately or wait for a while. Just then a waiter appeared, deciding the matter. She relaxed imperceptibly in her seat.

Having eaten at the famous restaurant many times, Briana ordered lobster salad without bothering to consult the menu. Drake asked for the same thing. He ordered a Scotch for himself, as well, and, after consulting Briana, a glass of white wine for her.

When their drinks arrived, Briana sipped her wine, hoping that it would still her anxiety. Drake's steady regard disturbed her. His mere presence seemed overwhelming to her, even more so than it had in the parlor the day before. He propped one elbow casually on the table and took a drink of his Scotch, then looked at her again.

Briana dabbed nervously at her mouth with her napkin. "Do you plan to live in the house?" she asked a little breathlessly.

A brief smile touched his lips. "My home is on St. John, and I'm comfortable there. If I lived on St. Thomas, I'd probably never get away from business. It's too easy for people to track me down."

She glanced across the room. "Like that man who stopped you as you came in?"

He nodded. "He heard the corporation is going to build a hotel on St. Croix, and he wants to bid on the carpeting. To get away from him, I had to agree to call him later."

"I didn't realize that would be a problem. Perhaps we should have met in your office."

"I'm glad we didn't." His voice was quiet and seemed slightly weary. It occurred to Briana that he might have postponed something important to meet with her, that in fact he must work very hard. She shifted in her chair. "I imagine you'll want to sell the house so that you can recoup the money Erik took. The house has been allowed to run down. It won't bring that much on its own, but there are some rather valuable antiques."

"I'm not knowledgeable when it comes to antiques," Drake replied. "I'll have to get someone to take inventory and make an estimate of the value of the furnishings. As well as check out the building itself.''

As he talked, Briana found her glance drawn to his mouth, the firmness of his lips and the flash of his white teeth. Then her eyes were drawn upward, following the angle of his scar. It was a moment before she realized what she was doing, and when she did, a flush tinged her cheeks.

"Actually," he continued, "I've given considerable thought to restoring the house and turning it into a museum. There are so few of the old great houses left in the islands. I think they're a part of our history that ought to be preserved.''

Briana looked at him with surprise, her interest engaged in spite of her own dire circumstances. "I certainly agree with you," she stated. "I'm writing my dissertation for my doctoral degree on the history of the Virgins, so I'm intrigued by all aspects of our heritage. It's... generous of you to want to do this, considering the total value of the property.''

He shrugged. "It's a tax write-off.''

Their meal arrived, and they ate silently for a few moments. Then he said, "What will you do after you have your degree?''

"I hope to teach at the college here.'' Taking a deep breath, she put her fork down. She couldn't wait any longer before broaching the plan she had worked out during the long hours of the night. "The research and writing of my dissertation will probably take a year. In the meantime I'll look for a temporary job. I...I was wondering—hoping actually—that if you're in no great hurry to start restoration of the house, you might agree to rent it to me. It would be much easier on grandmother if we could stay there for the time being."

Drake gave her a long assessing look, and she wished, as she had on the previous day, that his expression would give away more of what he was thinking. He ran his index finger along his left cheek, following the scar line, and she fought down an impulse to plead with him.

"You said yesterday that your grandmother isn't well. What's wrong with her?"

"She has a heart condition and hardening of the arteries. She hasn't been sleeping well lately, either. I talked to her doctor yesterday afternoon, and he agreed to prescribe a mild tranquilizer."

Drake sipped the coffee he'd ordered with his meal, setting the cup back in its saucer thoughtfully. "Have you told her about the house yet?"

Briana hesitated, then answered truthfully, "No."

"And you won't until you have to, will you?"

"No," she admitted, forcing herself to meet his steady look.

He laughed, the low sound rumbling in the quiet of the restaurant. "You're a lot more concerned about the old lady than your brother was.''

Briana flushed, her pulse quickening. ''I've no intention of trying to defend Erik. What he did is inexcusable, and I know it wouldn't do any good, anyway.''

''No, it wouldn't,'' he agreed tersely.

''I'm forced to deal with the mess he left behind,'' she went on. Her stomach was tightening into a knot. He had not yet answered her original question, and she feared that meant he would say no. ''About my renting the house—''

''I'll have to think about it.'' After gazing at her again for a moment, he turned his attention back to his meal. Briana picked up her fork, realizing that he wasn't a man who could be rushed into making a decision. He wouldn't be where he was if he'd been the sort to act impulsively.

They finished their salads, and Briana had a cup of coffee while Drake ate a piece of cheesecake. He talked little during the remainder of the meal, and she didn't try to keep a conversation going, either, for he was clearly preoccupied. As they were leaving the table, he said suddenly, ''Do you have anything important you have to do this afternoon?''

She looked up at him, startled. ''No, why?''

He put his hand under her arm to guide her toward the stairs. She felt a tingling where his fingers touched her skin, and she had to overcome an instinct to pull away. Every man wasn't like Ricardo, she reminded herself for the hundredth time, but there was a constriction in her throat, nevertheless.

At the foot of the stairs he released her arm, saying, "I'd like you to come home with me. I want you to meet my sister and my niece."

CHAPTER THREE

BRIANA STARED at Drake for a moment, trying to make sense of his request. What possible reason could there be for her to meet his sister and niece? She hadn't the vaguest idea why he had made such an odd suggestion. "But...but I thought you said you live on St. John," she stammered.

"I do. The ferry makes a round trip every hour."

"I don't understand why you want me to meet them," she said bluntly. "What has this to do with our business together?"

"There's a connection," he said, his expression maddeningly unreadable. "But I want you to meet them first before I explain it to you."

"I...I'd have to call grandmother and tell her—something."

"And I'll have to call my secretary. Well, what do you say?"

Briana looked up at him and nodded mutely. The whole idea seemed crazy. If there was the slightest connection between her going home with him and the fact that she wanted to rent the house, it was a mystery to her. But what choice did she have? If she refused to go, he might decide to refuse her request to stay in the house. He was holding all the cards for the time being, and though she chafed at the knowledge, there wasn't a thing she could do about it.

He touched her arm again, and she felt the same sensations that she had earlier. "Let's make our phone calls," he said. "We've less than a half hour before the ferry leaves."

They left Briana's car at the restaurant, taking Drake's black MG to Red Hook dock and boarding the ferry just before it began the twenty-minute trip to St. John. Their fellow passengers were mostly tourists, but a few native women laden with bags and boxes were returning home after shopping in Charlotte Amalie. Drake and Briana found seats and settled back just as the motor roared, and the ferry surged away from land.

The blue sea rippled in white-crested waves in their wake. Yachts and boats of many sizes and types floated by in the transparent waters around them. The sunlight washed everything with bright pure light, turning sails an unbelievable white and deepening the green lushness of the small islands farther away. The fine spray churned up by the waves slapping against the ferry touched Briana's face like the brush of an angel's wings.

"I love it here," she said softly. "All the time

I lived in New England, I wanted to come back.''

"I know what you mean," Drake responded. "After I left school, I decided to go to the mainland—Miami—to make my fortune. I fought off homesickness for six months, and then I came home. I'd always been aware of the beauty of the islands, but after being away, I saw it with fresh eyes. I realized that if I had to create a paradise, it would look exactly like this.''

His arm was resting behind her on the back of the seat. She was suddenly aware of its faint pressure, of the tingling feeling it aroused even with a layer of linen fabric between them.

She glanced furtively at him from the corner of her eye. He seemed totally relaxed, his eyes half-closed, the dark lashes almost resting on the prominent cheekbones.

She relaxed, too, and together they looked out over the ocean, murmuring together infrequently as the ferry plowed through the serene water. Unconsciously Briana leaned against him. She felt somnolent and at peace, and for those few minutes managed to banish her anxieties.

Only when the ferry slowed to approach the Cruz Bay dock did she remove her gaze from the incredible view and glance up at Drake. He was looking down at her, his eyes glittering like ebony between the fringes of his lashes, his mouth softened and sensual in a way that she hadn't seen before.

Briana's heart leaped erratically, and she sat up in the seat, moving away from him. She hardly knew Drake Rutledge. When she'd come to meet him today, she had been prepared to dislike him, to dismiss him as a small-minded provincial who had learned the secret of making money but had no conception of how to live well, with grace and discrimination. Yet here she was, uncomfortably aware of his vitality, his elemental masculinity, the confusing impact he was having on her senses. And he lounged against the seat so obviously in charge.

He did not fit her mental picture of an impoverished boy who had clawed his way to the top. He shouldn't be so at ease with the world, so sure of himself in every situation. It wasn't reasonable—and she found him far too exciting for her own good.

The ferry was shuddering up to the dock, and she got to her feet, following the other passengers into the aisle. Drake was close behind her. As the steersman turned off the motor, and the ferry jerked to a sudden stop, Briana lost her balance. Drake caught her from behind, his arms encircling her body just below her breasts.

For a moment she responded instinctively by leaning against his solid strength. As she did so, she felt a shudder run through him. Or was it emanating from her own flesh, which suddenly felt alive in every pore? His arms tightened around her, pressing her body against his. His mouth brushed her temple, and she felt his breath warm against her skin.

His reaction might have been unintentional, caused by the uncertain movement of the ferry. But, feeling the heavy thudding of his heart, she wondered with a flutter of fear what might have happened if they had been alone instead of surrounded by a crowd of tourists impatient to leave the ferry.

She made an effort to steady herself and pulled away from him, glancing over her shoulder. "I'm sorry. I lost my balance."

His eyes were impenetrably dark; they roamed her face with such intensity that her senses reacted as though he were still touching her.

"I've often wondered what kind of woman you'd grown up to be," he said with a soft gruffness in his voice. "I never imagined you'd be so beautiful."

He spoke as if he'd known her long ago. She remembered again that his mother had worked for her grandmother. Drake must have been around the house on occasion, and since he was older, he would remember things that she couldn't. She looked away from him. "We'd better get off, or they'll take us back to St. Thomas."

One of the ferrymen took her arm to steady her as she stepped onto the dock. Drake followed and, as they walked across the wood plankings, said, "I leave a car parked about half a block from here when I'm off the island. I never know exactly when I'll be returning, and it's easier than trying to have someone meet me."

The car was a Pontiac, a small maroon sports model with gold racing stripes down the sides. It was parked in front of a little gift shop, and the elderly woman who lounged in the open door waved to them and called, "Playing hooky, Drake?"

"Yeah, Dodie," Drake returned with a grin. "Aren't you jealous?"

"No, sir! I can close up anytime I feel like it. If you'd open a little store in Cruz Bay, you could, too."

"I'm giving it serious consideration," Drake told her, climbing into the car.

They had soon left the tiny village behind. Because two-thirds of St. John had been declared the Virgin Islands National Park in the 1950s, the little island had never lost the natural beauty and unspoiled atmosphere it had had in the nineteenth century. They drove along a narrow road that climbed rapidly through thick stands of trees and tropic greenery. Below sprawled Trunk Bay, one of the world's loveliest beaches, with its gently sloping white sand, still water and underwater snorkeling trail.

"I haven't been over here since I came home," Briana remarked after a long silence.

"It's just the same, isn't it? No wonder you prefer living here."

"We have the perennial water, electricity and phone problems," he said, "even more so than on St. Thomas. But it's worth such minor inconveniences to have all the other advantages. Not that my niece, Patty, would agree with me."

Briana turned to look at him and saw that a worried frown was etching a V between his dark brows. "How old is she?"

"Seventeen. A very restless seventeen. She thinks no place on the face of the earth could be as boring as St. John. She goes over to St. Thomas to school, of course, but she finds that almost as dull."

When it became obvious that he wasn't going to say anything more about his niece, Briana asked, "Does your sister like St. John?"

"As much as I do. Ruth had a pretty rough time while she was married. I think, since her divorce, she just feels grateful to be out of it. She spends a lot of time alone, beachcombing, gardening and reading. Except for worrying about Patty, she seems perfectly content."

Briana could understand only too well what a respite Ruth's present life must be after a bad marriage. It would be heaven. "I know how she feels," she said, unaware for a second that she had spoken the words aloud. She only realized it when he flashed her a question with his eyes.

It was a question she had no intention of answering.

Instead she gazed at his strong brown fingers gripping the steering wheel and said, "I think you have to be a born-and-bred islander to feel totally content here. I've heard visitors say they start to feel claustrophobic if they stay too long. But I'm surprised to hear that your niece is dissatisfied. Maybe it's just a phase she's going through."

His eyes probed her face again. "Did you feel dissatisfied at seventeen?"

Briana shook her head. "I wanted to go away to college, but I was sad about leaving, too. And I always meant to come back."

"But you married a man from Spain."

"Yes," she agreed in a low voice. "When that didn't work out, I returned to college and took courses the year round so I could come back here as soon as possible."

He changed the subject abruptly, perhaps sensing that she didn't want to talk about her marriage. "My property starts here," he said as they came to a pair of tall wrought-iron gates set into a beige stone wall. Drake got out to open the gates, then drove through.

"It's part of the old Sapphire Bay Plantation—just thirty acres and the house." They were driving slowly along a curving lane with poplars bordering it on both sides. "We're very private here, with the bay to the south and the national park to the east and west.''

Briana almost gasped aloud at its gracious appearance. Then the house came into view. It was made of the same beige stone as the wall they'd passed. The two-storied center section had a veranda running along the second floor, over a wide porch at ground level. Single-story wings spread out on both sides. The windows in front, made of many small diamond-shaped panes, were wide and arched.

Although it was old, the house had clearly been restored to its original beauty. And the manicured lawn surrounding it looked as if it required a full-time gardener to keep it. Drake must have been highly amused when she'd asked if he would be moving into the run-down Ivensen house.

"It's lovely," she told him as they got out of the car.

"It is," he agreed simply. "It was the first thing I bought when I could afford to indulge myself. I'd seen it as a boy and imagined how it would be to live here. It took almost a year to make it habitable again, the place had been vacant for such a long time. The man who owned it meant to turn it into a vacation home, but he had some financial reverses in offshore oil drilling in the Gulf of Mexico and had to sell." He smiled wryly as they started up the front steps. "I've always been grateful those wells didn't come in."

Inside, the rooms were large and bright, furnished with walnut and wicker and bright fabrics of yellow, white and green. A middle-aged sandy-haired woman heard them and came into the sunny room where they were.

"This is our housekeeper, Greta James," Drake said, and Briana smiled in response to the woman's inquisitive look and quick nod. "Where are Ruth and Patty, Greta?" he asked when he'd finished introducing them.

"Your sister is out back, Mr. Rutledge, and I think Patty went down to the bay to swim."

"We'll go out and find Ruth," Drake said. He gestured to Greta. "Will you bring us something cold to drink, please?"

He guided Briana through several other large rooms before they emerged on a flagstone patio. A plump woman with short dark hair reclined on a wrought-iron chaise. She wore a pink cotton shorts-and-halter set and was reading a paperback book. Briana guessed she was in her late thirties.

She looked up and smiled as they approached. "Drake! We didn't expect you so early."

"I know. I wanted to bring a...friend to meet you. Briana, this is my sister, Ruth Heyward. Ruth, this is Briana Ivensen."

"Hello, Briana." Ruth laid her book aside, her eyes curious. "Are you Frederik Ivensen's daughter?"

"Yes, I am." Briana felt a little uncomfortable under Ruth's direct and definitely probing gaze, but she didn't know what else to say. Just then Greta appeared with three tall frosty pineapple-coconut drinks, and Briana and Drake sat down on a wrought-iron settee, its cushions covered with a yellow-and-blue floral pattern.

Ruth was still watching Briana with interest. Finally she said, "Well, this is a first." She took one of the glasses from the tray, which the housekeeper had set on a low white patio table. "Drake simply does not leave work in the middle of the day to bring someone over here to meet me." Her gaze moved to her brother and back again before she sipped her drink. "He's an incurable workaholic, but I imagine you know that."

Ruth clearly assumed that she and Drake were well acquainted. Briana accepted a glass from Drake before she replied, "No, I didn't know. Actually we've only known each other a couple of days."

"Oh?" Ruth's dark brows shot up again.

Drake laughed. "There's a method in my madness, Ruth. Be patient and I'll explain later."

Briana had been told the same thing, and she was beginning to doubt that Drake could offer any plausible explanation for bringing her here. But there was nothing she could do about it at the moment. "What a spectacular view you have," she commented.

"Yes, isn't it?" Ruth continued to eye Briana with interest for a second before she turned to look out at the bay. "I never tire of looking at it. Uh-oh, looks as if Patty's coming back. I guess she decided not to swim after all. She's so restless. I'm glad school starts again next week. She's driving me crazy, wanting to go over to Charlotte Amalie two or three times every day."

"You haven't let her go, have you?" Drake asked a little sharply.

Ruth darted a glance at him. "Not since Monday, and I went with her."

A tall tanned girl with long brown hair appeared at the rim of the cliff on the path that led up from the beach. She looked too thin in her white bikini, but her legs were well formed, and she had a coltish grace that seemed to promise a mature attractiveness later. She came to the patio and tossed a beach towel across an empty chair.

"Hi, Uncle Drake." Her gold-flecked eyes slid over to Briana.

Drake got to his feet and planted a fond kiss on the girl's cheek. "Patty, I want you to meet Briana Ivensen. Briana, my niece, Patty."

Greetings were exchanged, and Patty flopped down on her towel, draping her long legs over the arm of the chair. "You live around here, Briana?" she inquired candidly.

"In Charlotte Amalie."

"Briana just moved back from New England," Drake said.

"Why?" asked Patty with perfect gravity.

Briana smiled. "It's home, and I plan to teach at the college as soon as I finish my degree work."

"Teach what?"

When Briana told her, history, the girl grimaced. "Yuck!"

Ruth frowned at her daughter. "Patty! Don't be rude."

"It's all right," Briana said. "I used to feel the same way until, as a college sophomore, I had a professor who could make the past come alive. That's what I want to do for my students."

Patty gave her a strange look but made no further comment. Drake seemed to be intrigued by Briana's remarks, though, and his brown eyes held hers for an instant until she looked away. She stared into her drink until the conversation drifted to other things—Drake's plans for the hotel on St. Croix; a leaf disease the gardener had discovered among the roses south of the house; Patty's desire to go over to Charlotte Amalie to buy some new magazines and books. Drake dispensed with his niece's request by telling her to make a list of the things she wanted, and he would pick them up for her.

For more than an hour the four of them sat there talking, and then Drake said, "We'd better be getting back, Briana."

She agreed readily and after saying goodbye to Ruth and Patty, they returned to the car. Drake was quiet as they drove back to Cruz Bay, and Briana didn't bother to question him about why they had come. She knew already that he would reveal nothing until he was ready. He filled his pipe and smoked thoughtfully, and Briana laid her head back against the seat enjoying the rather pleasant aroma of the tobacco.

They were seated on the ferry, churning through the water toward St. Thomas before he said, "You mentioned that you're looking for a job."

Perplexed, Briana nodded, and he went on, "I assume you'll want something part-time, if you're going to be working on your dissertation."

"That would be the ideal."

"How would you like to tutor Patty?"

She blinked at him. "You can't mean to take her out of school and make her stay home all the time!"

The censure in her tone was not lost on Drake, but he merely gave her a sardonic look. "No, she'll be going back to school next week for the last half of her senior year. The problem is she's failing most of her subjects. She simply has no interest in school."

"Then how can I help her? I can't force-feed an education. The notion that knowledge can be poured into a student's head like water went out ages ago." Briana was having trouble keeping the impatience out of her voice. Had he had this impractical scheme in mind when he'd asked her to go home with him?

"I was thinking of something a little more subtle than that," he said with a low chuckle. "I want her to go to college on the mainland. I haven't suggested it to her yet, but I think she'll agree—just to get away from the islands. At least until she's eighteen and no longer subject to her mother's or my guidance."

"When will that be?"

"December. She could have a semester of college in by then."

"By which time you hope she'll have acquired a thirst for knowledge?" Briana asked dryly.

"Right." He was serious, it seemed. "But she won't be accepted at any decent college unless she graduates from high school and makes respectable scores on the entrance exams." He pushed his wind-tousled hair off his forehead in an absentminded gesture. "I know you were only with her for an hour, but she seemed to feel comfortable with you. I think you could become friends with her. And I hope you could teach her what she needs to know to graduate and do well on the exams."

Briana couldn't hide her skepticism. "You have a lot of confidence in me, considering that we met only yesterday!"

"You're my last hope," he said flatly. "So

what do you say? She takes social studies and English in the afternoon, and I'm sure I can get her released for tutoring since those are two of the classes she's failing. The other is chemistry.''

"I was hopeless in chemistry!"

"I'll confer with her teacher. Maybe he can give her some extra tutoring in that subject if you'll take on the English and social studies. You could meet her at school three afternoons a week, Monday, Wednesday and Friday, and go over to St. John with her. Or if you prefer, she could come to your house.''

"No," Briana said quickly. Margaret would probably fret and complain about having Drake Rutledge's niece in the house. "I think she'd come to accept me more readily in her own environment.''

"You'll do it, then?"

"Well...."

"Your pay would be the use of the house rent-free and a small salary in addition.''

Briana hesitated. His narrowed eyes seemed to be issuing a challenge.

"That wasn't just talk at my place, was it?" he asked. "That business about wanting to be an extraordinary teacher?''

She drew in a deep breath. "It seems that I haven't much choice.'' She tucked a stray lock of hair behind her ear, her fingers trembling. She felt confused—angry and resentful, yet excited, too. He had maneuvered her into a position where she had to do what he wanted or else lose her home. At the same time she couldn't deny that she would probably enjoy going to Drake's home three afternoons a week. Of course, he would rarely be there. This was best for everybody concerned, she told herself firmly. She looked up at him. "Okay, I'll do it."

His body relaxed visibly beside her. Briana hadn't realized he was so concerned about her answer. In a spontaneous gesture he draped his arm across the back of her seat and squeezed her gently. His hand trailed over her shoulder, touching the bare flesh of her upper arm.

Briana moistened her lips with her tongue, a nervous reaction to his touch.

"That's great," he murmured. "Thank you."

They sat together in companionable silence for a while, then Drake's fingers started stroking her arm almost absently. An answering warmth immediately hummed through her veins, pulsing in her temples. *He's the sexiest man I've ever met,* she told herself, feeling dizzy with the admission. For the first time in years she felt like a woman again, and the experience was as dazzling as it was frightening.

Abruptly she sat forward on the seat, breaking the physical contact between them. "We're coming into the dock."

For a long breathless moment Drake gazed at her. Briana, held captive by his burning look, felt an unfamiliar weakness in her midsection. She gripped the edge of the seat as the ferry came to a stop, then stood up hastily. He followed her off the ferry, and they got into his MG without speaking.

In minutes they reached Sebastian's, where they'd left her car, and as she started to get out, he said, "I'll arrange everything with Ruth and Patty, and I'll call you in a day or two."

"Fine," Briana said breathlessly, chancing a swift look at his face. His eyes were once more unfathomable, and she turned quickly away, not glancing back as she heard the powerful motor roar and the car move off.

CHAPTER FOUR

IT WASN'T MANY DAYS LATER that Briana parked her car near Patty's school and waited for the tide of uniformed students to erupt from the building for lunch hour. She hadn't seen the girl since the day Drake introduced them, and she wondered how Patty had reacted to the news. Briana hoped Patty had been more amenable to the idea than her own grandmother had been.

When she had mentioned her new job, Margaret had stared at her as if she thought Briana had suddenly taken leave of her senses. "You've accepted a job with Drake Rutledge? Just as Erik terminated his relationship with the man! Why on earth, Briana?"

"It's a great chance to gain some experience teaching, even if I have only one student. The schedule, three afternoons a week, couldn't be better. In fact, for my purposes it's ideal." She had wanted to sound reassuring, but she couldn't resist adding, "And we can certainly use the money, now that Erik had left."

They still hadn't heard from her brother, not that Briana had expected to after learning the truth of what had happened. But Margaret knew nothing of her grandson's real reason for leaving. "I can't understand why Erik hasn't phoned," she said almost plaintively. "I seem to be losing track of time recently, but he's been gone a long while, hasn't he?"

"Only a week."

"Do you think something could have happened to him? Perhaps we should consider hiring a private investigator."

"I'm sure that isn't necessary," Briana said hastily. "Erik told me he'd call when he's settled. He has to find an apartment and a job. Don't worry about him, grandmother."

"At the moment I'm more worried about you," Margaret stated petulantly. "I don't care for the idea of your being in and out of that man's house. I don't like anything about this new job of yours, Briana."

"Well, I'm sorry about that." A trace of impatience slipped into Briana's tone at the old woman's stubborn refusal to see any viewpoint but her own. "I won't be seeing much of Drake Rutledge, though. I've been hired to tutor his niece, not him. There's nothing at all for you to be concerned about."

"Humph! You don't know Drake Rutledge as I do! He's got something up his sleeve, you can be sure!"

Briana wondered if paranoia sometimes developed with old age. Far from wishing her and her grandmother harm, as Margaret seemed to think, Drake had shown compassion in allowing them to stay in the house that he now owned. But she couldn't tell Margaret that. Instead she had excused herself, saying, "I have a conference with Patty's teachers this morning. I'll see you at lunch."

After that, Briana had avoided talking to Margaret about her tutoring job. It was futile trying to reason with her; she had already made up her mind about the subject.

Briana's thoughts returned to the present as she saw the first students emerging from the school building. She got out of her car and stood on the walk.

Patty was one of the last to come out. She trudged slowly toward Briana, her book bag slung over one shoulder. It was clear the girl wasn't enthusiastic about the afternoon's tutoring session.

"Hello, Patty," Briana greeted her.

"Hi. This your car?"

When Briana nodded, Patty opened the passenger door and got in without further comment. Briana got in, too, and started the car, keeping a watchful eye on the stream of youngsters as she pulled into the narrow street. She glanced at Patty, whose expression was sullen. "Where do you usually have lunch?"

Patty shrugged. "Sometimes I bring a lunch from home. Other times I eat in town with friends."

Briana was silent for a moment, then she said, "You'll miss having lunch with your friends, won't you? I should have thought of that. Maybe I could pick you up after lunch. I'll speak to your uncle about it if you'd like."

"It doesn't matter," the girl replied disinterestedly. "It wouldn't be much fun, knowing you were waiting. Anyway, Greta's making lunch for us at home. Mother usually eats a late breakfast and skips lunch. But she said she'd wait and eat with us today."

"I hope your mother doesn't feel she has to join us every time I'm there. I wouldn't like to inconvenience her."

Patty settled her book bag on her knees and laid her head back against the seat. "She doesn't have anything else to do. Her only interests are the garden and what I'm doing. Sometimes I wish I had six brothers and sisters so she and Uncle Drake would have somebody else's life to run besides mine."

Briana wasn't sure how to respond to the obvious resentment in the girl's words. Finally she said, "I can't speak from experience, of course, since I don't have children. But I imagine your mother realizes that you're almost grown-up, that she won't have you with her always. If she and your uncle seem overly protective, I'd bet it's because they love you and want what's best for you."

"Yeah, well maybe I don't want the same things they want. Aren't I allowed to live my own life?"

It was a loaded question. Briana had no wish to get into an argument with her belligerent pupil. She wouldn't be able to help Patty at all if the girl disliked her. She said judiciously, "Of course you are. Everyone is, sooner or later."

"It can't come soon enough for me!"

Briana smiled. "Most people feel that way at seventeen." She parked her car in an empty space near the dock and cut the motor. "We timed that perfectly. The ferry's about to leave."

They got out of the car and hurried aboard, finding seats on the shady side of the boat. Patty maintained her glum silence during the trip, and Briana didn't try to carry on a conversation. When they reached the Cruz Bay dock, Ruth was there to meet them.

"Drake had an extra key to his Pontiac made for you," Ruth told Briana as they walked toward Ruth's own car. "I'll give it to you when we reach the house. After this you can use the Pontiac whenever you come over."

"That's good," Briana said. "Then you won't be inconvenienced. Patty told me you changed your schedule today in order to have lunch with us. I hope you don't feel you must entertain me. I'm an employee, not a guest."

Ruth laughed. "Believe me, your coming over three afternoons a week won't be an inconvenience. We don't get many visitors. I know you're coming to tutor Patty, but I'll enjoy talking to another woman now and then. Putting the Pontiac at your disposal was a wise decision on Drake's part, though. He knows I'm inclined to let the time slip away, especially when I'm working in the garden.''

Patty had got into the back seat of the car and hadn't spoken since they left the dock. They were driving up a steeply inclined road when Ruth turned to look over her shoulder at her daughter. "So, how was school today, dear?"

"The same as always," muttered Patty. "Boring."

Ruth glanced at Briana with a long-suffering expression. To Patty she said, "Maybe you'll like it better when your grades improve." There was no response to this, and Ruth didn't try to draw Patty into the conversation again as they completed the drive.

They lunched at a small table in the glassed-in breakfast parlor overlooking the patio and beach below. Greta had prepared an attractive shrimp salad, which she served with a large tray of cheese and fruit.

As they were finishing, Briana said to Ruth, "I thought Patty and I might spend some time this afternoon getting better acquainted. We can put off the studies until next time."

Patty glanced up at her in surprise, then shot her mother a hopeful look.

"That's a good idea," Ruth said. "If you two

would like to go to the beach, I can lend you a bathing suit."

"I don't really want to swim," Briana responded, "but perhaps we could stroll along the beach. What do you think, Patty?"

"Okay. Let me get out of this awful uniform first." She left the table, and the two older women went out to the patio to wait for her.

"I think I should tell you that Patty and Drake had a heated argument about these tutoring sessions," Ruth said when they were alone.

Briana nodded. "She's already made it clear she'd rather be doing almost anything else."

Ruth looked troubled. "I hope you can help her. She's so incredibly headstrong. I don't know what will become of her if she doesn't change some of her attitudes."

"I'll do my best," Briana promised.

"I do want you to feel welcome here." As she spoke, Ruth looked at her with the same intense interest she'd shown at their earlier meeting, and Briana suspected the other woman was still determined to read more into her relationship with Drake than was there. But before she could frame a response, Patty appeared, wearing white shorts and a navy knit top.

Fortunately Briana had worn lightweight cotton slacks, a sleeveless shirt and comfortable sandals. She was appropriately dressed for walking, even though she had only thought up the idea during lunch. Since Ruth had confirmed her hunch—that Patty was totally averse to the tutoring sessions—she felt a couple of hours trying to get past some of the girl's defenses would be time well spent.

She and Patty followed the narrow path leading down to the beach. Two women and a young child were playing in the shallow water several hundred yards to the east. Otherwise Briana and Patty had the beach to themselves. They took off their shoes and began to stroll along the wet sand at the waterline.

"This is better than being in a classroom, isn't it?" Briana said lightly.

"It certainly is!"

"We could have our tutoring sessions on the patio or in the garden when it isn't too warm. Would you like that?"

"I guess so."

"Patty, your mother's right. You'll like school better once your work improves. People tend to enjoy what they do well. But you're going to have to cooperate with me for that to happen."

Patty looked out at the ocean. "It seems like a big waste of time to me."

"Why do you say that?"

The girl bent to scoop up a handful of water and watched it run back through her fingers. Finally she straightened up and met Briana's questioning look. "Going to college is Uncle Drake's idea, not mine. He broke the news to

me yesterday. But what college will have me
with my grades?''

"That's the purpose of the tutoring sessions,
to bring your grades up and prepare you for the
entrance exams. Almost anything is possible if
you want it badly enough.''

Patty sighed. "Well, I guess college would be
better than staying here after I graduate—if I
graduate. But it will only be until I'm eighteen,
so what's the point?''

"You might find you want to go on for a degree once you've started.''

"That's what Uncle Drake is hoping, isn't it?
I won't change my mind, though. I have other
plans for my life, and once I'm eighteen, there
won't be anything mother or Uncle Drake can
do to stop me.'' Patty's chin was thrust forward
stubbornly.

"Do you plan to get a job, then?''

The girl tossed her long brown hair over her
shoulder and with a trace of sarcasm said, "No,
and don't pretend Uncle Drake didn't tell you
about Abel.''

"Abel?'' Briana met Patty's skeptical look.
"No, he didn't mention anyone named Abel.''

Patty studied her silently for a moment as if
she were trying to decide whether to believe her
or not. "Abel Weldon,'' she said at length, "is
the man I'm going to marry the minute I'm
eighteen.''

"Oh,'' said Briana in as noncommittal a tone

as she could manage. "I'm not here to pass judgment on your personal life, Patty. I'm here to help you with social studies and English. I had hoped, though, that we could be friends."

Patty said warily, "Just don't think you can trick me into becoming a dedicated career woman like you. And don't think you can make me forget Abel. I know that's what Uncle Drake hopes will happen."

"If he does, he hasn't mentioned it to me."

"Well—" she tossed her hair again "—he's tried everything else to break us up." Her bravado slipped for a moment. "I...I haven't heard from Abel in two weeks now, and I'm sure Uncle Drake has told him to stay away from me. He won't, though." She glared at Briana defiantly. "Abel loves me, and somehow he'll find a way to see me."

Since it was the first Briana had heard of Abel Weldon, there was obviously no sensible answer she could give to this. Instead she said, "I'd like to tell you what I discussed with your teachers on Friday." And as they continued their walk, she outlined what she hoped to accomplish in their tutoring sessions during the next few weeks.

The teenager seemed to be listening, even though she showed no great enthusiasm for the task ahead. Then Briana deliberately diverted the conversation to other things. As they finished their walk much later and started climbing back up to the house, she told herself that she had at least made a start with her reluctant pupil. Patty would be less defensive when they met again—where her studies were concerned, anyway.

As much as she would have liked to reason with the girl, Briana knew she would be wise to remain silent about Patty's plans to marry. Perhaps at some level her charge sensed she herself was not being reasonable about the subject, and this increased her defensiveness. No matter what kind of man Abel Weldon was, it was obvious Patty was far too immature to be thinking of marriage. Briana could even see a little of herself in Patty. Although she had been twenty when she married Ricardo, she had not been any better prepared for marriage than Patty seemed to be; and certainly she hadn't been prepared to deal with a man such as her ex-husband had been. Her disillusionment had been deep and swift. She didn't like to think of that happening to Patty, who was in many ways still a child.

But Briana pushed these thoughts aside. She would stick to the task for which she had been employed and leave Abel Weldon to Drake and Ruth.

SHE FELT TIRED after the long walk, and later, on the ferry returning to St. Thomas, she put her head back against the seat and dozed lightly. When the ferry came to a stop, she waited until most of the other passengers were gone before stepping onto the dock. As she walked toward her car, she saws that Drake was lounging beside it.

"Hi," he greeted her.

"Hello, Drake. Are you waiting for me?"

"I want to talk to you."

It was inexplicable how her pulse had leaped at the sight of him. Now Briana's heart seemed to be thudding too loudly. She told herself she must stop such silliness and behave like the mature woman she was. Drake Rutledge was her employer, nothing more. Her voice was steady when she replied. "About Patty? I haven't much to tell you yet. I spent the afternoon getting better acquainted with her—and trying to get past some of her suspicion."

"There are some things I think you should know if you're to work effectively with her. It's too involved to go into here. Can you have dinner with me?"

"I . . . I'm not dressed for it." It was the only excuse she could think of. Somehow she knew it would be safer for her to avoid being with Drake in intimate surroundings—like dimly lighted restaurants.

"We can go to my hotel," he told her, his dark eyes commanding. "There are a number of private places where the owner can entertain a guest for dinner."

A superior sort of smile curved his mouth as

he watched her. Did he suspect the reason for her reluctance was that she felt confused and vulnerable when she was alone with him? It wouldn't do at all for him to get any wrong ideas about his effect on her.

She gave in as gracefully as she could. "All right, but I can't stay long. Grandmother is expecting me."

"My car's right over there. I'll meet you in front of the hotel."

She watched him drive away from the dock, then checked her appearance in her rearview mirror before following him. Being outside all afternoon had left her with a windblown healthy look. She ran a stick of lip gloss across her lips, then pulled the pins out of her hair and brushed it thoroughly, leaving it to fall loosely about her shoulders.

Drake was waiting for her at the entrance to the hotel, and his appraising eyes seemed to approve of the changes she had made in her appearance. It occurred to her then that she might have been wiser to come as she was. Did he think she had tried to make herself attractive for him?

She had expected their conversation to take place in some private corner of the hotel dining room. Instead Drake took her up in the elevator to a private suite.

"I sometimes have to stay overnight," he explained as she followed him into a sitting room attractively decorated in earth tones, "so I keep an apartment here."

A small table next to the glass balcony doors had been set for two. A serving cart held silver-covered dishes. Evidently Drake had had their food brought up while he waited for her.

"My office is through that door, and the remainder of my private quarters are on your left." She had stopped just inside the entrance, and he looked at her with a watchful expression.

"It's very attractive."

He shrugged. "It's convenient. We'd better eat now before our food gets cold."

He held her chair for her. As she sat down, his hand rested lightly on her shoulder for a moment. She had to stifle a desire to look up at him in response. She was far too aware of his nearness, of the warmth of his hand through the thin fabric of her top. She chastised herself for reading intimacy into his every word and gesture.

He served the food from the cart, his movements deft and unselfconscious. The meal featured leg of lamb and hot lemon pie, two dishes for which the Grand Reef's chef was justly famous.

"I had lunch with Ruth and Patty at your house today, and now you're giving me dinner," Briana commented. "You're paying me enough without feeding me, too."

He sat down across from her. "I invited an attractive woman to dinner, not my employee."

"But you said you wanted to talk about Patty."

He smiled crookedly. "That, too. How did it go today?"

"I'm not sure. She was so on guard with me when I picked her up that I decided not to start the tutoring sessions today. We went for a walk on the beach and just talked. I hope she'll be in a better frame of mind the next time we meet."

"Did she open up with you? What did you talk about?"

"She feels very. . .oh, hemmed in, I suppose. Things are decided for her, she thinks, without her opinion being asked. It was inevitable that she would view our sessions as something else over which she has no control."

"She can be so foolish sometimes," he muttered darkly.

"I don't think either of us will get far with Patty unless we try to see things from her point of view," Briana ventured. "She'll be eighteen in less than a year."

"But she's a child."

"Yes, she's immature and inexperienced. But she doesn't see herself as a child, and that's the reality we have to deal with."

"Did you have a chance to speak to her about college?"

"The subject came up. She explained to me

that it was your suggestion, not hers. I don't think she's totally rejected the idea, but she's not enthusiastic about it. She did say going to college might be better than staying here after high school. Until she's eighteen. Then, she informed me, she intends to marry someone named Abel Weldon.''

"Over my dead body," Drake stated, helping himself to more vegetables from the cart.

Briana smiled. "The way Patty was talking today, I don't think she would be totally opposed to that solution, either."

They ate in silence for several moments. At length Briana asked, "Who is Abel Weldon?"

"He's a smooth operator, always looking for a way to get his hands on a dollar without working for it. He's almost thirty, and, as far as I can tell, has never held a job for more than a few months at a time. He looks good without a shirt and has a way with the ladies. I'm sure his interest in Patty stems from the fact that there's money in the family."

Briana gave him a wry look. "Of course Patty thinks he's the most handsome, exciting, charming man she's ever met. It's very flattering to a seventeen-year-old girl to be treated like a woman by a man of that age."

"Evidently," he said quietly. After a pause he continued, "I saw Ruth throw herself away on a shiftless bum, and I'll do anything in my power to keep Patty from making the same mistake."

"Have you said that to Patty?"

"I've let her know what I think of Weldon."

"Maybe that wasn't wise."

A muscle in Drake's jaw tightened, and she thought she had made him angry. But it couldn't be helped. She had to make him see he was taking the wrong approach with Patty. "What would you suggest I do?" he asked tersely.

"Try being a little more subtle. Don't be so openly critical of the man. It will only have the effect of making him more attractive to Patty. She already suspects you're up to something. She told me today she hasn't seen Abel for a couple of weeks, and she thinks you've warned him away. She assured me he loves her too much to let you frighten him off."

He pushed his plate aside and rested his elbows on the table. "My God, he's really done a number on her, hasn't he? I wonder what she would think if she knew he'd traded their great love for five thousand dollars."

Briana stared at him, then put her fork down slowly. "Are you saying you bribed him? You paid him five thousand to stay away from her?"

"I told you I'd do anything to keep them apart. Yes, I paid him off. And he was only too eager to agree, particularly after I told him that if Patty married him, they wouldn't get a dime from me. For five thousand Abel Weldon would sell out his own mother."

"Oh, Drake...." Briana felt a shiver of alarm. "If Patty learns of this, she might do something crazy. She might run away with him. Are you sure you can trust him not to tell her?"

"He won't have a chance. Part of the agreement was that he would leave the Virgins for a while. He hasn't left yet, but I'm having him watched. He'll go—one way or another."

The steel determination in his tone made her feel grateful not to be in Abel Weldon's shoes. She shuddered slightly.

Noticing her reaction, he asked, "Is the air conditioning set too low?"

"No, it isn't that. I'd better be going, anyway."

"Let's have another glass of wine on the balcony. We'll talk about something else besides my niece and her problems."

Briana found herself agreeing, even though a part of her wanted nothing so much as to leave. She had relaxed as they discussed Patty, but she tensed up again at the prospect of a more personal conversation.

Drake filled their glasses again, and they carried them out to the balcony. A soft mauve tropic dusk had settled as they ate. Briana leaned against the balcony railing and gazed down at the harbor lights, sipping her wine. Drake stood close beside her. To Briana's surprise, the silence between them became almost companionable as they finished the wine, and he smoked his pipe. Then Drake took the glasses and his pipe and set them down on a small balcony table.

When he joined her at the railing again, Briana felt a prickle of awareness along her spine. "Thank you for dinner," she said. "It was delicious, but then I hear the meals here always are." She stole a sideways glance at him. It was at such a point as this that she always pulled back from a man and fled. But she was not feeling threatened now, though she had with every man who had tried to get close to her since her divorce.

She knew that he was going to touch her before he did, but she wasn't ready for his gentleness, or for the immobilizing response she felt. "I'm glad you're here, Briana," he said huskily. His fingers moved slowly up her arms to caress her shoulders, then, inevitably, explored the sensitive column of her throat. During the whole almost overwhelming experience Briana gazed into his face as if she were mesmerized. When his thumb dipped lower to brush her collarbone, the soft skin near the V of her shirt, she drew in a shaky breath. Part of her wanted to tell him to stop, but another part wanted him to go on touching her. His hand slid down to the buttons of her blouse, and she wasn't prepared for the explosion of sensations she experienced when it slipped inside and cupped the warm swell of her breast. He must feel the thud of her heart. It pounded beneath his firm strong palm.

"Drake," she breathed finally.

His hand continued its erotic invasion. "I've wanted to touch you like this since the first moment I saw you," he murmured, and she was surprised to hear unsteadiness in his voice. A tremor ran through his body.

"Have you?" Her own voice wavered dangerously.

He pulled her against him, then cupped her face in his hands, his warm fingers entangled in her silken blond hair. "Yes, and you want me, too, I know. I can feel it."

Although his words sounded assured, there was for just a moment that old guarded expression on his face. Then a look almost of relief softened his features as his gaze fixed on her mouth, which quivered in readiness and made no pretense of evading him. When his lips touched hers, she shivered once convulsively, and then her blood seemed to gush through her veins with a deep aching rhythm. His mouth tantalized and tormented as his hands slid slowly down her back to her hips where they fitted themselves to her curves and pressed her lower body against him. She felt every throbbing inch of him, and his masculine need aroused in her longings she had never thought she'd feel again. She was no longer thinking clearly, hardly thinking at all, when her arms went around his neck and pulled him to her, and her mouth opened beneath his in wordless, hungry invitation.

He uttered a husky moan as he swept her up into his arms and carried her easily through the sitting room into a bedroom that lay in deep shadow. With her head on his shoulder, she listened enraptured to his heartbeat, deep and strong.

Drake strode to the bed, swept the dark-patterned spread back with one hand and lowered her onto the cool sheets. Then he lay down beside her, gazing into her eyes, as his gentle but insistent fingers worked at the remaining buttons of her shirt. Impatiently he brushed the opened garment aside and unfastened the front opening of her bra, exposing her breasts to his ravishing look and touch.

"You're so beautiful," he moaned, caressing her with long feathery strokes that followed the contours of her breasts and brought the tips to taut erectness.

She was drowning in a sea of sensual pleasure as his mouth claimed hers for long moments, as his fingers took one aroused nipple and teased it gently, lovingly. Then his mouth trailed a path of fire slowly down one shoulder and over her breast, enclosing its swollen peak in the tantalizing warmth of his lips. Her body arched toward his as the exquisite stimulation of his mouth sent unfamiliar sensations pulsing through her. Her body was aflame with need, a fierce need she had never known before. Dear heaven, what was happening to her?

It was in that moment of passion that her mind began to flash long-repressed images across the mirror of her memory. She pressed her eyes closed, trying to block out the pictures. Drake's lovemaking was nothing like Ricardo's. Ricardo had been violent and twisted. Drake was sensitive, yet amazingly sensual; his long muscular body trembled with the effort he was exerting to keep his own passion in check. And yet it was Ricardo's face that she saw flashing so vividly in her mind; it was the pain Ricardo had inflicted on her that she remembered.

Without wanting to, she began to shake violently and whimper, "No, no. . . ."

As she did so, Drake lifted his head, abruptly responsive to her change of mood. He took her chin in one hand, turning her face gently toward his so he could meet her eyes. He was obviously stunned at what he saw in their blue depths. "What's wrong, Briana? Did I hurt you?"

She could only shake her head and swallow convulsively.

He tried to cradle her in his arms, to kiss her again, but she turned her face away. "No, don't!" Suddenly she couldn't stand to be touched, and she pushed him away. Sitting up, she started fumbling with her clothing, trying to pull her shirt over her nakedness. But her fingers trembled with the upheaval of her emotions.

He sat up, too, staring at her in confusion. "What is it? Talk to me, Briana! Tell me what's wrong."

But she had no words to describe the scars Ricardo had left on her psyche. Even if she had, it would have been too humiliating to reveal them to Drake. Instead she blurted out, "You're paying me to tutor Patty, nothing more."

He stiffened, and even in the dimness of the bedroom she could see the instant blaze of anger in his dark eyes. "Do you really think I'd try to use our situation to take advantage of you?"

She made herself meet his furious look. "Isn't that what you were doing?"

"Dammit, Briana, that's an insult!"

She slid over to the side of the bed and got to her feet, still fumbling with the fastenings of her clothing. "I know you have the upper hand here, Drake. You own the house where grandmother and I live, and you're providing the salary that helps feed us. But my body has nothing to do with the services I'm willing to exchange in this bargain." Her words were brutal and unfair, Briana knew. She had desperately wanted him to make love to her—until the memories had overwhelmed her, blocking everything else out of her mind.

"It wasn't like that!" He sounded coldly indignant, and he had every right to be. Knowing the heights of passion that they had just shared, he could only be utterly frustrated now.

Desperation had kept Briana together so far, but she felt tears gathering at the back of her eyes. "I...I don't want to talk about it. Good night, Drake."

Before he could stop her, she ran out of the apartment, grabbing her purse as she went. Not wanting to wait for the elevator in case he followed her, she took the stairs to the ground level and her car. She felt almost ill. She was as much at fault for what had happened as Drake was. He had every right to think she had deliberately led him on. Once she was behind the wheel, she sat, shaking violently for several minutes before she felt composed enough to drive home.

CHAPTER FIVE

"...And all our yesterdays have lighted fools
The way to dusty death. Out, out brief candle!
Life's but a walking shadow, a poor player,
That struts and frets his hour upon the stage,
And then is heard no more; it is a tale
Told by an idiot, full of sound and fury,
Signifying nothing."

Leaf-dappled sunlight fell across the open book on Patty's knees. She and Briana were seated on a bench in the garden beneath the shade of an African tulip tree. Briana had been gazing up at one of the large red blossoms on the tree as her pupil read aloud from the last act of *Macbeth*, her current English-class assignment. When Patty stopped reading and glanced up, Briana looked away from the bright blossom and smiled at the girl's gravely contemplative expression.

"Quite moving, isn't it? That's the famous speech in the play."

"It makes shivers go up my backbone," Patty admitted. "It's all so sad. Macbeth's such a butcher. It seems impossible that a man like that could love, but he really loves Lady Macbeth, doesn't he?''

"Oh, yes. By this point in the play it's about the only admirable thing left in him. Even at his worst, Macbeth isn't totally evil. That's the essence of many of Shakespeare's great characters. They're both good and bad, like real people.''

"Yes,'' Patty murmured, "that's true, isn't it? Macbeth does such inhuman things, yet he seems so human that you can't help feeling sorry for him.''

"That's a rather astute observation,'' Briana stated.

Her pupil looked away, as if the compliment made her feel shy. "I feel sorry for Lady Macbeth, too. She nagged Macbeth until he committed the first murder, then she lost control of him and went insane, seeing blood on everything. I guess she just couldn't forgive herself.''

"'Thus conscience doth make cowards of us all,''' Briana quoted. "That's Shakespeare, too. From *Hamlet*.''

"I never understood what people saw in Shakespeare,'' Patty mused. "To tell the truth, *Macbeth* is the only one of his plays I've ever got through so far—with your help. I'm beginning to see why he's so famous.''

"He did know how to turn a phrase, didn't he?''

Patty looked down at her book. "There are only two more pages. Shall I finish reading it?"

"Go ahead. Then we'll talk about the theme and try to guess what sort of essay questions your teacher will ask on the exam."

As the girl resumed reading, Briana looked at her delicate profile. This was their fourth tutoring session, and for the first time Patty seemed truly interested in what they were doing. She had been friendlier and more at ease today, too, which made Briana hope that she was coming to trust her. That, she knew, was the key to how much they could accomplish together.

After Patty had finished reading, they discussed the play for another half hour before quitting. Then Patty gathered up her books and papers and carried them into the house.

Seeing that they were through studying for the day, Ruth called to Briana from the patio. "Come and have a cold drink with me before you go."

Briana joined her gladly, and as she seated herself in one of the patio chaises, Ruth handed her a tall frosty glass. It was the same pineapple-coconut drink that Greta had prepared for them the day Drake had first brought Briana there.

She sipped her drink slowly, savoring the cold tangy flavor. "Mmm. Just what I needed after *Macbeth*."

"How is Patty doing?"

"Today I think she was interested in spite of

herself. We finished reading the play, and I was pleased at how well she seems to understand it. Patty is a bright girl. I guess she just hasn't cared to apply herself to her studies.''

Ruth set her drink aside and said with concern, "It's only this year that her grades have fallen so alarmingly. Her attention has been totally absorbed by things other than school, you see. When she's at home, she spends hours in her room, lying on her bed, mooning at the ceiling. Daydreaming.''

"Seventeen is the right age for it," Briana stated. "Some girls tend to do it more than others, I guess.''

Ruth nodded. "Has Drake told you about Abel Weldon?''

Briana hesitated, unsure as to how much to reveal. Did Ruth know about the money Drake had paid Abel Weldon? "He mentioned the man," she compromised. "He certainly disapproves of his seeing Patty. I assume you agree with him?''

"Absolutely! He's too old for her, and he's not reliable. Well, he's just all wrong for Patty. I know I'm going to sound like a prejudiced mother when I say this, but he's simply not good enough for my daughter. She can't see it, of course.''

"She's in love," Briana ventured, "or probably infatuated. But she thinks it's love.''

"She's sure to find out how wrong she is in

time, but I'm afraid it won't be soon enough to stop her making a mistake that might ruin her life.''

Briana gave Ruth a sympathetic look. The two women had fallen into the habit of talking for a while after each tutoring session. Briana liked Drake's sister and was coming to think of her as a friend. ''There seem to be some things we can only learn by experience,'' she said sympathetically.

Ruth was thoughtful for a moment. She glanced toward the house before she said in a low voice, ''Did you know that Drake paid Weldon to stay away from Patty?''

Briana took a long breath and nodded. ''Yes, he told me.''

Ruth got to her feet with a restless movement, and thrusting her hands into the deep pockets of her cotton wraparound skirt, she started pacing nervously. ''I'm not sure he's handling this thing in the right way. Patty can be as stubborn as a mule. If she ever finds out what Drake has done....'' She cast another furtive glance toward the house, then returned to her chair and sat down on the edge, toying with the straw in her empty glass.

''I have the same uneasy feeling about this that you do,'' Briana said. ''I told Drake so, too. Apparently he thinks it's worth the risk. He said he'd do anything to keep the two of them apart.'' She frowned slightly. ''Let's hope that Patty doesn't find out about it. But if she does, maybe she'll realize that Weldon doesn't really care for her, not if he can be bought off so easily."

Ruth's dark eyes were melancholy. "Drake's adamant about this because he saw me make the same mistake Patty seems determined to make. He knows what I went through in my marriage, and he's bent on saving Patty from a similar fate." She smiled ruefully. "I sometimes think that Drake is wary of marriage for himself precisely because of my mistake, because he saw how painful marriage can be when it isn't right. He once confessed that he has seen very few happy marriages in his lifetime." She studied Briana for a moment. "The day he first brought you here, I thought maybe you were the woman who would change his mind."

Briana felt her cheeks grow warm, and she gave a nervous laugh. "I can't think of anyone less qualified than I. My own marriage was a disaster. I was twenty, but not much less naive than Patty is now. The man I thought I married turned out to be a figment of my romantic imagination." She shuddered involuntarily. "It was a dreadful six months—until I got up enough courage to leave Ricardo."

"But you're making a new life for yourself," Ruth said. "And it didn't take you seven years to make the decision, as it did me. In fact, I didn't leave my husband; he left me. He simply disappeared one day."

"Did you ever hear from him again?"

"No. I heard via the grapevine that he'd gone to Australia to work on a sheep station. He's probably been a dozen places since then. He was a rolling stone."

"Does Patty ask about him?"

"Not anymore. I try never to criticize him in her hearing, and so I don't think she resents him. She hardly remembers him, really." She lifted her shoulders slightly. "But who can say what goes on in someone else's secret thoughts? I...I guess it's possible that Patty remembers more about her father than I realize. She might see something in Abel Weldon that reminds her of Tom."

"From what you've said, they're alike in certain ways."

Ruth frowned thoughtfully. "Maybe I should have been more open with Patty about Tom and why our marriage ended. Of course, it was a long time before I myself could see things with any objectivity. He'd been gone more than a year before I finally admitted that I had to divorce him and make a home for Patty and me. I had to stop hoping that he'd change, that he'd come back a different man. One day I'd decide to file for a divorce, and the next I'd decide to wait a while longer. I kept changing my mind for months. I'm not sure I could have done it even then without Drake's support. I wasn't as decisive as you, you see. When you saw your marriage wasn't going to work, you made a decision and left.''

"Maybe I had stronger reasons than you for terminating my marriage," Briana said quietly. "And there were no children involved.''

Ruth looked at her expectantly, but when Briana didn't elaborate, she said, "One thing's certain. If I ever marry again, I'm going to make sure I know what I'm getting into before I make any vows. One mistake like that makes you cautious. The fact that I failed once is always there in the back of my mind. Do you feel that way?''

"I've put that period of my life behind me," Briana said quietly. "I try to look forward, not back.''

Briana thought about that conversation with Ruth on the ferry returning to St. Thomas. Her own last words had been said as much to convince herself as in response to Ruth. But in all honesty she knew she had not fully succeeded in putting her marriage and Ricardo behind her. Her reaction to Drake's lovemaking that night in his hotel suite proved it.

Since her marriage, no man had aroused her, had made her feel any degree of sensual pleasure—until Drake. She had thought that it would never happen for her again, that Ricardo had killed that part of her forever. But those long dormant sensations had stirred when Drake had touched her. And they had come

fully, clamoringly to life as she had wanted
Drake that night. Yet her memories of Ricardo
had intruded, had made her freeze and turn
away. Would she ever be able to be warm and
trusting and giving with a man again?

With time and patience Drake might be the
man who could help her learn to love again. But
she probably wouldn't be given the chance to
find out. She hadn't seen him since that night in
his suite. She knew she'd been unfair to him,
that the things she'd said had been cruel and in-
sulting. He evidently meant to avoid another
meeting except on an employer-employee basis.
As for Briana, she was torn between wanting to
see him and the fear that when she did, there
would be only contempt for her in his eyes.

It was better not to dwell on what had happened with Drake, she told herself. She forced
her thoughts back to Patty and to their session
that afternoon. The next time Drake asked
about his niece's progress, she would at least
have something encouraging to report.

The next time she met with Patty, her English
exam on *Macbeth* would be behind her. Briana
felt optimistic about how her pupil would score
on the test, and a good grade would be some
much needed positive reinforcement for her.

WHEN SHE WENT to Patty's school on Wednesday, Briana felt as anxious as if she were the one
who had taken the exam. She found a parking

space near the front entrance. Students were already coming out of the building as she turned off the motor and searched the crowd.

Ordinarily Patty was one of the first to appear, but Briana didn't see her. She was probably chatting with friends and would be out shortly. Briana waited until the students had scattered in all directions, and the wide front steps of the building were deserted. After she had waited another five minutes and Patty still hadn't come, she got out of her car and entered the school.

There was no one in the hall. Finally she found a secretary in the main office and said, "I'm looking for Patty Heyward. She was supposed to meet me out front fifteen minutes ago. Have you seen her?"

The woman, who sat at a large cluttered desk, looked slightly harried. "Not this morning, as I recall. Wait a minute. I'll see what class she had last period and check with the teacher."

She looked quickly through a card file, then said, "Chemistry. Mr. Stapleton's probably in the staff lounge. I'll go speak to him."

Briana paced about the cramped office for a few minutes, glancing frequently out the window, from which she had a view of the entrance. Finally the secretary returned with a tall, thin middle-aged woman.

"Mr. Stapleton went home for lunch. This is Patty's English teacher, Miss Mallory."

"We've met once before, at the beginning of the term. How are you, Miss Mallory?" Briana extended her hand.

"Just fine, thank you. It's nice to see you again. Patty's work is improving, by the way. I've already corrected the test she took yesterday afternoon. She scored an eighty-eight."

"That's good news!" Briana exclaimed. "She studied hard for it. Does she know her results yet?"

"I wanted to tell her just before lunch," Miss Mallory said, "but she's absent."

"I didn't know that. I wonder why her mother didn't call to let me know she wouldn't be at school today?"

"Oh, she was here for a while. She told Emily Herr, her second-period teacher, that she wasn't feeling well and was leaving school for the day. That was more than an hour ago. Emily mentioned it to me before she left for the noon hour because she knew I'd been looking for her."

"Patty's mother may be trying to reach me now. I'm sorry to interrupt your lunch."

Briana left the building and returned to her car. Before starting the motor, she glanced once more up and down the streets. As she did so, she caught sight of a girl, still more than a block away, running toward her. It was Patty.

Briana settled back against the car seat and waited. For someone who supposedly wasn't feeling well, Patty was putting a great deal of energy into running. A flicker of suspicion ran through Briana.

Patty reached the car, opened the passenger door and sank into the seat, gasping for breath. Her face was red, and she was perspiring freely. Clearly she had been running for some distance.

When she could speak, Patty gulped out, "Thank goodness you're still here. I was afraid...I'd missed you."

"You almost did. I talked to Miss Mallory and found out you'd left school more than an hour ago. I was about to drive away when I saw you." She watched Patty push her long hair away from her face and slump back against the seat. "How are you feeling?"

The girl darted a quick look at her. Unaccountably she looked as though she were about to cry. "Okay."

"I thought you'd be home by now."

Patty's fingers made tiny pleats in the navy skirt of her school uniform. She wouldn't meet Briana's eyes. "I...I missed the ferry, and then...since I was feeling better, I thought I might as well come and meet you after all."

Briana knew instinctively that the girl was lying. "Where did you really go, Patty?"

Patty glanced at her a bit defensively. "I told you, I went down to the dock."

Briana pressed her lips together on a retort. Calling Patty a liar wouldn't accomplish anything. In fact, it would probably destroy the tentative rapport she had begun to establish with the girl. Patty's trust would be withdrawn, and Briana might not be able to win it back. She glanced at her wristwatch. "We've missed another ferry, it seems. We have time for a sandwich somewhere before the next one leaves. Any place special you want to go?"

"I like Arby's," Patty said as Briana started the car and pulled away from the curb.

When they were seated at a table in the fast-food restaurant, Briana said, "Miss Mallory told me you scored an eighty-eight on the *Macbeth* exam. I'm proud of you."

"That's nice," said Patty with a surprising lack of enthusiasm. "I thought I'd done pretty well on it. Several of the essay questions covered the things we talked about."

Nonplussed, Briana picked up her roast-beef sandwich and began to eat. Patty took a few bites of her own sandwich, then put it down and stared out the window as she sipped her cola. Normally Patty would have been excited over doing so well on the exam. She obviously had something else on her mind, something that was of more importance to her at the moment than school or grades. Whatever it was, she seemed deeply worried about it.

Briana tried to draw her out with questions about the exam, but Patty's answers were absentminded monosyllables. She acted like someone who had sustained a shock.

Only when they returned to the car did Patty seem to rouse herself from her absorption. "Briana, you're my friend, aren't you?"

Briana was instantly on guard. "I want to be. Why?"

The girl's brown eyes were wide and earnest. "I have to ask a big favor of you."

Briana drove toward the dock. After a moment she asked, "What favor?"

"Promise you won't tell mother or Uncle Drake that I left school early today."

"I won't lie for you, Patty."

"It wouldn't be lying," Patty pleaded. "I'm sure they won't ask. Just don't volunteer the information. Please!"

Briana parked her car, and they got out. "I'd feel better if I knew where you went," she said as they boarded the ferry. "I know you weren't here at the dock all that time."

"I can't tell you."

They found seats at the back. Patty stared glumly out at the water as they started across the bay. Briana watched her, knowing that if she told Ruth or Drake that Patty had left school early and gone somewhere alone, the girl would interpret it as a betrayal. Finally she said, "I won't volunteer anything, Patty, but I won't tell an out-and-out lie, either."

Patty turned to her with a grateful look. "Thank you, Briana. I'm sure you won't have to lie."

Still, when they arrived at the house and Ruth commented upon their lateness, Briana felt extremely uncomfortable as she said, "We decided to have lunch before we left St. Thomas. I hope you weren't worried."

"I don't worry as long as I know Patty is with you," Ruth assured her, increasing her feeling of guilt.

Perhaps to smooth things over, Patty cut in. "Guess what, mother? I scored eighty-eight on the *Macbeth* exam."

As she had known it would, the news diverted her mother's attention from their late arrival.

"That's wonderful, dear! I knew you could do it if you applied yourself."

Patty glanced at Briana. "Well, we'd better get to work. I want to go over my history assignment with you."

Ruth beamed at her daughter's apparent interest in her schoolwork and suggested they use the patio for their session since she would be in the kitchen with Greta.

During the two hours they spent on the history assignment, Patty remained distracted, however. Finally Briana's patience ran out. "That's enough for today. I hope you'll be more attentive next time."

Patty closed her book. "I'll try to be, and thanks for—" she glanced over her shoulder "—well, you know what for."

"I only hope," responded Briana pointedly, "that I never have cause to regret it."

Patty looked rather sheepish, but before she had to reply, she looked toward the house and exclaimed, "Hello, Uncle Drake! You're home early."

Drake strolled over to where they were sitting, his glance going from one to the other. He didn't smile as he held Briana's gaze. "I wanted to speak to you before you left."

"How did you get here?" Briana asked. "Patty and I brought your Pontiac to the house."

"I called Ruth from Dodie's shop, and she picked me up."

Patty gathered her books hastily. "Checking up on me, huh?" She was obviously eager to get away. "Well, I'll let Briana tell you how I'm doing. I still have some studying to do before dinner. See you Friday, Briana."

When Patty was gone, Drake said abruptly, "Let's walk."

Briana nodded and followed him along the path that wound through the extensive flower-and-shrub gardens east of the house. Then the path widened so that there was room to walk side by side. Drake's hands were thrust into the pockets of his cream-colored trousers as he walked. He looked almost grim.

His silence made Briana feel terribly self-conscious. Finally she said, "Patty's doing much better. She did well on her last English test."

"Ruth told me," he stated, cutting her off.

"She also told me you and Patty were late getting home today."

Briana darted a quick sideways look at his dark expression. "We ate lunch in Charlotte Amalie."

They had reached a secluded corner of the garden where four white wrought-iron chairs were arranged invitingly beneath a cluster of palm trees. He muttered something she couldn't hear, then halted abruptly to look down at her. His expression was tense. "Is that all you did?"

Briana's uneasiness increased as she gazed at him. "I don't understand what you mean. I picked up Patty at school, and we had lunch." She realized that she was clenching her hands in her nervousness and hastily relaxed them.

His expression grew even more serious, and Briana's heart leaped irregularly. Her eyes were drawn to the scar that slashed his cheek, and when her gaze returned to meet his, he smiled. It was not a pleasant smile. Suddenly she realized he knew she was trying to cover up for Patty. She took a step away from him and opened her mouth to say something, but she didn't get a word out before he caught her arm and pulled her back to face him.

"We haven't finished talking," he said silkily.

"You're hurting my arm," she gasped. He eased his hold slightly but didn't release her. His dark eyes were blazing, and she knew beyond a doubt that he was angry.

When she relaxed, he finally let go of her. But his fingers almost absently caressed her arm with an oddly gentle touch. "Don't lie to me, Briana," he said.

"I...I'm not." She fought down an irrational fear and strove to keep her voice steady. But it quavered slightly. His expression changed, became knowing, and she imagined she saw the contempt that she had feared to see in him. He pulled her slowly closer to him, a hint of triumph in his eyes. The tension between them altered subtly.

Her throat went dry. "Drake?"

His brilliant eyes followed the smooth clean line of her throat downward, and his hand came out to curve around the back of her head. She couldn't move, not that she wanted to. She stared into the velvet depths of his eyes and felt suddenly as if she were drowning in them. While he held her gaze locked in his, his fingers caressed the line of her jaw, then moved to trace her lips.

Drunk with the honeyed warmth that poured through her veins and her senses, Briana sighed helplessly. The tip of her tongue came out to moisten her lips, parting them in an unwitting invitation.

With a deep groan Drake pulled her toward him and covered her mouth with his own. Crushed against the firm lean maleness of him, she felt herself melting with desire, and instinctively she arched her body against his. Her breasts were instantly taut and aching to press against his flesh without the barrier of fabric that now prevented that more intimate contact.

His mouth continued its sensual plunder, deepening their searing kiss as one of his arms moved down to encircle her narrow waist, locking her against him. His other hand explored the nape of her neck beneath the curtain of her hair, then traveled along the ridge of her collarbone and slowly, irrevocably downward until it closed possessively over one breast. His palm stroked the taut tip, sending an electric response radiating outward from the sensitive aureole. The incredibly compelling, hypnotic sensuality in his lovemaking made Briana's whole body yearn to be possessed by this man. A soft incoherent plea escaped her.

"Briana," he whispered, his mouth leaving hers and moving hungrily along her flushed skin to her delicate earlobe. "What are you doing to me?" His arm tightened, pressing her almost fiercely against the warmth of his body.

"I . . . I don't know what you mean," she got out desperately.

"Don't you?" His mouth moved back and hovered tantalizingly above hers. "If I didn't know better, I'd swear you were enjoying this as much as I am."

"Oh, Drake!" she murmured helplessly. "Isn't that obvious?"

His dark eyes studied her for a long moment, then he released his breath in a sigh. "You've certainly changed your tune since the other night."

His mention of that evening in his suite made her spine stiffen, her cheeks burn. She lowered her eyes and stared at the crisp dark curls in the open neck of his shirt. "I...I'm sorry for the way I acted that night," she gulped. "I didn't really mean it when I accused you of taking advantage of the...the situation."

His dark brows rose. "Didn't you?"

"No...." She wanted desperately to make him understand, but she couldn't bring herself to tell him about her marriage and what it had done to her. "I don't know what came over me," she said finally.

He gave a laugh and she lifted her head to stare at him in surprise. A coldness had replaced the fire that had been in his dark eyes moments before; she was totally confused.

"Are you trying to tell me you aren't playing some kind of game with me?"

"Yes!" she gasped. "I mean, no, I'm not!"

"You merely...like me, right?" His tone was heavy with sarcasm. "You're even starting to trust me."

"I...I'm trying to."

Abruptly he let go of her, looking down at her with dangerously narrowed eyes. "You're a clever minx, Briana," he said. "You almost convince me you're telling the truth."

"When...when have I ever given you reason to think I'd lie to you?" she stammered.

"Just a few minutes ago," he grated between clenched teeth. "You lied to me about where Patty was earlier this afternoon."

"I told you we had lunch in Charlotte Amalie. That's the truth!" She gulped, swallowing her guilt.

"I wouldn't even dignify it by calling it a half-truth," he retorted. "Patty left school this morning and went to Abel Weldon's apartment. I told you I was having him watched. Did you forget that? She was with him for forty-five minutes before she returned to school and met you."

Briana was unable to meet the outrage in his eyes. She turned away from him, brushing back her hair from her face with hands that trembled. There was a long pulsing silence. Finally she said softly, "I didn't know. She wouldn't tell me where she had gone."

"But you decided to conspire with her against Ruth and me."

She whirled about, facing him. "It wasn't like that...." She faltered as a new thought struck her. "Oh, Drake, you don't think he told her about the money, do you?"

"I saw him just before I came here. He swore he didn't."

Briana felt sharp relief, even though his angry stance had not relaxed. "She...she begged me not to tell you that she'd left school early," Briana stated quietly. "She's beginning to trust me, you see. I didn't want to destroy that if I could help it."

"How touching."

"You're being unfair," she flared. "But since you obviously think I'm not to be trusted with your niece, I'll tender my resignation as of now." She turned on her heel, but before she had taken a step, his strong hands gripped her shoulders and pulled her back to face him.

"No, you won't," he said in a low inexorable voice. "I can't find anyone as suitable as you for this job, and you know it. And you need the money. So don't make any grand gestures." He gazed at her searchingly. "Maybe you're not so different from your brother and the other Ivensens after all. I warn you, Briana, don't lie to me again."

His words hit her with the force of a blow. She was shaking again, this time with fury. "My brother stole from you, but he repaid what he'd taken with our family home. I'm not trying to excuse him, but how dare you toss all the Ivensens in the same basket with Erik!"

"Because that may be where they belong," he snapped.

She stiffened. "Leaving Erik aside, what did the rest of my family ever do to you?"

"Why don't you ask your grandmother?"

Warned somehow by the flash of fire in his eyes, Briana seethed silently for a long moment. Then she said, "Let go of me, Drake. I don't want to hear any more of your groundless accusations against my family."

"She never told you, did she?"

"She?"

"Margaret. And even now I can see you'd rather not know the truth."

Briana pulled away from him, and he didn't try to hold her. His hands fell to his sides.

Without another word she turned and hurried down the path the way they had come. Drake Rutledge was an unreasonable, impossible man, she told herself fiercely. She almost hated him! Yet she had quivered with desire when he kissed her, when he held her in his arms.... There had to be something radically wrong with her. For the second time she found herself attracted to a man who was arrogant and self-willed. And even though she sensed that Drake would not be cruel in the way that Ricardo had been, he was nevertheless relentless. He had made it plain that he had something against her family—not just Erik, but all of them, herself included. She would have had to fight her own weakness around him. He wouldn't hesitate to use it to his own advantage.

CHAPTER SIX

BRIANA WAS STILL UPSET when she got home. She didn't know what had happened in the past to make Drake dislike her family so much, but she was convinced it went beyond what Erik had done. That, of course, would have been enough. Yet he had employed her to tutor his niece, so she had to assume he didn't hold her brother's actions against her. Maybe he had built up something that happened in his childhood into a major case against the family. She realized now that her grandmother was certainly not in his good graces.

She recalled he had wanted to see Margaret the day he'd come to the house. Had he been waiting all these years to strike back because of some imagined childhood slight? But if he was so bitter against the Ivensens, why had he employed Erik in the first place? Why had he employed her and allowed her and Margaret to stay on in the family house?

Clearly there was more to this than met the eye. Briana hoped Margaret was feeling well enough to have dinner with her, for she meant to question her about what Drake had said.

When she entered the house, Ida was setting two places at the dining-room table. "Oh, good. Grandmother's coming in to dinner, right?" she asked.

"Yes'm. She in high spirits this evenin'," the old woman replied.

"Any particular reason?"

"Mr. Erik called."

Briana bristled inwardly at the mention of her brother's name. "And how is Erik?"

"Jes fine, judgin' by the way Mistress Ivensen been actin' since he called."

Briana went to her room to freshen up, and when she returned to the dining room, Margaret was seated in her place at the head of the table. Briana kissed her cheek before taking the other chair. "Good evening, grandmother. You're looking well today."

"I'm feeling better, dear. I talked to Erik this afternoon."

"So Ida informed me. Is he still in New York?"

"Oh, yes. He's found a nice apartment and is trying to decide among several job offers."

Briana picked up her fork and stabbed a piece of lettuce from her salad, eating it with deliberate slowness. Erik hadn't changed after his brush with incarceration, it seemed. Didn't he realize that Drake Rutledge could have had him arrested? She wondered suddenly why Drake hadn't chosen that course of action.

In any case, she doubted seriously that Erik had several job offers to choose from. He was probably living on the remainder of the money he had embezzled from the Rutledge Corporation—and living well, if she knew her brother. With his spending habits the money wouldn't last long, though. When it ran out, would his inflated opinion of what the world owed him simply because he was an Ivensen collapse? She doubted it.

"What else did he say?" she asked.

"He contacted one of Frederik's old friends, David Schwitzer, and the Schwitzers have taken him under their wing. They've introduced him to people in their social circle and invited him for weekends in the country. Isn't that nice?"

"Wonderful," murmured Briana.

"I feel so much better having talked to him. I took him to task for waiting so long to call, but he explained it's quite a project, getting the phone company to install a new phone. He hasn't had access to one until today."

Why couldn't he have used the Schwitzers' phone, Briana thought sarcastically. But of course, she knew the answer to that. It had taken Erik this long to get up enough courage to talk to Margaret.

"I couldn't stay angry with him," Margaret was saying. "He was so worried that I'd never forgive him. I think he was even a little concerned that I'd be upset over his leaving his job here. Naturally I assured him I agreed wholeheartedly with his decision. He asked all sorts of questions about Drake Rutledge. When I told him you were now working for the man, he sounded quite surprised. He wanted to know how that had come about.''

I'll just bet he did, Briana told herself bitterly.

''I told him you had some notion about gaining teaching experience.''

''What did he say to that?''

''He said it might not be a bad idea, and that I ought to support you in it. Then he said something quite odd. He asked if you'd mentioned moving into a smaller place, that you'd once spoken of it to him. Whatever made you suggest a thing like that, Briana?''

''It was only a passing notion,'' she improvised, chafing at the knowledge that Erik was drawing her into his lies. He must have quickly surmised that their grandmother knew nothing about the transfer of ownership of their house. That must have taken a load off his shoulders. She might very well disown him if she knew the truth, and Briana suspected that in spite of his lack of concern for his grandmother's well-being, he still needed her good opinion of him, her assurances that he was special.

"Well, I should hope so! You know very well I'll never leave this house."

Never, thought Briana, *is a long time.* But she didn't say it aloud. There was no point in taking her anger at Erik out on her grandmother. "Speaking of Drake Rutledge," she said instead, "I had an interesting conversation with him today."

"I can't imagine what that man could have to say that would interest you in the slightest," Margaret said with a sniff. "He simply is not our kind, Briana. I wish you would reconsider and give up this job."

"Unfortunately I haven't several job offers to choose from as Erik has," Briana told her. "After what Drake said today, though, I'm rather amazed that he employed me in the first place. He seems to harbor some ill feelings against our family."

"Oh?" Margaret put down her fork and stared at Briana. "Well, surely it only proves what I've been saying all along. Your working for him is unwise. You're playing with fire, and you don't seem to realize it."

"I don't remember ever seeing Drake Rutledge until that day he walked in here, wanting to know where Erik had filed some important papers," Briana replied. It was the story she had fabricated to explain Drake's appearance at the house on the very day Erik had left. "He offered me a job that I needed, and I took it. I don't understand how that could be playing with fire.''

"You don't understand because you don't know him. Oh, you saw him as a child many times, but you were too young to remember." Margaret took a roll from the warming basket and split it open to add butter. "You should be glad you don't."

"Why? What happened that was so dreadful?"

Margaret's face had gone quite still. "He was a dangerously violent boy, and I'm sure he's a dangerously violent man."

Briana could see that Margaret was growing impatient with the topic, but she couldn't let it go. "That's your opinion, but it doesn't tell me anything that makes me agree with you. What actually happened between Drake and our family?"

"Surely he gave you his jaundiced version!"

"No, he didn't. He told me to ask you."

Margaret pushed her chicken casserole around on her plate for several moments before answering. She seemed to be trying to marshal her thoughts, and she was plainly upset. But Briana had to know what was behind Drake's inordinate resentment. "Grandmother, please tell me," she begged.

When Margaret looked up from her plate, two bright spots burned on her withered cheeks. "Drake Rutledge's father died when Drake was very young. After that his mother, Pearl, became a...a loose woman, little more than a prostitute.'' She enunciated each word distinctly, but she was so agitated that her fork trembled in her hand.

Briana felt a stirring of alarm. After all, Margaret was old and unwell. ''I didn't mean to upset you, grandmother. I'd just like to understand Drake better since I'm working for him.'' She hesitated, noticing that the ruddy color was leaving Margaret's face.

''I'm all right,'' the old woman said eventually. ''Exactly what are you asking?''

''Even if Drake's mother was as...as undesirable as you say, I don't understand what that has to do with his feelings about our family.''

''When I learned of Pearl's low morals, I fired her. That's the basis for Drake Rutledge's feelings. She...she was supporting her family, but there were some things I simply couldn't tolerate. I've no idea what Pearl told her children—a pack of lies, you can be sure—but they chose to blame your father and me for their loss of income.''

''They must have been frightened and desperate.''

''That wasn't my fault! Surely you can see why I had to let the woman go.''

''I'm not certain I do, grandmother. Was she behaving immorally here in the house?''

Margaret took a deep breath, then said, ''We

had several servants then, a number of them young men. I simply could not keep a woman like that in the house. It would have been asking for trouble.''

Just then Ida appeared with the dessert, a fresh strawberry tart. Briana watched her quick competent movements as she placed the tart and a pot of coffee on the table. "Nenie Ida, we were just talking about Pearl Rutledge," she said. "Do you remember her?"

"Yes'm. I remember Pearl, all right." Ida stopped beside the table, her hands clasped in front of her. She darted a glance at Margaret, who was looking at her piercingly. "She work here for a while, and then she leave. That's all I know," Ida concluded with a shake of her head. "If you need me, I be in the kitchen."

"I don't want you quizzing Ida about this," Margaret stated when the kitchen door had swung shut behind the black woman. "Since you seem determined to persist with it, I'll tell you everything. Then there will be no need for you to bother Ida with your questions."

Briana poured the coffee as Margaret transferred a small portion of the tart to her dessert plate. Finally the old woman continued, "A few days after I let Pearl go, Drake Rutledge came here with a knife and tried to murder your father. He was big for his age, as big as a man, and unbelievably strong. He came in here shrieking irrationally. He was completely out of control."

"My God!" Briana searched her grandmother's rigid face. The faded blue eyes met hers unblinkingly. She was telling the truth, at least the truth as she saw it. "He actually tried to kill father?"

The fuzzy image that had flashed across her mind the first time she saw Drake came back with more vividness. She must have seen Drake attack her father. She remembered their grappling for the knife, and in the struggle Drake's face had been slashed. Blood. There was so much blood. She remembered that now, too. And then someone—one of the servants probably—had grasped her hand and pulled her into the house. She had been crying, had struggled to get free and go back to her father. But she'd been carried to her room, told that her father was all right, and that she was not to worry about what she had seen.

"I remember," she said at last. "I was there, wasn't I?"

Margaret nodded. "You seemed to have forgotten it. You blocked it out of your mind, I suppose. I didn't want to bring it back. It was such a frightening experience, and you were only five."

"But I don't understand why Drake attacked father when you were the one who fired his mother."

Margaret's thin shoulders lifted slightly. "I told you, he wasn't rational. And who knows what reason his mother gave him for the loss of her job. I suppose she thought I'd discussed it with Frederik before I fired her, but I hadn't. Frederik didn't like being bothered with domestic problems. He left all of that to me. I saw no reason to discuss my decision with him before I spoke to Pearl, and besides, he was away on business when everything came to a head." Her expression was troubled. "You do see that I couldn't wait for his return, don't you?"

"I guess so," Briana murmured, trying to take in the situation as her grandmother had described it.

"Well, now perhaps you understand why I've been so opposed to your working for Drake Rutledge."

Briana nodded, wanting suddenly to be alone, to try to sort out her twenty-year-old memories.

Margaret took a single bite of her dessert, then laid her fork down abruptly. "I seem to have lost my appetite for strawberries. If you'll excuse me, dear, I think I'll retire early. I feel weary all at once."

Belatedly Briana regretted having pressed her grandmother to relate what must have been the most frightening experience of her life. "I've tired you with all my questions. I'm sorry," she said apologetically.

"It's all right. Maybe now that your curiosity has been satisfied, we shan't have to speak of it again." Margaret left the table, adding, "I'll see you in the morning. Good night, dear."

Briana sipped at a second cup of coffee before going to her own bedroom. It was still too early to sleep, but she showered and donned a thin short nightgown. Then she opened the long French windows in her room and pulled a wicker chair in front of them to catch the breeze that was blowing in from the harbor. She sat there in the dark for a long time, pondering over Margaret's revelations. Now she understood Drake's attitude toward her family. Undoubtedly Margaret was right, and Pearl Rutledge had blamed both Frederik and his mother for the loss of her job. Pearl's version of the event must have been extremely inflammatory to send Drake back here with a knife. Yet it was still hard to imagine even a proud, hot-tempered fourteen-year-old boy reacting so violently to his mother's losing a job, no matter what story she'd told him.

Briana no longer doubted that Drake had done what Margaret said he did. Her grandmother's explanation had jolted those fragile images in Briana's mind and settled them firmly in place in her memory. She had seen Drake attack her father. Even as a child of five, she had understood that Drake hated her father and wanted to kill him. She understood, too, that he resented Margaret and held Erik in contempt. All of which made her own situation inexplicable. After all that, why was Drake trying to help her? Surely he must have known there could be no worse revenge against Margaret than to force her out of her family home. So why hadn't he done it? Why was he allowing them to stay in the house, allowing Margaret to remain oblivious to the fact that its ownership had changed hands?

She had felt a strong attraction to Drake from the beginning, and she had sensed he was drawn to her, as well. But was he? Why had he really tried to make love to her that night in his suite? She had felt desire in him, but had it stemmed from a need to gain mastery over another Ivensen, a desire to humiliate her?

The thought came like a sharp pain. Drake was such a complex man. Could she never be absolutely sure of his motives? One thing was certain. She must be alert and on guard with him from now on.

THE OPPORTUNITY to put this decision to the test came sooner than she'd expected. On Friday, the day of her next tutoring session, she stuffed a towel and her bikini into a beach bag before she went to meet Patty. Ruth had told her repeatedly that she was welcome to use their private section of the beach anytime. She decided to take her at her word and spend an hour or so on the beach later that afternoon.

Even though their session lasted longer than

usual, she didn't abandon her plan. Neither Patty nor Ruth was in a mood to join her, so she changed into her bikini at the house and went down to the beach alone.

No one was in sight, even on the public sections of the beach. It was already dinner time for most people. Briana was grateful for the privacy. She felt a need to be alone, to try to release some of the tension that had built up in her recently. Deliberately she freed her mind of worry and focused it on relaxing her body. She'd left her wristwatch at the house by design; she didn't want to know what time it was. For a while she swam in the water close to shore, then she lay on her beach towel, letting the last rays of the day's sun caress her skin. It was getting late, and she knew she ought to be heading back before long. But still she lingered, giving in to the lethargy that slowly crept over her.

She was dozing when she sensed, more than heard, someone's approach. When she sat up, she saw Drake walking toward her over the sand. He was wearing yellow swimming trunks and had a beach towel draped over one broad tanned shoulder.

She was tempted to leave immediately, but she knew Drake would interpret a hasty departure as fear of facing him. She would have to stay for a few minutes before she could leave casually.

His dark eyes ran over her brief black bikini.

The appraisal, as it was probably calculated to do, made her feel naked. "Ruth told me you were down here," he said as he spread his towel beside hers.

"I'm sorry she had to pick you up. I've let the time get away." He didn't respond, and she continued, "Do you come to the beach often?"

"Hardly ever. I play tennis at the hotel, but that's about all the recreation I have time for."

"Then why are you here today?"

He sat down on his towel, his knees drawn up, his long arms circling them loosely. His expression, when he turned to look at her, was amused. "Do you think I'm following you?"

"Well, are you?"

He flicked her a teasing glance, then gazed out at the sea. "What if I am? This is my property."

It was impossible to carry on a civil conversation with the man. Briana suspected he was deliberately goading her. She didn't want to give him the satisfaction of becoming angry, however, so she got to her feet in one swift movement and ran toward the water. She waded in until the waves were lapping about her waist, then dove under. When she came up again, she floated idly, looking out across the sea to the crimson horizon. She heard Drake when he dove in, as well, heard him swim over to her side.

When he stood up, she couldn't help watching how the water ran down his muscled arms, his bronzed skin. Her gaze followed the tapering line of dark hair that began on his chest and traveled down his stomach, disappearing in the low waistband of his trunks. Quickly she glanced away again.

"Are you afraid of me, Briana?"

She stood up herself, flinging dripping strands of blond hair away from her face. "No. Should I be?"

He looked at her steadily. "That depends."

"On what?"

"On whether you're going to deny there's some rather potent electricity between us. If you are, I think I can prove otherwise."

She reacted instantly. "If that's a threat to renew your efforts to seduce me, forget it. You're not my type."

She saw the flare of warning in his eyes and edged away from him. "Ah, forgive me," he murmured in silken tones. "I forgot for a moment that a Rutledge is far too lowly for an Ivensen to take seriously."

Briana waded away from him until the water touched the underside of her breasts. She felt braver with more distance between them. "Oh, please," she retorted, "spare me the sorry tale of your destitute childhood. That's your convenient excuse for everything, isn't it? Did it ever occur to you that your background isn't unique?"

He dove into the water, his arms extended,

and came up next to her. His temper was clearly rising. She'd allowed him to goad her when she'd promised herself she wouldn't.

"But it is unique," he grated.

"I fail to see how."

"Apparently you didn't ask your grandmother what happened twenty years ago."

"I did ask her."

"Then she must have refused to answer." His voice was caustic. "I can just see her. No one in the world can be as haughty and unyielding as Margaret Ivensen."

Briana fought down a sudden desire to strike his face. "On the contrary, Drake. She told me everything."

"Indeed?" he asked curiously. "And what is Margaret's version of everything?"

"In a childish rage you tried to kill my father."

She saw a muscle in his jaw tighten rigidly, almost as if she had struck him. He said in a low voice, "Did she tell you why?"

"What's the point of this, Drake? I've no idea what was in your mind at the time, but the fact is that grandmother had to fire your mother. Apparently that touched off unreasonable anger in you." She looked away from him, wading farther out until the water came to her shoulders. She wished he would go back to the house and leave her alone.

But again he followed her, and this time he

got a grip on her shoulders and forced her to look at him. "Did she tell you why she fired my mother?"

Briana tried to twist out of his hands, but his fingers were like steel. She lost her temper completely. "Your mother was promiscuous! She was entirely to blame for losing her job. I know that would be hard for anyone to accept at age fourteen. But Drake, it's ridiculous to hang onto those old resentments after all this time. Grandmother wasn't to blame for what your mother was, and neither are you."

She knew before she had finished that she had said too much, but she couldn't seem to stop herself. He was staring at her with such intensity that she was actually afraid of what he might do. She watched him fighting for control and knew her temper was no match for his. Finally he flung his hands away from her as if that were the only way to prevent himself from doing her bodily harm.

"I . . . I have to go home." She started swimming to shore, but she got only a short distance before he caught her and pulled her up short, facing him. "Not until you hear the truth, Briana. No, don't try to leave until I'm finished. My mother was not promiscuous. She was merely foolish enough to fall in love with Frederik Ivensen."

Briana's heart lurched, and she shook her head in denial.

"Your father charmed her, dazzled her with gifts and promises. Then he seduced her."

"I don't believe a word of this," she whispered hoarsely.

"They were lovers for months," he went on relentlessly. "He promised to marry her, but he said he had to choose the right time. He told her that Margaret still had partial control of his inheritance, but that he'd soon have it completely in his own hands. He promised that when that time came, they'd marry and get a house of their own.

"It was a string of lies, of course, but mother was besotted. She believed every word. Then Margaret found out about their relationship. Naturally she blamed it all on my mother, accused her of beguiling poor gullible Frederik. She ordered her out of the house and told her never to come back."

Briana's face was buried in her hands as she tried to shut out the hateful words. But he wouldn't stop. "She thought Frederik loved her, that he'd find a way for them to be together. She went home and waited for him to come for her."

Briana lifted her head, her expression tortured. "He was away on business. Grandmother told me."

He stared at her for a moment. "I don't know about that, but if he was away for a while, he certainly came back. Mother saw him in town a few days later. He was with Margaret, and he pretended not to see her. When she came home, she was as pale as a ghost. I'd never seen her look so lost and hopeless.''

Briana sucked in her breath. ''Obviously you believe what you're saying, Drake. But I knew my father better than you did. He wasn't a cruel man.''

''With you he probably wasn't.'' He gazed past her across the tranquil bay. The telling seemed to have taken much of the fury out of him. Now he appeared more depressed than anything else. ''She wouldn't have told us what had happened if she'd been herself. But she was shattered. Ruth and I were there when she walked in. She started to cry and shake; it was a full-blown case of hysteria. We just sat there and stared at her while the whole story poured out between bursts of weeping. When she'd cried herself out, she went into the bedroom and shut the door. We thought she was going to sleep.''

A look of intense pain crossed his face. ''We had an old rowboat tied up down at the beach. None of us had used it in a while. Later, after Ruth and I were asleep, mother took the boat out. I don't think she meant to take her own life. She probably wasn't thinking about the danger at all. Maybe she thought the exertion of rowing would tire her so that she could fall asleep. Anyway, the wind was up that night, and the boat probably leaked. She...she never came back. Her body washed ashore two days later.''

Briana listened to the peculiarly toneless recital with growing horror. No wonder he blamed her father and grandmother for his mother's death! She couldn't bring herself to believe the things he had said about her father, but Drake's version of what had happened explained everything much better than Margaret's.

''Your grandmother's right about one thing. I was in a towering rage when I came to your house. We'd found mother's body the evening before, and I'd been picturing her like that all night. By morning I felt I had to do something to avenge her. So I decided to kill Frederik. I was beyond reason by that time. I didn't even stop to think about the houseful of servants who would come to his rescue. He was quicker than I expected, too. He fought me until the servants could drag me off him. In the process the knife slipped and cut my face. I passed out, and the next thing I knew I was in the hospital, and a doctor was sewing me up.''

His finger touched his cheek absently. ''He wasn't much of a doctor, or he'd have done a better job of it. But he didn't ask any questions, which was the important thing to your family. They didn't want any unsavory gossip getting out about Frederik.''

"Drake, I...I don't know what to say. It must have been horrible for you and Ruth."

"It was. We were very close to our mother. After my father died, she kept the family together, even though the only work she could get was as a housemaid."

Unaccountably Briana felt hot tears spring to her eyes. It was too much to accept all at once. The story couldn't be as black and white as Drake had painted it. If it were, Margaret and Frederik had deliberately contributed to Pearl's death and no telling how much emotional pain to her children. But Ruth didn't seem to harbor any resentment toward the Ivensens. That gave Briana a fleeting glimmer of hope.

At the moment she didn't want to think about it, however. She didn't want to hear any more. She had to get away. She made a sound of incoherent denial and began to swim away from him. Her arms sliced through the water with as much speed as she could generate. The only thought in her mind was to put some distance between herself and Drake Rutledge.

"What are you doing?" she heard his startled voice behind her. "It's getting dark! You're going too far out! Come back here, you little fool!"

Briana swam harder, wanting only to get beyond the sound of his voice.

CHAPTER SEVEN

SHE SWAM BLINDLY, determined to blot out Drake's hurtful words. If she swam long enough and hard enough she would be too tired to think.

The sudden sharp cramp in her foot took her unawares. She groaned as the same muscles pulled taut again, and she tried to keep herself afloat while she grabbed the cramping foot with one hand. She was amazed to see how dark it had become. She could hardly make out the shoreline. Apprehensive all at once, she looked around her. Then another cramp gripped her foot, and she went under.

She came up sputtering and gulping for air—and went under a second time. Real fear overcame her then. She began to fight the water in a panic.

"Briana! It's okay. Stop fighting!"

Drake's voice somehow penetrated the roaring in her ears, and her body was caught, confined, her head above water. It was a moment before she realized he was trying to rescue her, and she stopped struggling. She went limp against him and managed to calm herself down enough to let him grasp her under her arms and swim toward shore.

When they reached the shallows, he carried her out of the water and laid her on a towel. In the descending darkness she could barely make him out as he stood over her, his legs apart. He was breathing hard. "What the hell were you trying to do, kill yourself?" he finally managed.

She lay on her back, too spent to move, breathing as heavily as he was. "I got a cramp in my foot."

There was a long silence filled only with the sounds of their labored breathing. She closed her eyes, aware of the many unspoken things between them.

"Are you all right?"

"Yes."

He lowered himself finally to sit beside her, but she didn't open her eyes. His breathing was not as labored as before. "Briana, I'm sorry for telling you the truth about your father the way I did. I've never been known for my tact."

She was too tired to be really angry, but her eyes flew open and she retorted, "If our parents were lovers, your mother was as much to blame as father was."

He was half-reclining on one elbow, his wet hair-roughened leg touching hers. She couldn't see his expression clearly, but his tone indicated that he was scowling. "I might agree, had they been in any way equal. As it was, she was at your father's mercy.''

''Since you're being so open tonight, there's something else I'd like to know. Why did you employ Erik in the first place, feeling as you do about my family?'' she asked.

His hand touched her arm, his fingers began to knead her soft skin gently. ''Let it go now, Briana,'' he muttered, his fingers moving upward to thread through her wet hair.

''Drake,'' she began stoutly, ''don't try to divert my attention.''

He chuckled low in his throat and buried his face against her neck. ''Are you having trouble paying attention, Briana? Never mind? I know how to get it back—all of it.''

She made a halfhearted attempt to move away.

''I saved your life,'' he murmured against her skin. ''Don't I even get a thank-you?''

''Thank you,'' she managed to get out as her heart jerked with an erratic beat. The reaction wasn't from fear of him, she realized distractedly. It was prompted by something far more dangerous, something she could hardly define to herself. The more time she spent with him, the less certain she was of her own reactions, and especially of her ability to control them.

She turned her head from side to side as if to clear it and said persistently, ''Did it satisfy you, having Erik working for you? I suppose you saw some irony in turning the tables, so to speak.''

He tasted the skin of her neck with his lips and tongue. ''I admit there was some satisfaction in it,'' he told her huskily.

His hand glided down to her skimpy bikini top. With one tug he freed her breasts from the wet strip of black cloth. Lightly he brushed the back of his hand across one nipple. The night seemed to hold its breath with Briana as she waited for what he would do next. His fingers curved under the roundness of her breast, lifting it reverently while his mouth descended to savor its taste slowly. She drew in her breath with a great gulp and felt it lodge in her throat. The delicate tugging of his mouth made her quiver with delightful anguish. For a moment she was dizzy with the heat and longing he was generating in her blood. His hard length pressed against her, making clear his need, and her own body clamored to the heady fulfillment she knew he could give her.

Briana's hands clutched at his hair, her fingers caressing him restlessly. Then her fingers slid down over his hard high cheekbones to his mouth, which was filled with the sweetness of her flesh.

She couldn't let this go on, she realized dizzily. She had to have some answers before she could even begin to trust him. ''Drake!'' she gasped as his mouth slowly released her, slowly moved upward to draw further delights from her lips. She wrenched her mouth free. "Stop it! I'm trying to talk to you. You're making it extremely difficult!"

"Am I?" he murmured, tracing her full bottom lip with the tip of his tongue. "I don't think you really want to talk at all."

Her lips throbbed in response to the feathery kisses he was raining on them. "If you'd relax for once and stop fighting your instincts, we could communicate in a way that's far more enjoyable than talking."

"Oh, Drake...." She seemed to have forgotten why she had wanted him to stop. Her lips searched for and found his. He moaned as he savored the fierce sweetness of her response.

His hand moved on her soft skin, sliding down to rest against her flat stomach. Why, she wondered dazedly, did she find his touch so delightful? Her flesh beneath his was afire with longing.

His lips and tongue explored the hollow of her throat before he returned to the nectar of her mouth. Unconsciously her fingers wound themselves among the thick strands of his damp hair again, clenching fiercely as the sounds in her throat were muffled by his kisses. "You see?" he murmured against her lips. "This is so much better than talking."

As she felt the passion grow within him, she tried once more to fight her own wanton reactions. She had to think, she told herself in despair.

He had practically admitted that he'd felt some perverted pleasure having Erik in his employ. Had he had some vengeful scheme in mind when he hired him? A thought burst through her heavy languor and into her consciousness, and she blurted, "You...you're clever enough, Drake Rutledge, to have framed my brother for embezzlement."

He lifted his head, his mouth now inches above her own. "No framing was necessary." The vibrant quality of his voice was tinged with a hard edge. "Erik started stealing from me the day he started working. He wasn't even smart about it. I'm sure he had it planned when he took the job. Your brother is a lazy schemer, my lovely one. The auditor caught him within weeks."

She fought the rampant excitement still sizzling in her blood from his lovemaking. "'Schemer'!" she cried. "Isn't that the pot calling the kettle black?" She twisted from beneath him and sat up.

His body still entrapped her thighs, and she could feel his need. She stared into his eyes, dark with arousal, and hated herself for the impulse to reach out for him again.

"First you're hot, then you're cold," he said in a low husky voice. "Why the games, Briana? You want me as much as I want you. We both know it's only a matter of time until I have you."

The blatant possession in his words banished her tender impulses. He meant to have her, did he, as if she were a piece of candy to be devoured? *Have* her! The words echoed in her head. She would not be *had* by a man who hated all Ivensens! "I...I don't believe your accusations about Erik!" she cried. She had to say something to stop him from kissing her again.

She felt him grow still. "Are you calling me a liar?"

"Your story doesn't make sense," she raced on. "If you knew Erik was stealing from you from the first, why did you keep him around for eighteen months?"

"I wanted to see how far he would go."

He raised himself on one elbow, and she peered into his face, now level with her own, trying to read his expression in the waning light. "You what?" she whispered, stunned by the bald admission.

"I knew how much he owned in assets," he went on. "When he'd embezzled as much money as he was worth, I stopped him."

"You...you despicable—!" His admission pained her more than she would have thought possible. "You wanted our house all along, didn't you? You deliberately let Erik get in deeper and deeper until he'd have no choice but to sign it over to you!"

"What should I have done, Briana, slapped his hand and told him to be a good boy?"

"You... you should have fired him the moment you suspected what he was doing!"

Drake lay quite still for a moment, breathing deeply, then abruptly he sat up. She could feel the tension in him, and a part of her wanted desperately to ease it. But wounded judgment prevailed, and she felt about for her discarded bikini top. She found it finally and tried to put it on with clumsy, unsteady fingers.

"Listen to me, Drake. You may have maneuvered Erik into a corner, but I am one Ivensen you will never get a hold over!"

"Briana...." He was leaning toward her, the determined timbre of his voice spurring her to even more fevered attempts to cover herself. "You're whistling in the dark, and you know it. I don't force myself on women, ever. But you'll come around on your own when you've gathered enough courage to be honest about your feelings."

She finally got her bikini top fastened and scrambled to her feet. She wanted to deliver a final, crushing denial of his words, but nothing would come.

He got to his feet and reached for their towels. "Run along, little witch," he murmured, the hardness completely gone from his voice. "I can wait for you to come to me. I'll just keep reminding myself how wonderful it's going to be when you do."

Briana headed for the path leading up to the house, her insides quivering with humiliation and unfulfilled desire.

Ruth came out of the kitchen just as Briana slipped into the house through the patio door. She looked at her in surprise. "Briana! I thought you'd gone home."

"I lost track of the time. I'll change my clothes and be off."

The older woman glanced at her wristwatch. "But it's eight o'clock. The last ferry has already left for the day."

"Oh, no!" Briana exclaimed. She hadn't even thought about the ferry schedule.

"Well, no real harm done," Ruth was saying. "You can call your grandmother and explain what happened. We'll put you up for the night."

Knowing that she had no alternative, Briana slipped her cotton shirt on over her damp bikini and followed Ruth into the house, where she phoned Margaret to say she'd been careless and missed the last ferry. Not surprisingly, her grandmother was adamantly opposed to Briana's spending the night under Drake Rutledge's roof.

"I'm hardly in a position to be picky, grandmother," Briana told her.

"But isn't there a hotel in Cruz Bay where you could stay?"

Briana sighed. "No doubt there is, provided I

had the money for a room and my own transportation into town. Besides, what explanation would I give Ruth? She'd be insulted. Don't worry, grandmother. I'll see you tomorrow morning.''

Ruth came into the room just as she hung up. "I've asked Greta to make up the bed in the southeast room upstairs," she announced. "Come along, and I'll show you."

The room was large and furnished tastefully with French Provincial furniture of pale reddish brown fruitwood. The long windows were draped with sheer blue gray gauze curtains, the color matching that of the quilted coverlet. An armchair and footstool were upholstered in soft rose velvet. The Oriental rug, ringed with a floral design, repeated the blue, gray and rose colors, tying the room together beautifully.

"What a pretty room!" Briana exclaimed.

"Thank you. We had it redecorated recently. We're redoing the guest rooms one by one. I didn't want to rush, you see. I wanted time to work out the scheme for each room separately. When we started this project, Drake hired a decorator, who disagreed with every idea I had. Finally I let him go and did it myself.''

"You certainly made the right decision. The room couldn't be lovelier." It made Briana curious suddenly about the family bedrooms. What did Drake's room look like? None of your business, she told herself firmly.

"The bathroom's through that door," Ruth was saying. "You'll find towels, soap, everything you need in the linen closet in there."

Briana sat down on the vanity chair and picked up a comb lying on the fruitwood dresser. She ran it through her tangled hair slowly, waiting for Ruth to go.

The other woman moved toward the door, then hesitated. "Briana, have you and Drake had a disagreement?"

Briana looked up at her as she continued to comb her drying hair. "Did he say we had?"

"No. But you looked so strained, so tense or something when you came into the house a while ago. And Drake still hasn't come back from the beach. He did find you, didn't he?"

"Yes, he found me." She paused, then said, "Actually I've been meaning to talk to you about something, Ruth. The other day, when Patty left school and went to see Abel Weldon, I had no idea where she'd gone. She wouldn't tell me. I assumed Abel had already left the island, and I didn't know she had seen him until Drake told me later. Patty begged me not to say anything about her leaving school early unless you asked. I agreed because I wanted to keep her trust, and I couldn't see what harm it would do."

"Drake was upset with you, wasn't he?"

"Very. He accused me of lying to him, of conspiring with Patty against the two of you."

"Oh, Briana, you have to take that with a grain of salt. He's so worried about Patty. Is that what you argued about on the beach just now? Is that why you came back to the house alone?"

"No. We...well, I'm sure it's no secret to you that Drake has never really got over what happened between him and my father twenty years ago. We don't seem to be able to discuss it without getting angry."

Ruth chewed her bottom lip thoughtfully. "I've tried to tell him nothing can be gained by rehashing that old tragedy. We were all hurt by what happened. At first I blamed your family, too. But your father came to the hospital to see Drake after they scuffled and Drake was cut. Frederik tried to tell him how sorry he was, but Drake wouldn't listen. He got so agitated that Frederik had to leave. Before he did, he...he gave me money to pay the hospital bill. He wanted to pay for plastic surgery on Drake's face, too, but my brother wouldn't even consider it. He didn't find out for months that I'd paid the hospital with Ivensen money, but when he did, he was furious with me. I was a lot more practical and less proud than he was."

She shrugged her shoulders. "I was just seventeen, Briana. I had a job clerking in a tourist shop, but the money your father gave me got us over some rough spots. I'm not sure Drake could have stayed in school until he graduated, otherwise. He didn't know I was using more of Frederik's money. He thought my wages covered our expenses." She sighed. "As I grew older and had problems in my marriage, I became even more convinced that in most cases of misunderstanding, blame can be placed on both sides. More to the point, holding grudges only hurts the one who harbors them."

Briana relaxed a little on the vanity chair. "Thank you for telling me all this, Ruth. I don't know all the facts that led up to your mother's death. I've heard two different versions now—from grandmother and from Drake. My grandmother isn't well, so I don't want to press her about it. Anyway, as you say, it's in the past."

"I'll go and let you get dressed. Dinner will be ready in a half hour or so."

"If you don't mind, I think I'll skip dinner," Briana said. "I'm not hungry."

Ruth looked at her in silence for a moment. "Okay, if you're sure. I could have Greta bring you up something later."

"Don't bother—really."

Still looking somewhat doubtful, Ruth left, closing the door behind her. Briana went into the bathroom and ran warm water into the tub. She found a stoppered bottle of geranium-scented bubble bath and poured a generous portion into the tub as it filled. Then she stripped off her bikini and got in, sliding down until the bubbles covered her to her chin. She sighed tiredly and closed her eyes, savoring the sensuous warmth of the water against her skin and the lovely scent of the bubbles. She didn't move again until the water cooled completely.

As she toweled herself dry, she realized for the first time that she had forgotten to ask her hostess for something to sleep in. Ruth had evidently not thought of it, either. Oh, well, she wouldn't see anyone until morning, she thought. She'd just sleep nude.

She brushed her blond hair thoroughly before turning out the light and crawling into the wide bed. As she slid down between the cool crisp sheets, she tried to ignore the hunger gnawing in her stomach. She'd lied to Ruth when she said she wasn't hungry. The truth was she didn't want to see Drake again that night. She preferred missing a meal to being subjected to his provocative glances.

She shifted restlessly, remembering his challenging remarks on the beach. Did he really believe she would come to him, begging him to make love to her? He was such an arrogant beast!

Unwanted, the memory of his hands, his lips on her body intruded and sent a shiver through her. What was wrong with her? She would be crazy to let another man into her life. She never meant to marry again, not that Drake had ever hinted that he had marriage on his mind. What he obviously wanted was something far less per-

manent than that. She ought to be insulted. Unfortunately that hadn't kept her from enjoying
his fervent lovemaking.

SHE COULDN'T SLEEP. It must have been almost
an hour later when there was a light tap at her
door. She sat up in bed, drawing the sheet up to
cover her nakedness, and reached over to turn
on the bedside lamp.

"Yes? Who is it?"

The door opened, and Drake came in, carrying a tray. "I brought you something to eat," he
said, approaching the bed and placing the tray
on the table beside her. His eyes grazed over
her, from her tousled hair, down the slope of
her bare shoulders to the hem of the sheet
tucked beneath her arms, on down over the outline of her body beneath the sheet and back
again.

Pride demanded that she maintain she wasn't
hungry and send the tray back. But the glistening bowl of fruit salad and the club sandwich
with its crisp green lettuce and wafer-thin slices
of chicken and beef peeking out between thick
layers of homemade bread made Briana's stomach contract. Her mouth actually watered.

Not meeting Drake's eyes, she anchored the
sheet more firmly around her. "Thank you. I
wasn't hungry earlier, but this looks good." She
reached for a small wedge of the sandwich and
tried not to appear too eager as she bit into it.

He continued to stand beside the bed, looking down at her. She heard him chuckle softly as she reached for another wedge of the sandwich.

"Talk about cutting off your nose to spite your face," he drawled. "You'd actually let your blue-blooded pride make you go hungry, wouldn't you?"

She lifted her lashes and gazed at him. "I have no idea what you're talking about."

He laughed outright this time, then handed her the paper napkin from the tray. "There's a drop of mayonnaise on your chin. Slow down. I'm not going to take the tray before you're through eating."

She swiped at her chin with dignity. "You needn't wait for the tray at all. I can take it down to the kitchen when I'm finished."

His dark brows rose. "Wearing what? A sheet?"

He was looking at her with intense interest, and when she glanced down, she saw that her breasts were clearly outlined beneath the sheet. She shifted and pulled the sheet higher, making a fold over her bosom. Her cheeks burned.

"Must be tough, handling that sheet and eating at the same time," he remarked in a teasing tone. "Maybe I can help."

She glared up at him. "No, thank you. I know what kind of help you have in mind!"

He gave her a slow sexy smile. "Yeah? Now

that you mention it, that bed is plenty big enough for two."

She almost choked on her iced tea. "You're impossible, Drake! Why are you doing this?"

"Doing what?" he inquired innocently.

"Talking in this...this suggestive way. Are you trying to embarrass me, rub it in because I missed the ferry? I was busy trying not to drown, if you'll remember."

"Are you referring to your little mishap in the ocean, my lovely Briana? Or do you mean you were trying not to drown in the delightful sea of love," he taunted.

"Love!" she sneered. "You mean sex, don't you?"

He shrugged carelessly. "Call it what you will. It was delightful, though, wasn't it?"

His mouth smiled as if he were teasing, but his dark eyes burned into hers with such brilliance that she felt hot under his gaze. She knew there was too much color in her face, and she despised herself for it. Why did she allow him to disconcert her so easily? Why did she feel as exposed as if there were no sheet protecting her body from his aggressive eyes.

"You have the most inflated opinion of yourself of any man I've ever known," she told him as she dug a spoon into the sweet fruit salad.

He continued to look at her with his enigmatic half smile. "You aren't going to tell me you didn't enjoy our intimate little scene on the beach, are you? Ah, Briana, don't bother. I know when a woman wants me."

"God, you're conceited!"

He laughed again.

"You don't fool me, either, Drake," she went on, wanting to goad him. "You'd like nothing better than to haul me off to a cave somewhere by my hair and ravish me—isn't that the word? It would give you the greatest pleasure to get even with an Ivensen in that disgusting way. You're nothing but a barbarian at heart for all your money and your modern trappings. Unfortunately this is the twentieth century. Men can't get away with such savage behavior anymore."

"What vivid fantasies you have, my beautiful blond witch," he commented. "I'm sorry I can't stay and help you make them all come true, but I have an appointment. We'll continue this provocative discussion later."

"That's what you think," she muttered, swallowing the last bite of salad. As she set the dish back on the tray, she looked at him with an expression that held a deliberate challenge.

Drake reached out and brushed the tousled hair back from her face, then ran his hand slowly, gently across her cheek. "Good night, beautiful Briana. Pleasant dreams."

She stared into the depths of his eyes for a long moment before he withdrew his hand with an audible sigh of reluctance. Then he picked up the tray and left the room.

Briana touched her cheek where his hand had been. She lay quite still for several moments before she switched out the light. What appointment did he have, she wondered? It must be on St. John, since there would be no ferry until the morning. Was it business or pleasure? For the first time she wondered if he had a relationship with a woman. A woman who lived on the island? Was he going to be with her now?

She groaned and turned over in the bed. She hadn't wanted him to come into her bedroom. She hadn't wanted to see him. She'd made it plain she wanted him to leave, and he had. It was stupid to feel disappointed.

CHAPTER EIGHT

"PATTY, THANK GOODNESS! I thought you'd run out on me again," Briana exclaimed as her pupil got into the car.

"I had to make a phone call. The only phone at school is in the office, and there was a lineup to use it," Patty replied, slumping back against the seat as if the effort had exhausted her.

Looking more closely, Briana saw that her bottom lip was trembling perceptibly. She started the car, and Patty turned her head to stare out the side window.

Something's happened, Briana thought and debated with herself whether to offer a sympathetic ear or pretend not to notice. By the time they'd reached Red Hook dock, she had decided to act as if nothing were amiss. Patty would confide in her when and if she was ready.

On the ferry Briana chatted about an intriguing sidelight on St. Thomas history she'd uncovered in the von Scholten papers. She knew Patty wasn't very interested in the islands' history but hoped a little of her own enthusiasm might communicate itself to the girl. Patty muttered a bored response now and then, and finally Briana gave up trying.

After lunch with Ruth, during which Patty talked hardly at all, Briana suggested they go out to the garden for their tutoring session. When they were seated on a couple of wrought-iron chairs, a small table between them, Patty announced, "I passed the history test."

It was said in the same dull tone that had characterized her speech ever since she'd got in the car at school. Briana found that she was a little put out with the girl for not showing more pride in her recent scholastic accomplishments.

"Why, that's wonderful! What was your score?"

"Eighty-two."

"Good."

"I should have had a hundred. We'd gone over every topic covered on the test and talked about it. Three of the questions that I got wrong I knew the answers to." She shrugged. "I guess I wasn't in a test-taking mood that day."

"Eighty-two is nothing to be ashamed of," Briana said stoutly. "You'll do better next time."

"Maybe." Patty gazed out over the garden, but Briana had the feeling the tropic beauty of the trees and flowers was lost on her. "The problem is I just don't care that much."

Briana sighed. "Patty, I wish you would try to look into the future a bit. It's true that a few years from now it won't matter one whit whether you made an eighty-two or a hundred on a history exam. If you can't find enough satisfaction in the learning itself, think of passing your courses as a means to an end.''

The girl grimaced. ''College, you mean.''

Briana hesitated, thinking of Drake's determination that his niece enter college in the fall. Finally she said, ''Not necessarily. You don't even have to decide now. The point is, graduating with a respectable average opens doors in your future. You'll have choices that you just won't have otherwise. Don't you see what I'm saying?''

''I guess so,'' responded Patty disinterestedly.

''You can't possibly know what you'll want to do a year—five, ten years—from now. Don't close all the doors before you know what's behind them.''

Patty tossed her long brown hair behind her shoulders and looked at Briana with bleak eyes. ''The thing is, I thought I knew what my future would be. I thought I would marry Abel and have a home and children to take care of.''

''No one is saying you can't have a home and children. In fact, you undoubtedly will in time.''

The girl drew in a long leaden breath. ''Not with Abel,'' she said finally. Then she swallowed convulsively.

Briana gave her a few moments to compose herself before she said, "Patty, I don't know what happened, but I'm sorry you're feeling unhappy."

Her pupil looked at her, her brown eyes glittering with unshed tears. "Don't say that everything will work out for the best in the long run. I'm so sick of hearing adults say that!"

Briana smiled. "Okay, I won't. But it might help to talk about it. Want to? I don't think we're going to get much studying done, anyway."

With a sudden movement Patty buried her face in her hands. Her slender body began to shake with silent tears. Briana instinctively moved her chair closer and put her arm around the girl. Then she waited in silence.

At length Patty gulped down her sobs and lifted her tear-stained face. After giving her a comforting squeeze, Briana opened her purse and pulled out a tissue. "Here," she said, pressing it into her hand.

Patty wiped her eyes, then crumpled the damp tissue in her fist. "That day...when I left school early and was late meeting you...I went to see Abel."

Briana tried to make her voice neutral. "I see."

"I know I shouldn't have. Men don't like girls who chase after them, do they?"

"It depends on the man, I suppose."

"Well, Abel didn't like me coming to his apartment. I could tell. He...he acted nervous, like he was expecting someone else or something. But when I asked, he said he wasn't. I... I even asked if he was seeing another woman, someone older. But he said no. He said he had a lot of things on his mind."

Briana waited as Patty wiped away fresh tears, as she straightened up and gazed before her. "I...I asked him why he hadn't called me. He used to call me at school, and we'd have lunch together sometimes. I first met Abel on my lunch period...last year. I'd gone to Arby's with a girl friend, and he asked if he could share our table. After that he began to call me at school, and we finally started dating."

She glanced over at Briana. "Sometimes I skipped out of school in the afternoon and went out with Abel. Until Uncle Drake found out and threatened to send me away to boarding school if I played hooky anymore."

"That helps explain why you were failing your afternoon classes," Briana remarked.

Patty twisted the tissue in her lap. "We talked about getting married when I became eighteen. I was so happy. I thought...I *know* Abel loved me. He told me he did all the time."

"Sometimes people have different definitions of love," Briana ventured carefully. "Some people use the word more loosely than others." *Some aren't even capable of such a giving emo-*

tion; they're only able to take, she added silently to herself.

Patty looked at her dully. "All of a sudden he stopped calling me. I didn't see him for weeks. I phoned his apartment house and left messages with his landlady, but he never returned my calls. So I...I went to see him." Her throat worked visibly as she swallowed down more tears. "He...he acted different, as if he felt uncomfortable with me. When I asked why he hadn't called, he said he'd been busy. I said I bet Uncle Drake had done something to make him change. He denied it. He...he acted as if I was practically a stranger, as if I was making a nuisance of myself, and that he wished I'd leave. So I did. But I thought that he would change his mind, that whatever it was that was making him act so odd would go away."

"The phone call you made from school today—did you call Abel?"

Patty nodded. "I couldn't believe he really didn't want to see me anymore. I was sure he was sick or worried about something that day in his apartment." She closed her eyes, as if she'd seen something she couldn't bear to look at. "He...he's leaving St. Thomas. He was packing when I called. I wanted to go with him. I begged him to take me." She shuddered suddenly. "Do you know what he said, Briana? He said I was just a kid, that we'd had some good times together, but that I was taking a little fun too seriously. He said he had a job in Texas, and that he'd probably never see me again.'' Her voice broke and she couldn't go on.

Briana hugged her tightly, swallowing a lump in her own throat over Patty's broken heart, even though she knew the girl was well out of it. She only hoped that Patty never found out Drake was responsible, that he'd bribed Abel Weldon to get out of his niece's life. ''Honey, I'm sorry,'' she murmured finally. ''I know you can't believe this right now, but you'll get over it.''

After some moments Patty managed a bitter-sounding laugh. ''Will you swear to that?''

''Yes, I will.''

Patty turned and looked probingly into her face for a moment. ''Did you love your husband when you married him?''

''Yes. At least I thought I did. Let me put it this way—I loved him as much as I was capable of doing at the time. I was awfully immature.''

''But you don't love him now—not even a little?''

''No,'' Briana replied emphatically.

''What happened? How can you fall out of love?''

''It doesn't happen overnight. People change. Or maybe it's more accurate to say that sometimes, after you get to know someone well, you find out he isn't what you thought he was.''

''Is that what happened to you?''

"Yes."

"Gosh, that must have hurt."

"I wouldn't try to tell you it didn't," Briana admitted. "But part of the hurt was wounded pride. I thought I'd made such a wise decision, and it turned out that I...I had a lot to learn. After the divorce I went back to college. I buried myself in my studies. I didn't have time to feel sorry for myself. Keeping your mind occupied is wonderful medicine. A person can't think about two things at the same time, you know." She smiled encouragingly at the dejected girl.

Patty frowned. "And you're completely over it now?"

Was she, Briana wondered. Would she ever be over the disillusionment and pain? She didn't know. But for years she had been over the feelings she had thought were love. And that was really what Patty wanted to know. "Completely. I'm looking forward to a teaching career. Part of it is the feeling of independence it gives me, the feeling that I can take care of myself, come what may."

"It's not very smart to be dependent on a man for everything, is it?" Patty murmured. "I guess every girl thinks her marriage will last forever, but look at what happened to my own parents. Look at you. Uncle Drake takes care of mother, but I'd rather be independent, like you."

Briana was tempted to remind Patty that she had once vowed she'd never be a career woman like Briana. But an I-told-you-so attitude was the last thing Patty needed now.

"You can be," she said instead.

Patty took a deep sigh and smiled faintly. "We're back to college again, aren't we? What was it like at your university?"

"Nice," said Briana. "Vermont's a beautiful state. The campus buildings were old and gracious—faded brick with ivy climbing all over them. And in the winter, when snow covered everything, it looked like a Christmas card. I loved to curl up in front of a roaring fire in my one-room apartment and sip hot chocolate and watch the snow come down. Having been raised here, I never quite got over the magic of snow. I used to go skiing on the weekends. There were a number of good slopes nearby."

Patty looked interested for the first time that afternoon, so Briana didn't mention the stranded cars, sitting through class with wet feet, how near the end she had longed for the tropics. "Would you like me to send for catalogs—from my old university and others in New England?"

"I guess it wouldn't hurt to look at them," Patty conceded. "Go ahead and send for them if you want to."

"I'll do it tomorrow," Briana promised. "Now, is there any possibility you could concentrate on that Faulkner short story for a while?''

Patty opened her literature text. "I'll try."

IN THE WEEKS that followed that tearful session, Patty seemed to treat her studies more seriously. She evidently took to heart Briana's advice about keeping her mind occupied and even turned in extra essays to her teachers for additional credit. Early in March she admitted to Briana that she could actually think about Abel without bursting into tears.

Her success with her pupil was balm to Briana's spirit. She needed all the strokes she could get, she told herself cryptically as she traveled back to St. Thomas one March evening on the ferry. She was a good teacher, even though she seemed to be lacking in skills in the other areas of her life. Her relationship with Drake had certainly not improved since that night she had been forced to spend in his house.

They spoke when it was necessary, but the strain between them seemed to grow worse rather than lessen. Only the day before yesterday she had been sitting alone on the patio, having a glass of iced tea before going home, when Drake had appeared unexpectedly. She had almost jumped out of her chair.

He'd smiled that knowing smile of his and said, "You seem a bit nervous, Briana."

"You startled me." She dabbed at the damp

spot on her slacks where her tea had spilled. "How did you get here?"

"I caught a ride from the dock."

"My using your car is proving to be an inconvenience for you."

"Never mind that." He sat down facing her and helped himself to tea from the pitcher that Greta had left on a table. "I thought, the way you jumped just now, that you might be under a strain."

"Well, you're wrong."

"Am I? You look a little hollow eyed lately. Aren't you sleeping well?"

"I sleep like a log," she lied. "Except for one or two really hot nights. Our air conditioning isn't working. Other than that there's nothing to keep me from sleeping."

He lifted his broad shoulders in a shrug. "There's tension. Are you having problems with your dissertation?"

"No," she snapped.

"How is your grandmother?"

"As well as anyone is at her age. Don't tell me you're concerned about poor grandmother's health!"

He ignored this. "Of course, it could be sexual frustration."

She shot to her feet. "You have a one-track mind! Excuse me."

"I'll drive you to the dock."

During the drive she refused to respond to his

continued banter, saying, "I have more important things to do than to listen to this."

AND SHE DID, she told herself staunchly as she left the ferry on St. Thomas and walked toward her car. Having gone through her grandmother's family papers thoroughly and filed them with the other printed material she had been gathering for more than a year, she was ready to do an outline for her dissertation. She planned to start on it that very evening.

She was still absorbed in thinking about where to begin when she reached the house. Entering the foyer, she heard voices coming from her grandmother's apartment. She went down the hall to the sitting-room door, which stood open.

Margaret turned at her entrance, a smile on her face. "Briana, come in and welcome the wanderer back home."

Erik, who had been sitting on the Victorian settee, got slowly to his feet. In pale blue trousers and a hand-embroidered white on white silk shirt, his blond hair gleaming, he looked rested and self-confident. "Hi, sis. I hear you're a working woman now."

Too shocked to respond immediately, Briana merely stared at him, wondering if her eyes could possibly be deceiving her. Did he actually have the nerve to show his face here after what he had done?

To gain a little time she walked to Margaret's chair and patted her shoulder. "I don't need to ask how you're feeling. You look in fine spirits."

Margaret tilted her head and looked up at Briana curiously. "Why wouldn't I be? I have both my grandchildren home with me again. Aren't you going to say hello to your brother?"

Briana turned toward Erik, who had sat down on the settee again. "What are you doing here?"

She heard Margaret's gasp of surprise and reminded herself not to say too much in her grandmother's hearing. Somehow she had to hide her outrage until she had Erik alone.

Erik laughed nervously. "I live here."

"Oh? What happened to the apartment in New York? What about those job offers you were trying to choose from?"

"Briana!" Margaret was clearly stunned and heartily disapproving of her reaction to Erik's return. "What's wrong with you? If you've had a trying day, there's no need to take it out on your poor brother. He hasn't even unpacked yet."

Still looking at Erik, Briana asked, "So you're back to stay?"

Erik bristled at her obviously hostile stance. "For a while. I wasn't aware that I had to have your approval."

"I shouldn't have to remind you, Briana," put in Margaret, "that this is Erik's house." And Erik sent her a challenging smirk.

"I am only too aware," Briana said, glaring at her brother, "who owns this house."

"For goodness' sake," Margaret fretted, "sit down. I'll ring for Ida to bring you something to drink. What's put you in such a cross mood? It isn't like you."

Biting her tongue to keep from blurting out the real reason for her mood, Briana sat in one of the Queen Anne chairs. "I don't want anything, grandmother. We've less than an hour until dinner time."

"I was scolding Erik about dinner before you came in," said Margaret, flashing him a fond smile. "This naughty boy is going out for dinner on his first night back." She reached out to pat his hand. "But I'll forgive you, dear. I know you're eager to see Jane again."

"Thank you, grandmother. I promise I'll be home for dinner tomorrow evening."

"Jane knew you were coming?" Briana asked. "She might have warned us."

"She didn't know," said Erik, his lips thinning in irritation. "I phoned her from the St. Thomas airport. I didn't know I was coming myself until yesterday."

"What happened yesterday?"

"Nothing, except I finally admitted what I'd known for weeks, that I wasn't going to be satisfied in New York. Even though one of the job offers I had was quite appealing," he added.

"It was in a bank, I presume," Briana muttered.

Erik's look was sharp and angry. "Actually it was with a brokerage firm."

Briana couldn't sit and listen to Erik's drivel and watch her grandmother hang on his every word any longer. She got to her feet. "If you'll excuse me, grandmother, I think I'll go and shower. I'll see you at dinner."

As she left the room, she heard Margaret trying to make excuses for her behavior. "I don't know what's come over her. She's not usually so rude. No doubt working for Drake Rutledge is proving to be more unpleasant than she will admit."

Briana hurried to her room, clenching her teeth in frustration. She wasn't finished with Erik, not by a long shot. But she would have to confront him when they wouldn't be interrupted by Margaret. It had been clear in his manner that he knew she was aware of his embezzlement, the loss of their home. She wondered if his dinner date with Jane Fitzcannon was a tactical delay in having to face her. If it was, it wouldn't put off the confrontation for long. She intended to work on her dissertation in the study after dinner—with the door open, so she would hear him when he came home. She would wait up as late as necessary to see him.

At dinner Margaret took her to task again for her behavior with Erik. Briana mumbled an excuse about being tired, an excuse that didn't satisfy her grandmother. But Margaret was too ebullient over Erik's return to allow Briana's unexpected reaction to deflate her. She talked throughout the meal, mostly about Erik and how wonderful it was to have him home again, hardly noticing Briana's noncommittal responses.

As soon as she could, Briana excused herself and went to the study. Seated at the old oak rolltop desk, with papers and books stacked about her on every available surface and her notebook open in front of her, she began to write. She had learned after her divorce the discipline of single-minded concentration on the task at hand. Within minutes she had forgotten Erik and the outrage his return had stirred in her.

SHE WAS STILL WORKING at midnight when she heard the key turning in the front door. Closing her notebook, she went out to intercept Erik in the hall.

When he saw her, he hesitated briefly, then came toward her. "You're up late, Briana."

"I want to talk to you."

She indicated the study, and he sauntered past her. She shut the door behind them. He sprawled in an armchair and looked up at her, his mouth quirking. "You weren't too interested in talking to me in grandmother's sitting room earlier. What changed your mind?"

Briana paced across the floor and leaned against the desk, her arms folded in front of her. "I can't believe you had the gall to come back here!'' she blurted out, unwilling to engage in word games with him.

"Oh, come off it, Briana! Where else would I go? I've made grandmother happy, haven't I?''

"Don't pretend that you've ever given a second thought to grandmother or anyone besides yourself! I'm paying the rent on this house now, and I have a say in who lives here.''

He eyed her warily for a moment. "If I move out, I'll tell grandmother it's at your request.''

Briana's blue eyes were brilliant with indignation. "You...you're a selfish, lazy, despicable...embezzler! Don't sit there and threaten me!''

He startled her by smiling a slow, ugly smile. "Tell me, Briana, how long have you known about my agreement with Rutledge?''

"He came here the very day you left and told me what you'd done! Did you think he'd be reluctant to serve us with an eviction notice? Ha! If you thought that, you don't know Drake very well!''

"Not as well as you, evidently,'' he drawled. Suddenly he sat forward in his chair. "So it's 'Drake' now, is it?'' He smirked. "Well, I know a few things about Rutledge myself. He wanted revenge. He has no use for an old plantation house in need of major repairs from roof to foundation. He's already got a mansion on St. John and a swank suite at the Grand Reef. No, he wanted this house because he knows how much it means to grandmother. You're not naive enough to think he accepted the deed in lieu of having me arrested out of the goodness of his heart, are you? No, way, little sister. He wanted to walk in here and throw us out on the street." He raked her with a mocking look. "Why didn't he, I wonder? It's obvious grandmother knows nothing. How did you get Rutledge to set aside his plan?"

"It wasn't easy! I asked to be allowed to rent the house so we could stay here, and grandmother needn't know what you'd done. Fortunately he needed someone to tutor his niece, so we made a bargain. My services as a teacher in return for being allowed to stay."

His lips curled. "You did all that to protect grandmother?" He laughed. "How marvelously touching. Only I'm not buying it, Briana. I admit, though, I had no idea you had it in you."

"What do you mean by that?"

He got to his feet and leaned toward her. "Nobody but our old-fashioned grandmother would buy that story about Rutledge hiring you to tutor his niece."

"He did hire me!"

"I don't doubt that. But the tutoring is just a smoke screen, isn't it?"

"I have no idea what you're talking about!"

"Then I'll spell it out for you. You're Drake Rutledge's whore, little sister." He threw his head back and gazed at the ceiling for a moment. "How ironic! His mother and our father, and now you and Rutledge." His narrow-eyed regard came back to her face. "How would you like grandmother to learn about the real services you perform for your employer?"

Briana was gripping the edge of the desk behind her so tightly that her knuckles were white. "Then it's true," she whispered, "what Drake told me. Father and his mother were lovers."

"Of course it's true."

"Father must have loved her. He promised to marry her."

"What difference does it make what he told her?" The words were filled with contempt. "She was stupid to believe him. Hell, she was a *maid*! But you, Briana, don't even have that excuse. How can you lower yourself to Rutledge's level just to stay in this crummy house?"

"That's too ridiculous even to deny! Even if it weren't, I have no intention of defending myself to you of all people. My personal life is none of your business."

"Right," he spat out. "If you enjoy crawling into that scum's bed, that's your business—until you start ordering me around."

She knew what he was threatening and didn't doubt for a moment that he would carry out his threat if she pushed him too far. If she insisted that he move out, he would go to Margaret with his filthy lies. He had her in a corner, and he knew it.

She was staring at the face of the man who was her brother. They had been children together. Yet she wondered how she could ever have thought she knew him. Finally she said in low measured tones, "Even if I agree to your staying, what makes you think Drake will allow it?"

"I'm sure you can use your influence to make him see it your way," he said with heavy sarcasm.

He had won, and she could hardly contain her fury at the knowledge. "If you stay here, Erik," she said when she could do so with some semblance of calm, "you'll pay your share of the expenses. If you refuse, I'll be forced to tell grandmother everything—and have Drake throw you out, if necessary." She was bluffing, of course. She couldn't tell her grandmother the truth.

Having faced her down, Erik seemed inclined to be a little more agreeable. "Fine. I've hit a streak of luck at cards. I'm quite able to pay my own way."

"Well," she said, brushing past him to leave the study, "that's a switch."

His triumphant laugh followed her all the way to her bedroom.

She knew she would have to tell Drake that Erik was back and was staying at the house. Charlotte Amalie wasn't large enough for anyone to remain ignorant of Erik's return for long. Given that, Briana preferred to be the one to tell him.

AFTER TAKING THE RETURN FERRY following her next tutoring session with Patty, she waited at Red Hook dock for Drake to put in an appearance. Ruth had said she expected him home for dinner, so Briana didn't think she would have to wait long. She bought a can of cold soda and found an empty bench beneath the shade of a tree. About a half hour later Drake's MG pulled up near where she was sitting. He got out and came toward her.

"Waiting for someone?" he inquired.

"You," she said. "I have to tell you something, and I didn't think it could wait."

He was wearing tan trousers in the trim belted style that he wore often. The summer fabric molded itself to his muscled thighs in a way that emphasized his lean masculine build. His cinnamon brown knit shirt fit snugly, as well, and was opened at the collar to reveal his dark chest hair and the tan skin of his neck. Briana's senses were instantly aware of his physical attractions as he strolled to the bench and sat down beside her.

"I think I know what you're going to say. Erik is back."

She pushed absently at a strand of her hair as she searched his face for his reaction. As usual his expression was difficult to read. "How did you find out so quickly? He only arrived Wednesday afternoon."

He grinned. "You know how gossip travels on this island."

"Yes. I...I guess I should have let you know sooner."

He cocked his head. "Why?"

"We *are* living in your house," she murmured. "Considering what Erik did to you, I wouldn't blame you for wanting him out of there immediately."

"Briana, you're paying the rent on that house by tutoring Patty. It's your affair if you want to let him move in on you."

She hadn't expected such a reasonable attitude. "It isn't that I want him there. But if I insist that he leave, he says he'll tell grandmother why he has to go."

Throwing back his head, Drake made a harsh sound in his throat. "Why," he asked with irony in his voice, "doesn't that surprise me?"

"You know that I've told grandmother nothing about why Erik left your employ, or that you hold the deed on the house. It...it might kill her, Drake, and I simply can't take the chance. I have to let Erik stay. He's promised to pay his own way."

"No need to tell you how much faith I have in Erik's promises." He faced her with a pondering look. "You're still looking tired," he went on after a moment. "Are you sure you're getting enough rest?"

"Yes, I am."

"Well, don't let Erik get under your skin." His intent look was making her feel nervous. She shifted uneasily.

"I won't."

"Promise?"

She nodded. "Thanks for being so understanding. I'd better get home now."

"Wait a minute. I want to warn you to expect an air-conditioning repairman at the house in the next few days. How long has the cooling system been out of commission?"

"For months."

"Why didn't you tell me sooner?"

"The other day I merely mentioned it in passing. I wasn't hinting that you should have it fixed."

"I know you weren't, but I'm glad you told me. I like to keep up my property. I'd do more if you'd agree."

She shook her head. "No, Drake, please don't. Grandmother would be suspicious. I can make her believe I called the air-conditioning repairman, but if a whole crew of workers show up, she might start to wonder how I'm paying for it. Her mind wanders occasionally, but not all the time."

"I'm still surprised at the way you're determined to protect your grandmother. Which brings up another point. I want an inventory of the house's furnishings, particularly now that Erik is back. It occurred to me that you might like to make it, rather than have another out-sider come in for the job.''

Briana found that she was rather unsettled by Drake's sudden concern for her. "Yes, I would. I'll get started on an inventory this weekend.''

He didn't speak for a moment but merely looked at her as if he were debating something with himself. Then he said, "If Erik starts to pressure you—in any way—I want you to tell me.''

"I will,'' she promised. Then, getting to her feet, she added, "Thank you, Drake.'' She turned and walked away from him.

For the rest of the evening she recalled again and again that curious meeting. Every detail of his appearance came back to her, as clearly as when he had been sitting on the bench beside her. She was amazed to realize that she hardly noticed his scar anymore. In her mind it had be-come just another facial feature, as much a nat-ural part of him as his brooding dark eyes or the chiseled angles of his nose and jaw. He wasn't handsome, she reminded herself—but so virile, so exciting to her feminine senses. And regard-less of his feelings about her family, she admit-ted a grudging respect for him, for what he had made of himself.

CHAPTER NINE

IT WAS LATE AFTERNOON. Briana was working in the study when she heard the hall telephone ringing. She was engrossed in going over her dissertation outline, so she ignored the phone. Ida would get it in the kitchen. It was probably Jane Fitzcannon, anyway. She had called Erik almost every day since he'd come home a week ago.

With the detailed outline in front of her, Briana could see some thin spots that needed additional research. For one thing, she would like to have more information about the early sugar plantations on St. John and the conditions that had led to the slave rebellion in 1733. She wondered if Drake knew any descendants of pioneer families who might have original records in their possession. Her grandmother's family papers had proven to be a rich source of anecdotes and sidelights on early St. Thomas history. Primary sources—particularly those that hadn't been used by previous historians—were always more exciting to research than secondary materials such as articles and books.

She leaned back in her chair and gazed out the window. Lengthening afternoon shadows made a gray blue contrast to the bright green of the lawn. The grass needed cutting again, she noticed, and she wondered how much longer their ancient mower would be up to the job. Maybe she could talk Erik into cutting the grass since he hadn't yet contributed any money to household expenses as he had promised. She sighed, not wanting to think about Erik, and returned her mind to Drake. He seemed to know everyone on St. John, and it was possible he did know someone from one of the old families. Still, she hated to ask him for another favor.

The air conditioner had been repaired, and Briana was sure her grandmother was sleeping better as a result. Margaret had accepted without question Briana's explanation that she had arranged for the repairman. With her usual disregard for their financial situation, she hadn't even wondered, apparently, if it had been difficult for Briana to pay for the repairs, which had come to over two hundred dollars.

Working in a cool study was certainly more pleasant than working in a stuffy one, although Briana's nights were still restless. But that merely proved what she had already suspected—that the temperature had nothing to do with her insomnia. Not that she was willing to accept Drake's diagnosis, either.

"Miss Briana." Ida thrust her head around the study door. "Telephone for you."

Briana came back to earth. "Thank you, Nenie Ida. I'll get it in the hall." As she hurried toward the wall niche where the old-fashioned black instrument rested, she reflected again upon the inconvenience of having only two phones in the rambling old house. But additional extensions would be an expense that they couldn't afford, and one they could manage without.

She picked up the receiver. "Hello."

"Briana." It was Drake. "I hope I'm not interrupting your work. I waited until after four to call, thinking that you'd be finished for the day."

"I was going over my outline, so it doesn't matter."

"How's the air-conditioning system working now?"

"Perfectly. I appreciate your getting the repairman out here so quickly."

"There's something I'd like to discuss with you, but not on the telephone."

"Oh. Well, I'll be tutoring Patty tomorrow afternoon. I could meet you at the dock about five."

"I'd rather make it this evening if you're free."

Briana hesitated. "I could meet you somewhere in a half hour," she said finally.

"Briana...." His tone was slightly exasperated. "I'm trying to arrange to take you out to dinner. Don't you think we could do it properly this time? I'll call for you at seven."

"But you can't come here!"

"Why not? Don't tell me you're afraid of what people will say. I'm fairly respectable, in spite of what your grandmother thinks." She could tell from his voice that he was smiling.

"It isn't that, and you know it. But what will I tell grandmother?"

"How about the truth?"

He was right, Briana realized. She wasn't a teenager who had to account to her elders for where she went and with whom. "All right," she said. "I'll be ready at seven."

She went immediately to her bedroom to look through her closet. Tonight, she sensed, would be different from the other times she'd been with Drake. This was their first real date, and she wanted to dress appropriately. She wanted to look attractive without overdoing it.

Finally she settled on a bright turquoise peasant blouse and a triple-tiered skirt. She added the bold accent of a multicolored braided belt along with gold neck chains and high-heeled straw sandals. And she wore her hair loose, falling in shining golden waves away from a center part.

She was ready by six-thirty and went in search of Margaret. She didn't want Drake's arrival at

the house to come as a surprise to her grandmother. Both Margaret and Erik were in the
front parlor having tea. Or rather Margaret was
having tea; Erik was drinking a piña colada.
Like their father he had cultivated a taste for the
rum distilled in the islands. He must have pur-
chased a supply, for their liquor cabinet had
been virtually empty for months. Briana wondered wryly if rum was Erik's idea of a contri-
bution to the household.

Both Margaret and Erik looked at her curiously as she entered the parlor. "You look lovely, dear," Margaret said. "Have you gone to so
much trouble to have dinner with Erik and
me?"

Briana smiled. "Not that I don't think you're
worth it, grandmother, but I'm going out for
dinner."

"How nice." Margaret gazed upon her fond-
ly. "Is there a party? Tell me who the guests will
be."

"There's no party. I'm having dinner with
Drake."

Erik lifted his glass and eyed her scornfully.

"Don't you see enough of that man when you
go to his house to tutor his niece?" Margaret
asked, her manner much more chill.

"I hardly see him at all when I'm working
with Patty." Briana started to add that Drake
had something to discuss with her, probably
Patty's progress, but she stopped herself. She

would not be put in the position of making excuses, particularly when she had done nothing to warrant it.

"What time is he due?" inquired Erik belligerently.

"Seven," Briana told him.

"I suppose you mean to play the proper hostess and invite him in," Erik went on.

"I may," said Briana, bristling.

"Then I'm sure you'll excuse me." Erik drained his glass and got to his feet. "Seeing Rutledge is bound to spoil my appetite. See you at dinner, grandmother." He left the room quickly.

"I shall sit in my own parlor and finish my tea," said Margaret with haughty disdain.

Briana had hoped that Margaret, like Erik, would wish to avoid Drake. Evidently her grandmother's pride wouldn't allow her to retreat. "As you wish, grandmother." She gazed out one of the long narrow front windows, restless all at once and eager for Drake to come and take her away from Margaret's disapproval.

"Is this a social engagement?"

Briana turned away from the window. "I'm going out to dinner with a man. I think you could call that a social engagement," she retorted.

"Don't be impertinent," said Margaret. "I can hardly be blamed for wondering. After all, Drake Rutledge isn't our...."

"Our kind?" Briana finished for her. "What is our kind, grandmother?"

"You know perfectly well what I mean," Margaret sniffed. "I don't like to say I told you so," she continued, "but I warned you that working for such a person would lead to other...even more unacceptable things."

Briana couldn't help laughing. "Oh, grandmother, it must be so comfortable to have such unshakable opinions on everything."

"If you mean that as a criticism, Briana, I'll overlook it. I've surely never doubted my opinion about Drake Rutledge!"

Dull red spots appeared on Margaret's cheeks, and Briana was on the verge of apologizing for her curtness when the doorbell rang. Not waiting for Ida, she went into the foyer and opened the door. Drake looked very attractive in a three-piece gray suit worn with a white shirt and a gray-and-blue striped tie.

"Hello, Drake," Briana said. "I'm ready to go." Politeness forced her to add, "Unless you'd like to come in for a few minutes."

The irony of her inviting him into his own house was not lost on Drake, who smiled wryly. "Thank you. I'll come in, if you don't mind. Our reservation isn't until seven forty-five."

She led the way into the parlor. "Grandmother, you remember Drake Rutledge."

Margaret, who sat erectly on the brocade sofa, her tea tray on a table in front of her, looked past Briana to Drake, who had paused in the archway. Meeting her look, he came forward. "Good evening, Mrs. Ivensen."

Margaret's lips were clamped together in a disparaging line. For one horrified moment Briana thought that her grandmother would refuse to acknowledge the greeting. Margaret's blue eyes locked with Drake's brown ones, giving Briana the apprehensive feeling that a battle line had been drawn. Finally she said, "Hello, Drake." Somehow she succeeded in filling those two words with censure.

Briana was surprised to see a hint of unease in Drake. "Sit down, Drake," she offered. He took the chair nearest the front door, and Briana chose a seat beside her grandmother.

"I won't offer you tea," Margaret stated, "since Briana tells me you're going directly to dinner from here."

"Would you like a drink—a martini, perhaps?" Briana put in, knowing that Margaret wouldn't suggest it.

Drake glanced at Briana with a faint smile. He sensed her apprehension. "Never mind. I don't want anything." He returned his attention to Margaret. Briana had the feeling that he had looked forward to this meeting, that he was now trying to reconcile the Margaret Ivensen who sat before him with the Margaret Ivensen of his childhood memories. "How are you, Mrs. Ivensen? Briana says you've been a little under the weather.''

"Briana exaggerates," snapped Margaret. "My health is excellent."

Drake suppressed a smile. "I always thought you had a strong constitution."

She glared at him, wondering, Briana was sure, what he meant by that remark. "I don't approve of my granddaughter working for you, Drake," she stated bluntly. "I don't know whether she told you, but I want that clearly understood."

Briana stirred uneasily, but Drake's quick looy stopped the embarrassed disclaimer she might have made. "I suspected that you wouldn't like it, Mrs. Ivensen. You might try looking at it from your granddaughter's point of view, though. She enjoys teaching, and she's very good with my seventeen-year-old niece. You should be proud of her."

Margaret sniffed disdainfully. "What I am proud of is my granddaughter's background. She has breeding and social standing, and she's been trained to fit into our world." She emphasized the word "our," making it clear that Drake was not part of that world. "We may not enjoy the financial resources we once did, but Briana has the grace and bearing of her ancestors. Her intelligence permitted her to acquire an excellent education by winning scholarships. I can't say I entirely approve of her having a career, but I'm proud of her scholastic achievements. Not that I expected less of an Ivensen. She'll be accepted on the faculty of the college here, if that is her desire—and without the dubious recommendation of tutoring your niece. Why, the president of the college is a family friend. I am personally acquainted with most of the members of the board of directors. The Ivensen name means something in the Virgin Islands!''

The old woman was becoming agitated, but Drake's voice was perfectly calm when he replied, ''No one is doubting that for a moment.''

Margaret cut him off. ''Look around you, Drake Rutledge. This house was once the center of St. Thomas society. It was photographed for the best decorating magazines published in New York City. That lamp at your elbow was ordered from the finest glassmaker in France by my grandmother. It's the only one of its kind in the world. This settee came from the country home of the Prince of Wales. My father-in-law bought it at auction in England. That carpet is from Morocco, handwoven from my mother-in-law's own design.'' Her gaze drifted to Briana's worried face for a moment, and she seemed to falter. ''Oh, why do I bother telling all of this to someone who can't possibly appreciate the value of fine things being handed down in a family?''

"My family left me no heirlooms," Drake said quietly, "but that doesn't mean I can't appreciate the tradition or that I don't want to leave a better legacy to my children than my parents were able to leave me."

Margaret's outburst had tired her. She looked at Drake in silence for an instant, then said, "I'm going to lie down a bit before dinner. I see, Briana, that you are going ahead with this...this...." She couldn't seem to find an appropriate word. As she looked from Briana to Drake, she seemed to shrink visibly. "Good evening." She stood up and walked slowly toward the door.

"I'll see you to your room, grandmother," Briana said.

"No," Margaret threw over her shoulder. "I'm quite capable of finding the way to my apartment without help."

When she was gone, Briana looked at Drake. "I'm sorry. I was afraid she would be rude to you. That's why I hesitated before asking you to come in."

He had stood up when Margaret did, and now he said, "Don't apologize for her. You aren't responsible for your relatives' behavior. Let's go to dinner, shall we?"

He was unusually quiet as they drove to Sebastian's. Briana wondered what he was thinking as she watched Charlotte Amalie's shops slip by. When they were seated at their table, having ordered veal Calvados as an entrée, Drake said, "Patty tells me you've sent for catalogs from some of the New England universities."

This seemed to confirm Briana's earlier suspicion that he had asked her to dinner to discuss his niece's progress. She brushed aside a tinge of disappointment and replied, "Yes. She asked me what my university was like and seemed to be interested in what I said." She smiled. "I confess I told her all the good parts. Anyway, when I suggested that we send for some catalogs, she agreed."

"That's encouraging. I think we can breathe easier now that Weldon has left St. Thomas."

"She was heartbroken," Briana told him. "She phoned Weldon just before he left. He was pretty rough on her—he told her she was still a child, that she'd taken their relationship too seriously."

"It'll only hurt for a brief time," he said tersely. "One day she'll thank her lucky stars that it turned out as it has."

"In time, yes—provided she never learns the real reason Weldon left the island."

He looked grave. The waiter appeared with the wine Drake had ordered, and they were silent as it was served. Then Briana said, "Thank you for your restraint with grandmother. When she was going on about the house, you must have been tempted to tell her that you own it now."

"Briefly," he agreed. He sipped his wine, looking thoughtful. "To tell the truth, she threw me off balance. I wasn't quite sure how I wanted to respond."

"Off balance? How? She reacted exactly as I expected she would."

"It wasn't her reaction to me. I expected that, too. I guess it was seeing her after so many years. When I was a boy, she seemed so powerful and untouchable. So strong. I was still carrying around that image of her in my mind. When I walked in there and saw her tonight, I was so taken aback I could hardly think of anything else." He uttered a low self-derisive laugh. "I actually feel sorry for her. Not because she's grown old and weak necessarily, but because she's so caught up in the past. I had the feeling that, as far as she's concerned, time has never progressed beyond 1950."

"Grandmother would hate it if she knew you were pitying her," Briana said dryly.

"I know. Fortunately she would never suspect it." He shook his head. "It's going to take a little while for me to get used to the Margaret Ivensen I saw tonight."

As he talked, Briana realized that, even though he had been surprised by Margaret's appearance, it didn't wipe out his unhappy childhood memories. Twenty years of bitterness and resentment could not be erased so easily. Again she remembered her confrontation with Erik on his first night home. Her brother had insulted and angered her, but upon calmer reflection she had to admit that there was some truth in the things Erik had said about Drake. She thought it was probably accurate that Drake had been looking for some means of revenge against her family. Employing Erik had provided that means. Now, in spite of his seeming willingness to postpone taking action, he had at his disposal the potential for humiliating Margaret and destroying her pride, if not her life. He could exercise the option anytime he chose. This didn't make Briana feel exactly secure in his company. On her side, there was always an element of wariness when they were alone together.

She was reflecting upon this fact as they finished their meal, and he said, "Let's go to my hotel suite for a nightcap."

Briana was inclined to refuse. "I think I'd better get back to the house and check on grandmother."

"You can phone from the hotel," he said quietly.

Still she hesitated, and he regarded her with a slanting look. "Coward," he said softly.

"Nonsense," she retorted. "But I don't see why we can't have a nightcap here." She hated the cynical way he was eyeing her, and felt called upon to add, "If you insist, we'll go to your hotel."

She couldn't let him go on thinking she was

afraid to be alone with him, she told herself as they drove toward the Grand Reef. He smoked his pipe and they said little. Once they had entered Drake's suite, however, the evening began to deteriorate rapidly. For one thing, she kept remembering that other night they had come here, and she began to tremble noticeably.

When Drake handed her a martini glass, he felt the tremor in her fingers. "What's wrong with you?" he asked, looking askance.

She turned away quickly. "Nothing. I'd better call home." She rang the house, and Ida told her that Margaret was asleep. Fumbling, she dropped the receiver on the tabletop before managing to replace it.

"Everything all right?"

She nodded, slowly turning to face him again. "Grandmother's asleep."

"I wasn't referring to your grandmother."

She took a swallow of her drink, then set the glass down beside the phone. "I'm all right." To her humiliation she was shaking harder than ever.

He stared at her pale face and lowered eyes intently. "I can tell." That was barbed. "My God, my effect on you is really something, isn't it? You seemed all right in the restaurant, but the minute we walked in here. . . . I've never had a woman react quite so violently to me before. Are you allergic to my after-shave or what? You aren't going to faint, are you?"

Briana's face burned with sudden color. Blast him, she thought. She should have known better than to come here with him.

"I never faint," she said, pushing away from the telephone table. She was horrified to realize that her knees actually did feel weak. Maybe she was coming down with flu. Was it something she'd eaten at the restaurant?

"Come here." Drake took her arm firmly and led her to the couch. Placing his hands on her shoulders, he pressed her down against the plush cushions. He retrieved her half-full martini glass and handed it to her. "Drink," he ordered curtly.

She sipped at it obediently before setting the glass on the coffee table. "I feel like an idiot," she began hoarsely.

He looked down at her intently while he finished his drink. His towering height looming above her made her feel at a horrible disadvantage until he discarded his jacket, stripped off his tie and sat down beside her. "Why are you afraid of me, Briana?"

There was a peculiar tension between them. She shivered slightly. "I'm not afraid. I'm fine," she answered distantly.

"Good." He sounded as uncertain as she felt. "Fear is the last thing I want you to feel."

She glanced around the room, refusing to meet his look. "This is a nice apartment. It's so different from your house. Did you decorate it yourself?''

"No, I left it to a decorator. I don't spend enough time here to take much notice of how it looks. It's only a convenience, for business purposes.''

She glanced at him, wondering how to take that. Did he mean that he never brought other women here? "I assumed you kept it for privacy, for entertaining people you didn't want to take to your house.''

"You mean women. I don't bring women here...ordinarily.''

She looked at her hands clasped in her lap rather than at him, then glanced up to find his eyes wandering over her in a way that made her breath catch in her throat.

The neckline of her peasant blouse was low, giving him a tantalizing view of the smooth slender column of her throat and the beginning of her rounded breasts and shadowed cleavage. His eyes lifted to her face, skimmed over it. "You look lovely. I like your hair loose like that.''

"I know. That's why I wore it this way.''

He looked at her oddly. "I don't understand you. You do your hair the way I like it, yet you put up a barrier every time we're alone together.''

She didn't answer. The silence between them seemed to expand and contract with its own beat.

"Sometimes," he said, "I think you despise me as much as your grandmother does."

She looked away hurriedly. "I don't despise you. I . . . I just feel unsure when I'm with you. I always wonder what you're thinking."

Drake smiled and touched her face gently, cupping her chin in his hand. His fingers felt warm against her skin. "I'm very drawn to you," he whispered. "But you know that, don't you? You're a beautiful woman, and lately I find that what I'm thinking about more and more is you."

The lamplight behind him outlined his head, softening the harsh angles of his face and blurring the scar on his cheek. His mouth was warm, sensual, curving in a faint smile.

"I don't mean you any harm, Briana," he told her gently. "I don't know what else I can do to prove that to you. Trust me."

His mouth moved closer, and she knew he was going to kiss her. Yet she didn't turn her head aside. The kiss began tentatively, and quickly deepened as desire flared between them. Gradually, he eased her down beneath him on the couch. When he finally lifted his head to look into her eyes, his expression was filled with a sort of wonderment.

"I've been wanting to touch you all evening," he confessed unsteadily. She stared up at him as his hand stroked the soft skin of her throat, as it moved in a slow caress along her shoulder and down to the rise of her breast. Her heart leaped in response. She lay watching him, trying to read in his face what he was really thinking. Could she believe him as he wanted her to? Could he separate her in his mind from her family? Even if he could, could she truly trust him—or any man—again?

With a feather touch he ran his fingertips along the swell of one breast and then the other. Nobody spoke, and Briana slowly shut her eyes, letting him explore her body without protest. For long moments she surrendered herself to the slow caress of his fingers and enjoyed what he was doing.

She didn't even object when, much later, he slipped off her blouse and skirt, and finally, impatiently her lace bra. By then her own fingers had moved to undo the buttons of his shirt, had pushed it aside so that her hands could touch him so much more intimately.

"Briana..." he murmured thickly, his lips tasting the fevered responsive skin of her neck, her breasts, her stomach.

Her fingernails dug into the smooth muscles of his back, and she shuddered beneath him. When his lips came back to take hers again, she met the searching probe of his kiss without reserve, giving way to the hunger throbbing deep inside her body.

He felt her responding to him and deepened the kiss until it was a deliciously erotic demand.

His lips trailed fire down her neck, and her head fell back against the cushion. She moaned with desire, obeying her instincts and arching her body against his. She wanted this, wanted him, wanted—

"I want you, Briana," he was murmuring, his face buried in her hair.

Until that moment Briana had been lost in the sensual sorcery that he practiced so skillfully. But now that they were ready, now that they were on the brink of fulfillment, she couldn't go on. She tried to turn off her memories, ignore them, but they were too strong; behind them there was unutterable pain and the scars left by that pain. She struggled up through the roiling sea of passion, her hands clutching convulsively at his shoulders.

"I can't," she whispered. "No, don't. I can't!"

Drake looked down at her, his eyes vulnerable, impassioned. "I need you, Briana. I won't hurt you; you can trust me. Oh, my darling, let me love you, please. Don't push me away again."

The very urgency in his voice made her shudder and go cold beneath the fierce heat of his body. She had once felt the same need in Ricardo. He, too, had always said he didn't mean to hurt her—when it was too late. When he was trying to calm her so that she wouldn't tell anyone the truth about him.

Drake's arms tightened around her, and he began to kiss her again, trying to break through to the passion he had felt in her only moments before. In a panic, she thought he wasn't going to listen to her. He was going to force her.

She wrenched her mouth free of the suffocating demand of his and cried out over a sudden rise of hysteria. "No! No, please don't—Ricardo!" She was so frantic to stop him that she was not even aware of what she had said.

His body went rigidly still, and she felt his passion leaving him. He lay unmoving for a moment, then he levered himself off the couch. He walked to the balcony doors and stared out for a while. The silence between them lengthened as Briana slowly sat up and started fumbling with her clothes. Hot tears stung her eyes and trickled down her face. When she was dressed, she huddled in the corner of the couch, watching him through her tears. She wanted to say something to break the silence, but what could she possibly say?

Finally, without turning around, he said tensely, "You're still in love with him, aren't you?"

Confused, she ran a hand over her wet cheeks. "Who?"

"Your ex-husband," he grated.

It was the absolutely last reaction she had expected from him. The ludicrous misconception forced a hollow-sounding laugh from her, and she realized she must be still on the verge of hysteria. She felt exquisitely fragile, as if she might fly into a thousand pieces. "Love him! No, I hate him!"

Slowly he turned. His hooded eyes raked her huddled form, and then he came back to the couch and sat beside her. "Then why did you call his name?"

"Did I?" Briana couldn't stop her tears. After trying unsuccessfully to wipe them away with the hem of her skirt, she gave up and let them fall. Through the watery haze she looked at the confusion in Drake's face. "He...he was sick...in his mind. I never saw that side of him before we were married. He was always so polite, so correct—and I was an ignorant child. I was a virgin, and after we were married... he...."

Drake uttered a soft curse. "He abused you? Is that what you're saying?"

She hesitated, appalled at herself. Then she nodded reluctantly, looking down at her clenched hands. She had said too much to stop now. "Sex with Ricardo was never anything but punishment for me. At first—" She faltered, forcing down a sob. "I was so inexperienced that I wondered if that's how all men were. And later I kept thinking I must be doing something to make him treat me that way, that it was somehow my fault." She hugged herself almost desperately. "After six months I couldn't take it anymore. I—'' she looked at him quickly, then looked away ''—I can understand your wanting to kill my father. I wished many times that Ricardo would die. I even wished that I had the courage to kill him.''

Drake reached out for her, pulled her against him. His embrace was fierce and protective, but she needed the comfort too much to protest. ''Oh, Briana, I'm so sorry,'' he murmured as he rocked her back and forth.

She pressed her face into his shoulder and went on talking, her voice muffled against his warm skin. ''I ran away while he was out of the country on business. I didn't dare come back to St. Thomas because I knew he'd look for me here. So I went to Vermont. Finally I saw a lawyer and told him the whole story. The lawyer handled everything for me. Ricardo agreed to the divorce because he didn't want his...his eccentricities brought out in court. I never saw him again.''

They were silent for long moments. Drake's hand stroked her hair. Then she said, ''Aside from my lawyer, I never told anyone the truth about my marriage...until now.''

He continued to hold her for long minutes until her trembling had stopped, and she relaxed completely against him. ''I could kick myself,'' he said softly, ''the way I've been badgering you. All the stupid, insensitive innuendos.''

"It's all right. You couldn't have known," she mumbled.

With careful hands he smoothed her hair off her forehead, stroking it gently. After a moment he said, "I'll wait, Briana." Quietly he got to his feet and helped her up. "I'll take you home now. But I want you to think about something. You have to let go of the past if you're ever going to trust a man again. I want you to give me a chance to prove I'm not like your ex-husband."

CHAPTER TEN

BRIANA THREW BACK THE SHEET and felt for the
sheer silk of her robe. Finding it, she slipped it
on, tying the belt as she walked to a bedroom
window. Since the air conditioning was on, the
window was closed and the curtains drawn. She
pushed back one of the soft curtain panels and
looked out at the night. Stars twinkled brightly
in a clear sky. The moon provided enough light
for her to discern the outlines of the yard and
driveway.

She'd been in bed for a long time—hours, it
seemed. But she couldn't sleep. Ever since
Drake had brought her back to the house, she'd
been having second thoughts about telling him
so much. Looking back on the evening, she
feared she'd made a spectacle of herself. The
incident in his suite had caused her to forget
caution and common sense, and now he knew
things about her past that no one else knew.
Once she'd told him she'd never allow him to
have a hold on her. Yet tonight she'd gone back
on that vow. He had information that could be
used against her now, although she couldn't in

these long night hours think how. She was sure that if there was any way to use information to manipulate someone, however, Drake would recognize it.

Why couldn't she trust him? He wanted a chance to prove that he wasn't like her ex-husband, he'd said. She knew Ricardo *had* made her more distrustful than most women. The problem with Drake was that she knew too much about his past relationship with her family. She found it very nearly impossible to believe that he could forget she was an Ivensen. She paced the floor restlessly, castigating herself for giving Drake another weapon to use against her if he should choose to do so.

After a while she went back to bed, still wide-eyed. Eventually she slept in fitful dozes until morning.

ERIK WAS ALREADY AT BREAKFAST when she entered the dining room. "You're up early," she commented.

"I noticed the grass needs cutting. Thought I'd see if I could get the mower running."

Briana looked at him in surprise. Erik offering to make himself useful around the house without being asked? What had come over him? More to the point, what did he want? She helped herself to scrambled eggs from the warming tray and one of Ida's homemade biscuits. "I was thinking yesterday that the yard needed tending.

I'm glad you're going to do something about it."

"If I'm to live here," he said lightly, "I'd better do my part to keep things going. Incidentally I gave Ida some grocery money so you won't have to worry about that for a couple of weeks."

"You're being terribly helpful all of a sudden. What's behind it?"

He grinned at her suspicious look. "I don't blame you for wondering." He shrugged good-naturedly. "Maybe being away all those weeks made me appreciate home and family more. I've been meaning to apologize to you, and this is as good a time as any." It was as if he were a split personality, and she was getting a rare glimpse of his good side.

"Apologize? For what?"

He laughed. "For which one of my many sins? The truth is I've been feeling rotten about the things I said to you in the study the first night I was back. I admit I was feeling defensive. No matter how chummy you get with Rutledge, I doubt that I'll ever be able to feel friendly toward him. Still, I had no right to say what I did."

"No, you didn't," she agreed. "Those accusations you made—they aren't true."

"If you say so, that's good enough for me. The point I'm trying to make is that your private life is none of my business. You were right about that."

Briana gazed at him doubtfully. "When you went to New York, you left me in a dreadful bind. I wanted to strangle you."

"Don't blame you," he said with seeming earnestness. "You may not believe this, but the main reason I left as I did was that I simply couldn't face you and grandmother and tell you I'd lost the house. It was cowardly, I know, but I couldn't help it." He frowned. "What I could have helped was taking that money from the Rutledge Corporation in the first place. I meant to pay it back, honestly. I kept thinking I'd hit a lucky streak on the horses or cards, and I'd put it all back without anyone being the wiser."

"Oh, Erik, don't you know most people who steal from their companies start out thinking that? You were fooling yourself."

"I understand that now. You'll never know how sorry I am about losing the house. I admire you for the way you've handled everything, the way you're protecting grandmother. I still don't know how you got Rutledge to go along with you. The only side of him I ever saw was the hard-bitten self-interested business magnate."

"He isn't that single-minded," she said. "He works hard, but he has a selfless side. For one thing, he's very fond of his sister and niece. They live with him. It was just lucky for me that I met him at a time when Patty was doing poorly in school, and he was extremely worried about her. When I told him that I'm planning to teach, he thought I might be able to help Patty. He offered me the use of the house as a part of the remuneration, so I could hardly turn down the tutoring job.''

Erik helped himself to strawberry preserves from a crystal dish. "His sister's divorced, isn't she?"

"Yes. Her husband deserted her when Patty was a small child. She told me she wouldn't have known which way to turn if Drake hadn't been there."

"Hmm," he said thoughtfully. "I've seen her around. I think I've seen the niece, too. Isn't she a tall girl, slender with long brown hair? Has a Rutledge look about her."

"Yes. Where did you meet her?"

"I haven't met her, but I used to see her during noon hour at one restaurant or another around town. She was usually with girl friends. Once or twice I saw her with an older man, though. I didn't recognize him."

"That was Abel Weldon," Briana told him. "Patty was seeing him against the wishes of her mother and Drake. They were both terribly worried about it when I first started tutoring Patty. He's something of a ne'er-do-well, from what I've heard."

Erik poured himself more coffee. "I can see why Rutledge was worried. He must have thought the man was interested in his niece because of his money. He was probably right, too."

"Yes, but Patty couldn't see it. Weldon has left St. Thomas for a job in Texas, so that's no longer a problem. We all breathed a sigh of relief when he left."

"All except Patty?"

"She's young. She'll recover."

"How did Rutledge get him to leave?"

Briana looked up from her plate, startled. "I didn't say he did."

He gave her a long look. "I'll bet that's what happened, though. To men like Rutledge, money is power. And they use that power to get what they want. It wouldn't surprise me if he paid the man to get rid of him." He saw her troubled look and gestured carelessly. "Hey, that's the way the world works. I'm not criticizing Rutledge. Our ancestors did the same kind of thing." He uttered a short laugh. "Maybe I'm just envious because I don't have the money to make me a man of influence, in spite of the Ivensen name."

"I wouldn't know about that," Briana said warily. "Maybe Drake did talk to Weldon. Anyway, he's out of Patty's life."

"You've become fond of the girl, haven't you?"

"Yes," Briana admitted. "Her mother, too. Ruth had a hard life before she came to live with Drake. Both of them want Patty to have more advantages than they had at her age. Now that Weldon's gone, she's thinking of going to college in New England. We're all pleased about that."

"Lucky kid," he remarked. "Not every girl has an uncle who can afford to send her anywhere she wants to go to college."

They were silent for long moments, and Briana watched Erik from the corner of her eye as he finished a hearty breakfast. It had been a long time since they had talked together comfortably like this. For the first time in memory, he seemed to be taking an interest in her and Margaret. Maybe his brush with the law had changed him after all.

"Erik," she said at length, "you've known about father and Drake's mother for a long time, haven't you?"

"It seems I've always known it," he replied readily. "I was eight when it all happened. Everybody in the house knew they were having an affair, except you—and for a long time grandmother. When she found out, grandmother fired the woman. You were too young to understand what was going on. I used to hide in that hall closet near the kitchen and eavesdrop on the servants' gossip."

Briana remembered that her brother, as a child, had been good at slipping up on people unnoticed. She could imagine him skulking around the house to listen in on the servants' conversations. "What did you overhear?"

"Actually I learned all the details from

the servants. Grandmother and father would never answer my questions about Rutledge's attack. Generally the servants resented Pearl and thought she had delusions of grandeur. They didn't think father was interested in a permanent relationship with her. They thought she was naive to imagine otherwise."

"According to Drake, father asked Pearl to marry him. She loved him very much."

He shrugged. "That shows how deluded she was. Her suicide certainly proved her instability."

Briana shook her head. "Drake is convinced her drowning was accidental. She cared too much for her children and what would happen to them to take her own life. I think father really did love Pearl. He wasn't the kind of man to take unfair advantage of a servant. You know that, Erik."

"Well, I can't believe he meant to marry her. Grandmother would have thrown a fit."

Briana sighed. "I know he hardly ever opposed her. She's so strong willed, and I guess he preferred peace to family turmoil. But surely for the woman he loved he would have been willing to do the right thing, even if it meant standing up to grandmother."

Erik regarded her with amused tolerance. "Briana, you always were an idealist. Don't you know that 'right' is whatever is expedient and what doesn't interfere with one's creature comforts?''

"Only cynics believe that," she retorted.

He chuckled to himself. "Realists, little sister."

With a feeling of helplessness, she watched him leave the table. Erik actually believed what he had said. He also believed that background and bloodlines gave a person certain privileges not permitted to other people. Perhaps that belief was what had made it possible for him to embezzle money from his employer without a twinge of conscience. Her brother, she thought sadly, was short on compassion, as well as conscience.

But she wasn't ready to give up on Erik quite yet. He had given Ida grocery money, and he'd offered to take care of the lawn. And he hadn't asked for anything in return. He seemed to want to help her, if belatedly. Surely there was some good in him.

AT MIDMORNING she went in to see her grandmother, who was dressed for the day in pale blue crepe.

"I'm glad to see you ate all your breakfast," remarked Briana, eyeing the tray that still sat on the secretary. "Did you have a restful night?"

"Yes, thank you." Margaret motioned her to a chair and sat facing her. "I'm glad you came in before going to work. I want to talk to you about Drake Rutledge.''

"Yes?"

"I don't like your having dinner with him. Working for him is one thing, but it ought to end there.''

"Why, grandmother?"

"Don't be obstinate," Margaret said impatiently. "You've led a sheltered life. You've never had any dealings with a man like that.''

Sheltered, thought Briana dryly. *If you only knew!* "Aren't you forgetting that I'm twenty-five years old? I've been married. I've been on my own for the past five years.''

"Then consider what people will think.''

Briana shook her head helplessly. "Grandmother, I don't give a fig what people think. Besides, anyone who sees me with Drake will probably think I'm fortunate. Don't you know he's considered one of the best catches in the islands?''

"Catches!" Margaret's expression was distasteful. "I despise that expression. Surely you aren't trying to 'catch' Drake Rutledge! You can't possibly be seriously interested in that man—in any personal way. Why, after being married to someone like Ricardo, the very idea is laughable.''

Briana was tired of having Ricardo held up to her as the perfect husband. "Drake is worth ten of Ricardo.''

Margaret stared at her. "I can't believe you said that, Briana. Has your divorce made you so bitter?"

"I'm merely stating a fact, and I'm in a better position to know than you are."

Margaret's cheeks were pink. "Drake Rutledge is common!"

"By your standards, maybe. But don't upset yourself. There's nothing serious between Drake and me, anyway. I doubt that there ever could be."

Margaret did not appear to be entirely satisfied with Briana's response. She changed the subject crossly. "Where's Erik?"

"Working on the lawn mower, I believe. He's going to cut the grass."

"We've always hired someone to do that. I don't know why you can't see that we need a gardener, at least part-time."

Poor Margaret would never accept the truth of their financial state, Briana realized. "He doesn't have anything else to do," she said. "And doing your own yard work is in vogue, didn't you know?"

Briana's facetiousness was lost on her grandmother, who merely lifted her shoulders in a way that said she would never understand her grandchildren's generation.

"I'm going into town to pick up a few things before I meet Patty. Anything you need?"

"No, thank you. Would you remind Ida to

come for my tray before you go? I rang the bell, but if she heard, she chose to ignore it. Servants are so cheeky nowadays. In my time, we wouldn't have put up with it for a moment.''

"I'll take your tray," Briana said, getting up. "Ida was scrubbing the kitchen floor the last time I saw her."

AFTER TAKING CARE of her errands, Briana drove to the school. She arrived a few minutes early and was sitting in her car, glancing absently through a college catalog that had come in the mail, when another car pulled up behind her. The driver honked, and she looked back to see Erik getting out of his car. He came forward and leaned down to speak through the open window on the passenger side.

"I was driving by and saw you sitting here. Waiting for your pupil?"

"Yes, she's due any minute. I thought you were mowing the lawn."

"Couldn't get the mower going. I took the engine apart and after two hours figured out what was wrong. I'm not the world's best mechanic, I fear. I've just come from the hardware store. They're out of the part I need, but they expect a shipment this afternoon. That's why I stopped. I was wondering if you could pick it up when you return from St. John. It would save me another trip."

"Sure." She glanced toward the school. "Here comes Patty now."

The girl approached the car, her gaze fixed on Erik. "Hi," Briana said to her. "This is my brother, Erik. Erik, meet Patty Heyward."

Erik straightened, smiling. "Hi, Patty." He opened the car door for her.

"Hello," Patty said, ducking her head shyly. She got into the car, and Erik shut the door, leaning down again with his hands on the window opening. His eyes rested on Patty's face.

"I just had a great idea," he said, looking from Patty to Briana. "Let me take you two gals to lunch before you leave. I was planning to grab something in town, anyway."

Patty glanced quickly at Briana. "Could we? Mother's visiting a friend and won't be home until later."

"Won't Greta be expecting us?" Briana asked.

"She's making jam today. We'd probably only get a sandwich at home. Oh, let's stay!"

Since Abel Weldon's departure Patty had shown little interest in anything besides her schoolwork. Briana knew she could use the diversion of a leisurely lunch in town. Since Erik seemed to be on his best behavior today, Patty would probably enjoy it. So she gave in.

"Good, I'll meet you in ten minutes," said Erik, naming a sidewalk café in Palm Passage.

He was already there when they arrived, sitting at an umbrella-covered table in the cobbled passageway. He waved to them, then stood up to hold Patty's chair for her.

Briana smiled to herself when Patty blushed. Erik was certainly putting himself out to be charming.

"How come I've never met you before?" Patty asked, looking at Erik from beneath lowered lashes.

"I've been living in New York, and I just got back a couple days ago. But I used to see you around town. I always notice pretty girls."

Patty looked a little flustered and opened her menu. After they had ordered, she asked, "What did you do in New York?"

"Business—you'd probably find it boring. I'd rather talk about you. Briana tells me you plan to go away to college next year."

"I might," she answered. "Briana's helping me prepare for the entrance exams. I hope I don't disappoint everybody after all the time she's spent with me."

"You'll do fine," Briana told her.

Erik's blue eyes rested on Patty's flushed face. "Don't tell me she's got brains, as well as beauty. That's a fascinating combination."

The girl laughed self-consciously.

Erik winked at her. "Just stating the facts, ma'am."

He continued to charm Patty as they ate, and Briana was content to sit back and watch her pupil blossoming under such flagrant flattery. She would have to thank Erik later for paying so much attention to her. He couldn't know how much she needed a little male attention right now.

When they had finished their meal, Erik said, "This is too good to end. I have another brilliant idea." He glanced at Briana. "I could borrow the Fitzcannons' motorboat. We could take a spin, maybe stop at one of the uninhabited islands for some beachcombing. Would you like that, Patty?"

Patty's dark eyes widened in delight. "Oh, yes! Let's do it, Briana."

"Now, wait a minute," Briana said. "We have work to do this afternoon. You have two tests to study for. It's a nice thought, Erik, but we can't. Maybe some other time."

Patty's face fell. "Don't you ever feel like forgetting all that for an afternoon?"

"I certainly do," Briana said, "but then I remember what your uncle is paying me for. We'd better go now, or we'll miss the one-o'clock ferry."

She pushed her chair back, and Patty reluctantly followed her example. Erik stood up and threw a casual arm around Patty's drooping shoulders. "Don't look so sad, honey. Briana's right. Maybe we can do it another day."

Patty looked up at him and smiled. "Okay. Thanks for lunch."

He bowed over her hand playfully. "The pleasure was all mine, Miss Heyward."

Patty talked about him all the way to St.

John. "Gosh, he's so handsome, Briana. Why didn't you ever mention him?"

Briana laughed. "The subject never came up."

Erik certainly seemed to have made a conquest. She tried to see her brother through Patty's eyes and decided that he probably would seem sophisticated and handsome to a seventeen-year-old girl who didn't know him. She decided Patty's interest in Erik was harmless enough. At least it had taken her mind off Abel Weldon for a little while.

"Has he ever been married?" Patty was asking.

"No, not even engaged."

"Does...does he have a girlfriend?"

"He dates Jane Fitzcannon occasionally."

"Oh. It was her boat he was going to borrow, then?"

"Uh-huh."

Patty was silent for several moments, then asked, "Is he in love with her?"

Briana glanced over at her sharply. "With who, Jane? I don't think so." She felt a small twinge of concern. She had wanted Patty to be diverted, not infatuated. *Oh, well,* she told herself, *she'll have forgotten Erik by tomorrow.*

This assessment seemed to be true, for Patty didn't mention Erik again that afternoon nor during Briana's next few sessions with her.

Nor did Drake put in an appearance at the

house while she was there. She hadn't seen him since the night she had talked too much in his suite. She felt certain he was avoiding her. He'd probably decided she was a bundle of emotional hang-ups.

She didn't know whether to feel glad or sad about that. When he left her alone, she didn't have to deal with the mixed feelings his presence stirred up in her. On the other hand, she found that she missed him constantly. When she was working with Patty, she often glanced toward the house, half expecting to seek Drake coming toward them. When he wasn't there, she always felt a twinge of disappointment.

She told herself she wanted to see him again just to overcome the last memory he had of her, that of a hysterical female.

CHAPTER ELEVEN

A WEEK LATER Patty met Briana at school, full of enthusiasm about the college catalogs that had been arriving in the mail.

"Gosh, I'm really starting to get scared about the entrance exams," Patty confided when they were seated on the ferry. "Before, when I wasn't interested in college, I didn't care that much. Reading those catalogs has got me excited about going away to school, though."

"Even if you score low on the exams," Briana told her, "most colleges will let you attend one semester on probation to see if you can do the work."

Patty's face perked up. "Really? That makes me feel a lot better."

"I think you're going to be surprised at your scores," Briana said. "You've made amazing progress in your grades since we started working together. I have a book at home that will help you prepare for entrance exams, by the way. I'll bring it with me on Friday. If nothing else, it'll give you an idea what kind of questions to expect."

"Good." Patty smiled at her. "There's a small

liberal-arts college in Connecticut that sounds great—in the catalog at least. They have a good drama department, and I think I might like acting."

Briana was delighted with Patty's enthusiasm and encouraged her to talk about her college plans until they reached the house. The two of them were laughing as they entered the breakfast parlor. Ruth was already seated at the table, and Greta began to serve the food as soon as they had taken their places.

"I've been telling Briana about that college in Connecticut," Patty informed her mother. "I want her to see their catalog. Do you know where it is?"

"I've been reading it. It's in my room," Ruth said. "I'll bring it down later."

Briana noticed suddenly that the woman looked troubled. "Aren't you feeling well?" she asked in concern.

Ruth shook her head, but she was gazing at Patty, whose attention was fixed on the date muffin she was buttering. "I'm fine. A little worried about my daughter, though."

Patty looked up in surprise. "What? I don't look sick, do I?"

"No. You've never been healthier, as far as I know. That's what I told Mr. Edelson when he called me this morning."

Patty put down her knife. "Mr. Edelson? The high-school principal?"

"The very one," responded Ruth dryly. "He

called to find out why you were absent yesterday afternoon. He wanted to know if you were ill, or if there had been a change in the tutoring schedule.''

Patty looked down at her plate. "What did you say?"

"That I didn't know you'd been absent."

"Oh, mom," Patty groaned, "did you have to say that?"

"What else could I tell him, Patty, since you didn't see fit to inform me that you left school at noon yesterday? Where did you go?"

Patty met her mother's look with a defiant lift of her chin. "I wanted to be alone for a while to think about college. I felt too restless to sit in a classroom all afternoon. So after lunch I walked down to the harbor. I just sat and thought and then read a book until it was time to board the ferry."

Ruth shook her head, disappointment in her eyes. "Oh, Patty."

"It's true!" Patty declared. "That's what I did."

"Why didn't you tell me yesterday? Did you think Mr. Edelson wouldn't call? That I'd never find out?"

"I would have told you. Honest."

Ruth looked at Briana and shrugged helplessly.

"I'm going up to look for that catalog," Patty said, placing a muffin and a piece of chicken in a napkin. Her chair scraped on the shining floor tiles.

"You haven't finished your lunch," Ruth said to her retreating back.

"This'll be enough."

Ruth sighed, then turned back to Briana. "She'll pout all afternoon now. How does she manage to make me feel in the wrong, when she knows she's at fault?"

"It's her defense. She's feeling guilty."

Ruth shook her head sadly. "She's been in such a good mood the past few days, talking nonstop about the colleges she wants to apply to. Last night we went through a stack of fashion magazines and discussed what new clothes she should get. I was feeling so good about everything, and now this...."

"Don't make too much of it, Ruth," Briana advised gently.

"Do you think I shouldn't have told her about Mr. Edelson's call?"

"You had to tell her, of course. Does Drake know?"

"No." Ruth pursed her lips. "I wanted to talk to Patty first."

"Her grades have improved so much," Briana said tentatively. "Maybe she deserved an afternoon off."

"Maybe," Ruth agreed. "At least we know she wasn't with Abel Weldon."

"She was probably at the harbor, just as she said."

"Hmm," mused Ruth. "Tomorrow Mr. Edelson will make her stay an hour after school in study hall. Don't you think that's punishment enough?"

Briana nodded. "I doubt that she'll do it again now that she knows the principal will be checking up on her."

"I don't think there's any point in telling Drake, do you? He'll just get angry and upset. Why bother him with it?"

"I couldn't agree more."

Greta came in with an apple cobbler. "Where's Patty?" she asked. "This is one of her favorite desserts."

"She'll probably want some later," Ruth said. When Greta had returned to the kitchen, she continued, "I have a favor to ask of you, Briana."

Briana dipped her spoon into the warm cobbler. "Anything. You know that."

"I want to spend a few days on St. Croix with a friend of mine from school days. She's married, but her husband is away on business. She phoned yesterday. I hadn't heard from her in more than a year, and I really would like to see her again. Besides, I think it would do me a world of good to get away from home for a bit."

"I'm sure it would. If you want me to encourage you to go, I will. I think it's a great idea."

"I've already decided to go. Drake says I should. The thing is, I don't want to leave Patty here with no one but Greta to keep an eye on her. Drake might have to work late, and I don't like the idea of her being here alone. I know she's practically grown-up, but she can be so unreliable. Skipping school yesterday afternoon is a prime example of what I mean."

"I'm sure if you talk to her—"

Ruth shook her head. "I don't want her to think I don't trust her. But I'd feel much better if you could stay here at the house while I'm gone."

"Me, stay here? Ruth, I don't really think that's necessary." She made a wry face. "Besides, grandmother wouldn't like it at all."

"Didn't you say your brother is back home? She won't be alone. Please, Briana. I don't think I'll enjoy myself unless I know someone I trust is here with Patty when Drake's gone. If I asked anyone else, Patty would throw a fit and accuse me of thinking she needs a baby-sitter. But she likes you, and since you're here three afternoons a week, anyway, she won't think of you as a guard."

"Well. . . I do need to do some research on St. John. For one thing, I want to visit the sites of some of the old sugar plantations and take some snapshots. Patty might like to come with me."

"Then you'll stay with her?"

"When are you leaving?"

"Friday afternoon. I'll only be gone three or four days."

"All right," Briana said. "I can't say no because I'm sure you won't have a minute's peace if you leave Patty here alone."

Ruth smiled happily. "I don't know how to thank you."

"You already have," Briana said, finishing her cobbler. But as she thought about spending several days and nights in Drake's house, she had to fight down an urge to tell Ruth she had changed her mind. It was silly to feel uneasy, she told herself resolutely. Patty and the servants would be there. It wasn't as if she would be alone with Drake.

As SHE'D EXPECTED, Margaret voiced adamant disapproval. "If Drake Rutledge is as wealthy as people say, why can't he hire a woman to stay with his niece while his sister is gone?" she wanted to know.

They were at dinner. Briana responded, "He could, of course. But Patty knows me. She'll be happier with me there than if Drake brought in a stranger. Besides, I've been wanting to do some research on St. John. This will give me a perfect opportunity."

"What kind of research?" Erik put in, his tone rife with innuendo. Apparently he'd given up playing the understanding brother. It had been a nice few days while it lasted.

Briana looked at him sharply. "On the sugar plantations, particularly Annaberg."

"I see." His grin was mocking. "Well, you're getting very cozy with the Rutledges—practically one of the family."

"Don't be absurd," Briana snapped.

"Erik's right," said Margaret. "It does look as if they're your social equals. Drake Rutledge always did think too highly of himself."

"It may surprise you, grandmother," Briana said, "but Drake *is* our social equal. In fact, he probably bypassed us long ago. His name is on every hostess's preferred list. It's time you got over thinking of him as a servant's boy."

"Ridiculous!" sniffed Margaret. "There are still a few of the old order left who know the importance of breeding and background."

"I don't want to argue with you," said Briana tiredly. "I'm going to stay with Patty while Ruth's gone, and that's that." She left the table, pretending to be oblivious to Margaret's outraged stare and Erik's smirk.

ON FRIDAY, Drake had a late luncheon meeting with a business associate visiting from Arizona. Two years earlier the man had been looking for a partner to invest in a Phoenix condominium complex and had been put in contact with Drake by his broker. The partnership had proven to be quite profitable, and now Drake had offered the Arizonan, Bill Drummond, a block of shares in the St. Croix hotel he planned to build. Drummond had come to Charlotte Amalie to discuss the deal and to enjoy a short vacation with his wife at the same time.

The two men met for lunch at two o'clock, and their discussion lasted until after four. When Drake left Drummond, he decided not to return to the Grand Reef. Instead he went home early. He would be able to say goodbye to Ruth before she left for Charlotte Amalie, where she would be met by the Rutledge Corporation's pilot and flown in the company plane to the neighboring island.

In the back of his mind the past few days had been the knowledge that Briana would be staying in his house while Ruth was gone. He was looking forward to her presence far more than he would have admitted to anyone except himself. The revelations Briana had made about her marriage that evening in his suite had made him see her in a different light—at least part of the time. Her reluctance to become intimately involved with him was more understandable now; at the same time he couldn't quite shake the feeling that her reserve with him was partly due to their very different backgrounds. He would find himself forgetting that she was an Ivensen, and then the knowledge would come back to him with a jolt. Could she really be so totally different from the rest of them?

Whenever he thought about Briana's staying

on St. John, he cautioned himself to play it cool. But his blood sang with anticipation as he left the restaurant Friday afternoon and walked along the busy Charlotte Amalie street, whistling.

At the corner he caught sight of Tom Edelson, the principal of Patty's school, coming toward him. Drake halted on the curb and called out, "Edelson!"

The principal looked up, saw Drake and made his way around a group of tourists to his side. "Mr. Rutledge, how are you?"

The men shook hands. "Fine, thanks. Good to see you again. How's my niece doing in school?"

"Better, much better. If she continues to improve, I see no reason why she can't graduate with a B average."

"Good. I always knew she was capable."

"Now that we've settled that little matter of her unexcused absence the other day, I'm sure she'll think twice before doing it again."

"Oh?" Drake's smile faded. "What day was that?"

Edelson looked a little hesitant. "Why, Tuesday. Patty played hooky in the afternoon. Didn't Mrs. Heyward tell you?"

"I haven't had much chance to talk to Ruth since Tuesday," said Drake.

"I kept Patty in study hall yesterday, and we had a good talk. She promised not to do it again."

"Well, nice seeing you," said Drake abruptly. "I'm on my way to the ferry, and I haven't much time."

By the time Drake got off the ferry at the Cruz Bay dock, he felt indignant, as well as worried. Why hadn't he been told? How could Ruth cover up for Patty? Didn't she realize that wasn't the way to help the girl? He found one of the young men who regularly hung around the dock looking for odd jobs, and paid him to drive him to the house in his battered Jeep.

"You give your Pontiac to that sexy blond I see drivin' it, or what?" inquired the young man as the Jeep roared away from the dock.

"She's Patty's tutor," said Drake in a clipped voice, "and I haven't given her the car. She's only using it."

"Neat little package," the fellow grinned slyly at Drake. "You got somethin' goin' with her?"

Drake turned to him coldly. "Such as?"

"Nothin'. I didn't mean nothin'." He didn't open his mouth again during the rest of the drive. Drake often gave him temporary jobs, and he obviously didn't want to press his luck.

At the house Drake found Ruth in her bedroom, packing. Briana was with her, sitting at the vanity table, talking.

Ruth looked up as he entered the room. "Oh, hello, Drake. Have you come to see me off?"

"Yes." He eyed the suitcase speculatively.

"You're taking enough clothing for a month. How long did you say you're planning to stay?"

His sister laughed. "Only a few days, but I'm not sure what we'll be doing. I want to be prepared for anything."

"I've never seen her so excited," Briana put in.

"Hmm," Drake murmured. "Does Dorothy's brother still live on St. Croix?"

"Oh, hush!" Ruth blushed prettily. "Sam and I have been friends for years. There's not a smidgen of romance between us."

"So you say," Drake remarked.

Briana watched him teasing his sister and wondered what was wrong. Now that she knew him better, she was sensitive to his moods, and she felt that beneath his bantering tone he was upset about something. Surely he didn't begrudge Ruth this holiday?

"There." Ruth took a last look through her bureau drawers. "I think that's everything."

Briana zipped the suitcase closed, and as she turned it upright, Drake said, "I ran into Edelson this afternoon."

Both Ruth and Briana looked up at him. "He mentioned that Patty had played hooky again," Drake went on. "He naturally assumed I'd been informed of it."

"We didn't want to bother you," Ruth said.

"Bother me! What's going on here?" He glanced from Ruth to Briana. "Ruth, you knew

I should be told. It seems Patty hasn't given up her old habits after all.''

"She wanted to be alone to think about college,'' Ruth said defensively. "She didn't do anything really wrong.''

"Except leave school without permission,'' Drake reminded her. "You do recall that Patty has lied to us before about where she goes and with whom?''

"Abel Weldon is gone!'' Ruth said impatiently. "We don't need to worry every time she's out of our sight now. She's promised not to do it again.''

Drake thrust his hands into his trouser pockets, scowling darkly. "Ruth, you know how much Patty's promises are worth!''

"Well, I think you're overreacting,'' she told him. "She had to spend extra time in study hall as punishment. I thought that was enough, and Briana agreed with me.''

Drake's gaze swung to Briana's face. "I might have known.''

Briana bristled. "What do you mean by that?''

"I mean that you've always been inclined to take Patty's side.''

"Drake, there are no sides in this!'' Briana flared. "Patty is seventeen and planning to go away to college. You can't follow her around checking on her for the rest of her life. Or do you intend to have her tailed when she goes to New England?''

"Don't get on your high horse with me, Briana!" he grated.

Realizing she was only making him angrier, she tried to modulate her tone. "She's been working hard recently, really she has. Skipping an afternoon's classes once is nothing to worry about."

"Oh, yes? You aren't particularly qualified to judge, are you? You haven't made such wise decisions in your own life—" Drake broke off abruptly.

Briana stared at him. "How dare you!" she exclaimed. "How dare you judge me, and how dare you barge in here and...and try to spoil Ruth's vacation before she even leaves the house. She hasn't been away from you and Patty for years. She's been looking forward to this, and you have to ruin it, don't you?"

"Briana, it's okay," Ruth intervened.

"No, it isn't okay! Who does he think he is, anyway?"

Drake made a furious sound in his throat. "I see I'm getting nowhere with this whole subject. We'll discuss it later, Ruth. I'll carry your suitcase to the car."

He lifted the case and walked out of the room. Ruth looked at Briana worriedly. "I'm not sure I should go now, with you and Drake at odds like this."

"Go," Briana said, shaking her head. "Your brother and I seem to rub sparks off each other whenever we talk. Don't worry about it. I'll go about my own business while I'm here and leave him to his.''

''Well, if you're sure....''

''I'm sure.''

Ruth hugged her quickly and left the room. After a moment Briana wandered to the guest room where she would be sleeping. She got out some of her research materials and read them over until it was time to go down for dinner.

THE MEAL WAS DEFINITELY STRAINED. Even Patty seemed aware of the tension at the table and didn't chatter as she usually did. Apparently Drake hadn't mentioned his meeting with the principal, though, for she frequently glanced at her table companions with a quizzical look.

After dessert Patty murmured, ''Excuse me. I'm going to my room to wash my hair.''

Briana pushed her own chair back hastily. ''I'll go up with you. I want to get back to work.'' Drake slid a cool glance toward her, but she ignored it and walked away from the table.

''What's wrong with Uncle Drake?'' Patty asked as they climbed the stairs.

''Must be business problems.'' They had reached Briana's door, so she said, ''Good evening, Patty. Sleep well.''

In her room, however, Briana found it hard to get back to her research. She wondered worriedly if her entire stay here was to be as uncomfortable as dinner had been. She almost wished Drake would stay at the hotel while Ruth was gone. Finally she succeeded in bringing her attention back to her dissertation and spent the next couple of hours working.

The house was quiet when she put her folders and books aside and stretched her muscles, which were stiff from sitting so long at the desk. It was still too early for bed. She flipped on the small television set beside the bed. The Virgin Islands received only one channel clearly, and it carried a rerun of an old Western movie. She shut off the set and decided to go down to the patio for a while. She couldn't, she told herself, stay shut up in this room whenever Drake was in the house. Since she hadn't heard any sounds from below for some time, she assumed that he was in his study or in his own bedroom.

She tucked her knit shirt into the waistband of the khaki slacks she was wearing and left the room. Her steps were muffled by the carpeting. Downstairs the only lights turned on were at the front of the house. She slipped through the darkened kitchen and out the door leading to the patio.

The night was lovely, clear and with a lazy breeze blowing in off the water. She passed through the roofed patio and out into the garden where the narrow stone-cobbled paths were clearly visible in the moonlight. Throwing back her head, she gazed up at the sky. The stars looked near enough to touch. How beautiful it was in this part of the world. How could anyone want to live anywhere else?

She walked slowly along the nearest path for several yards, then stopped abruptly when she caught a whiff of tobacco. It was a familiar odor, the sweet aroma of the brand Drake used. She couldn't see him, but since she didn't want to stumble into him in the dark, she reversed her direction and started back toward the house.

"Briana." Drake stepped out of the shadow of a tall shrub on her left.

She started at the sound.

"Sorry. I didn't mean to frighten you. I came out to have a smoke and saw you leaving the house."

"Why didn't you say something sooner?"

"I was watching you. You look beautiful in the moonlight."

"I . . . I didn't mean to disturb you. I'll go back to the house and leave you to your smoke."

She heard him tapping the bowl of his pipe against his shoe. Then he came a few steps closer. "Don't go. We need to talk." He stuffed his pipe into a hip pocket, looking down at her. She could see his face quite clearly in the moonlight.

"What about?"

"Let's sit down." He touched her arm and led her to one of the low stone benches that were scattered about the garden.

When they were seated, he said, "I owe you an apology for what I said earlier in Ruth's room. I didn't mean to bring up your personal life."

"The things I told you," she said curtly, "were in confidence. I wouldn't have mentioned them at all if I hadn't been overwrought."

"I know, and I won't betray your confidence. You needn't worry about that."

"Fine," she murmured. "Anything else?"

He drew in a deep breath. "I still don't think you and Ruth should keep things from me. I can't help Patty if I don't know what's going on with her."

"You're making far too much of a simple adolescent impulse."

After a pause he muttered, "Maybe I am."

"I felt it was up to Ruth to tell you if she wanted you to know," Briana continued. "And I think we've exhausted that topic, don't you?" She started to stand up.

He reached out and touched her arm, effectively halting her movements. "I agree," he said. "I was only trying to keep you here by whatever means. But I can think of far better ways to spend our time." When she didn't resist, his arm moved around her, drawing her against him. His lips touched her forehead, the wing of her brow, her cheek, before settling with a warm sigh against her own.

Even as she wondered how she could be so

lacking in pride after his rudeness earlier, Briana gave in to the temptation of the moment. She inhaled the familiar scent of him—tobacco mingled with the clean masculine odor of his skin—and her lips softened willingly under his. She could enjoy his sensual magic without fear, she told herself. As long as Greta and Patty were in the house, she was safe against his going too far.

"Ah, Briana," Drake whispered, his mouth moving hungrily across her cheek toward her sensitive earlobe. "I've been counting the days until you came to live here with me."

"I'm not living here," she retorted in a desperate little voice. She should go back inside, she knew, but for a few more moments of pleasure she would have given anything. "I'm only keeping Patty company for a few days."

"So much can happen in a few days." His mouth moved back to hover over hers. Desire was burning in his eyes as he gazed down into her face.

"You...you promised not to rush me," she told him breathlessly. "You said you would wait."

"How long do you mean to keep me waiting?" He brushed his lips across hers seductively, then lifted his head and studied her for a long moment. "I've warned you before, Briana, not to play games with me."

"Drake, you mustn't get any ideas about my reasons for coming here."

"No games," he said a little roughly. The corner of his mouth quirked upward as he watched her tense expression. Then his lips descended, causing a swift, staggering impact on her senses. He parted her lips easily, exploring the warm sweet moistness as if he had laid claim to it. She trembled in his arms, which only made him press her more thoroughly against his hard length.

"Drake," she whispered despairingly as his lips left hers to trace a tantalizing trail back to her earlobe. "We can't always settle our differences this way. It...it isn't fair."

In reply he pushed her down beneath him on the bench, cushioning her body with his arms. "You like the way it makes you feel, though, don't you?"

"Yes, I do!" she confessed in a whisper, "but—"

He silenced her with another kiss, then held her wrists above her head on the bench. His grip was light; she could have freed herself if she'd tried, but she didn't. With deliberate boldness his other hand went to the waistband of her slacks, tugged at the knit of her shirt and freed it from its confinement. By the time he had slipped his fingers beneath the fabric and had caressed her lingeringly, she was quivering under his touch.

"You're driving me crazy, Briana, teasing and tempting, then pushing me away." His tone was deep and vibrant as he moved his palm along the warm softness of her skin, pausing to unhook the front clasp of her bra. "My touch gives you pleasure. I can make it even better for you if you'll let me."

"Oh, Drake," she murmured as he deliberately exposed one pink-tipped breast and bent to kiss it tenderly. "What is it you really want?" she quavered. "Do you want to punish me for who I am?"

"I want you, period," he said, his voice thick with desire, his tongue toying her taut nipple until it throbbed with exquisite pleasure. "And you want me. Don't fool yourself about that any longer." His breath fanned her heated skin as he removed her bra completely, freeing her other breast for his delight. Cupping its fullness in his hand, he brushed his thumb in agonizing circles around its peak until Briana squirmed in pleasure beneath him.

"It isn't enough," she panted at last. "I... I'm not a car or a hotel that you can have just because you want it. I know there are...are women who could meet you on your terms, but I can't! Not after what I've been through."

"Oh, Briana, Briana!" he groaned, pressing her body against him. His face was so close to hers that even by moonlight she could see the brooding of his dark eyes. He freed her wrists, and his hands came up to frame her face, his thumbs moving seductively along the line of her jaw. "Are you using your ex-husband as an excuse to keep me dangling?"

Her hands gripped his shoulders, and her voice was pleading as she said, "I don't toy with men. You of all people know how devastated I was by my marriage. I can't shrug off those memories so easily."

"So you continue to lead me on," he added ruthlessly, "until you're sure of what you want. And you may or may not decide that what you want is me."

Her fingers gripped fiercely, digging into the flesh of his shoulders through the loosely woven fabric of his shirt. Despite herself her body arched against him. "I've made no promises," she said desperately. "I'll not be pressured into anything. And I'm *not* leading you on."

"Then prove it," he muttered. He bent and dropped fiery kisses along her throat, down to the cleavage between her breasts. "Come inside with me, come into my bed. We'll spend the night exploring each other. I want to discover what pleasures you most, what will make you tremble for me. I'll make you forget that perverted ex-husband of yours, I promise you. Please, Briana." He lifted his head, and his gaze locked with hers, challenging and pleading at the same time.

Everything within her told her to give in, to lose herself in Drake's lovemaking, to try to banish all the painful memories in the sweetness of his arms. She squeezed her eyes shut in defense, and after a long moment she shook her head.

"Let me try!"

"No, Drake. I can't," she whispered sadly, looking at him once again.

She saw the bitterness take over his expression. He wouldn't beg, she knew that, and she almost said she was sorry, that she wanted more than anything for him to make love to her. But then the comforting weight of his body left hers as he levered himself to his feet. She sat up, too, staring up at him.

When he spoke, there was no longer any tenderness or even kindness in his voice. "It's going to be a long few days until Ruth gets back."

"You can always stay at your hotel while I'm here," she replied dully.

"Not on your life," he exclaimed. "I won't make it that easy for you."

In spite of herself Briana winced as he strode away from her.

CHAPTER TWELVE

THE WEEKEND was weighted with tension that seemed to fill every room in the house. True to his word, Drake didn't try to make it any easier for Briana by leaving. It seemed that every time she went into one of the sitting rooms or out to the patio, Drake was there ahead of her, smoking his pipe, sometimes reading. And every time he glanced up as she entered and scanned her with a mocking clinical look.

Meals were bearable only because Patty was there. Briana concentrated on talking to her, ignoring Drake unless he spoke to her directly. By Saturday evening she had decided it was easier to stay close to her room except at mealtimes. She explained to Patty that she had to work on her dissertation, which was true. The problem was she couldn't seem to concentrate on her work and found herself instead watching television or trying to read a paperback novel that failed to hold her attention.

Monday morning, when Drake had left for work and Patty for school, she felt as if she'd been let out of prison. She moved about the house at will, had breakfast in the open sunshine, then carried her paperwork down to one of the patio tables where she worked until noon.

She might have gone on working through lunch, unaware of the time, if Greta hadn't called to her from the back door. "Miss Ivensen! Patty's on the phone for you."

Briana went to the extension in the kitchen. "Hello, Patty? Where are you? Did you miss the ferry?"

"No. Listen, something has come up. I know you were going to help me with my English composition this afternoon, but the chemistry teacher told us today we're having a lab test tomorrow. Lissa Grey—she's a friend from school—wants me to go home with her this afternoon so we can study together."

"Where does she live?"

"In Charlotte Amalie, a few blocks from school. Lissa's a whiz in chemistry, Briana, and I really need her help. Besides, that English composition isn't due until Friday."

"You can stay as far as I'm concerned, but I think you'd better call Drake and let him know."

"Okay," Patty agreed cheerfully. "I'll call him right now. See you later."

"Don't stay too late," Briana cautioned, but she wasn't sure Patty heard her before she hung up.

She told Greta she wanted only a sandwich

for lunch and ate it on the patio as she continued with her work. By midafternoon she'd been at it for six hours and needed a break.

"That's enough history for one day," she murmured to herself as she gathered up her papers. She carried them back upstairs to her room. Then she changed into her bikini, grabbed a towel and headed for the beach.

As far as she could see in either direction, she had the beach to herself. She spread her towel on the sand, then swam vigorously for a while before returning to her spot and lying down on her stomach. With her cheek resting on her forearms, she sighed contentedly and closed her eyes. There was a slight cloud cover, just enough to filter the sun's heat to a wonderfully warm relaxing caress. It was one of the few times since Friday, she realized, that she had felt completely at ease.

Her mind began to drift disconnectedly, going back to the afternoon she had been there at the beach with Drake. Glossing over the harsh words they had exchanged, her thoughts dwelled instead on what had happened later as they lay on the sand. Against the darkness of her closed eyelids, she could see his tanned angular face as it had looked hovering above hers, his scar cutting across one cheek, his thick dark hair still wet and tangled from swimming, his brown eyes burning with a hunger that both excited and frightened her.

She remembered the way his lips had felt against her skin, how his fingers had touched her with intimate tenderness, and a drowsy sigh escaped her lips. *If only I could trust you, Drake,* she thought fervently, and then she slept....

She awoke later, completely disoriented. Raising her head, she stared around her, then she rolled over. (Almost immediately she rolled back again;) her backside felt as if it were very tight. She groaned and sat up very slowly.

The sun was much lower than it had been when she'd come to the beach. She'd left her watch at the house, but it must be five-thirty at least. She'd been asleep in the sun for two hours! Thank heaven, she had a good base of tan to begin with, or she would be in agony.

For a moment she had the dreadful feeling that she was incapable of getting up, the effort of moving was so severe. But she had to. Groaning aloud, she placed her palms on the towel and pushed herself upward until she could stand. She couldn't believe she had been so stupid as to fall asleep in the sun—she, who had been raised in the islands. Only tourists behaved with such ignorance. Many of them simply couldn't believe how fast their skin would burn, no matter how often they were warned, and they insisted on staying out too long. Then they suffered the miseries of sunburn for the rest of their vacations.

But she didn't even have the excuse of ignorance, she chided herself as she slid her feet carefully into her scuffs. Even the backs of her heels were a little tender. She picked up her towel and moved slowly toward the path that led to the house. The walk that ordinarily took three or four minutes required a quarter hour, since she had to be careful how she placed her feet. She felt exhausted by the time she reached the house.

She had wrapped her towel around her shoulders, and grateful that none of the servants was in sight, she slipped up the stairs and into her bedroom. Knowing that cool water was good for a burn, she ran the tub half-full and sat in it for a while. At first even the cool water felt sensitive on her skin, but it felt better after a bit. It was six o'clock when she stepped out of the tub and dried herself wherever she could stand the touch of the soft terry towel.

As she entered the bedroom from the bathroom, holding the towel in front of her, there was a knock at her door.

"Briana, are you in there?" It was Patty.

She opened the door, being careful to stand behind it in case anyone else was passing by. The girl came into the room, clearly in a cheerful mood, and Briana closed the door.

"You're a mind reader," she told her. "I was wondering who I could get to rub lotion on my back." She turned around so that Patty could see.

"Good grief!" the girl exclaimed. "You're cooked!"

"I fell asleep at the beach," Briana admitted. "Don't bother telling me how stupid it was. I've already told myself." She found a bottle of moisturizing lotion on the dresser and handed it to Patty. "Here, and be careful."

"Can you lie across the bed?"

"I think so. Most of the burn is on my backside." She discarded the towel and lay down.

Patty got on her knees on the bed and touched her shoulder lightly. Briana gritted her teeth as she squeezed the cool lotion over her back and began to rub it in.

"I'm sorry. Do you want me to go on?"

"Yes. Maybe it'll help. At least it's cool."

She bit her bottom lip as Patty smoothed the lotion over her back and arms, and finally over her legs. Afterward Briana put on shorts and a loose-fitting cotton shirt without a bra, since she was sure she couldn't stand such a snug-fitting garment.

Patty sat on the side of the bed and watched her get ready. "Better?" she asked.

"I believe so. Thanks." Briana sat on the vanity stool, trying not to wince, and picked up her hairbrush. "Well, how did you and Lissa get along?"

Patty smiled. "That's what I wanted to tell you. I had the greatest time. I can't remember when I've had so much fun."

Briana's brows lifted. "Studying chemistry?"

"Of course we did that, too. I think I'll do fine on the test. But after we finished studying, we just sat around and talked."

"Have you and Lissa been friends for a long time?"

"Yes—well, sort of casually. But after today I feel much closer to her. I learned some new dance steps and...." Patty faltered, as if she had said something she hadn't meant to.

"You and Lissa danced together?"

"Well...not exactly. What I mean is...there was this boy who studied with us. He's in our class at school." Patty smiled sheepishly. "You won't tell Uncle Drake, will you? We really did study first, honestly."

Briana's expression was amused. "I'm beginning to understand why you came home in such a good mood. This young man must have made quite an impression on you."

"He's really nice and so good-looking."

And he's Patty's age, Briana added to herself. The girl actually seemed enamored with a boy from school. That was a very good sign; it meant that she was getting over Abel Weldon. "I'm glad you had a good time. You did call Drake before going to Lissa's, didn't you?"

"I called, but he wasn't at the hotel. I meant to call later from Lissa's, but I was having so much fun I forgot."

"I don't suppose it matters. We'll work on your English tomorrow evening."

"Thanks, Briana." Patty jumped up and

headed for the door. "I'm going to shower before dinner. If I get a phone call, yell at me, will you?"

"You think the young man will call, do you?"

Patty grinned. "Maybe." She left the room, and Briana got up to stand at the window until dinner time. She was too sore to lie down.

She was glad she'd let Patty go to Lissa's house that afternoon. During the past few weeks she had seen some dramatic changes in her pupil. Her grades were up, she was forming a close friendship with a girl her own age, and now there was a young man in the picture. It was all so normal and right that surely Drake couldn't object to any of it. Still, she decided not to mention to Drake that Patty had stayed in Charlotte Amalie all afternoon. Patty could bring it up with him if she wanted to. But Briana didn't think she would. Patty saw her uncle as far too strict and old-fashioned.

Briana's lips curved wryly at the thought. Old-fashioned? It was hardly the term she would use in describing Drake Rutledge. But then she had seen a side of him that she was certain his niece had never dreamed of.

DRAKE SEEMED RELAXED at dinner, more talkative than he had been since Ruth left. As for Briana, it was all she could do to sit gingerly on the edge of her chair.

"Now," said Drake after Greta had served their dinner, "tell me how you occupied yourself this morning while we were gone, Briana."

Briana caught Patty's look and read her thoughts perfectly. She was afraid that if Drake found out she'd stayed in Charlotte Amalie instead of coming home for her tutoring session, he'd be suspicious and ask a lot of questions. She couldn't help sympathizing with the girl. Drake had to let go and allow Patty some freedom before she went away to college.

"I worked on my dissertation. Which reminds me of something I've been meaning to ask you. Do you know anyone on St. John who is descended from one of the old plantation families?" She sensed Patty relaxing as she steered the conversation in another direction.

"Maybe I do. Let's see, I think Dodie Gundersen—she runs that little shop in Cruz Bay—is descended from an old family on her mother's side."

"I was wondering if I could interview her. I'd like to know if she has any old family papers that might be useful in my dissertation."

"Want me to mention it to her?"

"Would you? She'd probably be more agreeable to seeing me if you asked her."

He shrugged. "Okay, I will."

"If you could set up a meeting for Wednesday or Thursday, I'd really appreciate it. I'll make a day of it and go on to the Annaberg ruins afterward.''

"Make it Wednesday, will you, Uncle Drake?" Patty asked. "I'll be home that afternoon, and maybe I can go with Briana."

"You're given three afternoons a week out of school to study," Drake reminded her.

"I know, and I just had a brilliant idea. I have to write a composition for English class, and I could do it about Annaberg. I could work on it Wednesday night after Briana and I get back."

Drake grinned. "Briana is actually going to get you interested in our history if you aren't careful."

"It's not so boring when you can see the places where things happened in the past. I've lived right here on St. John most of my life, and I've never thought of going to look at the Annaberg ruins before. You don't mind if I go with you, do you, Briana?"

"I'd love to have you," Briana assured her. "Mmm, this French onion soup is delicious." The soup was thick with melted cheese.

"It's one of Greta's specialties," Drake said. "I think she regrets the fact that we don't entertain guests more often. She doesn't have much chance to show off her abilities in the kitchen on a grand scale."

"What you need is a wife," commented Patty.

Drake quirked an eyebrow at her. "Oh, you think I can't entertain without a wife?"

His niece shrugged. "You could, I guess, but you don't. All you do is work. If you had a wife, she'd want to have parties and dinners and things like that. Haven't you ever even thought about getting married, Uncle Drake?"

Drake's dark eyes rested on her face. "What I might or might not have thought about is none of your business, young lady." His amused glance swung to Briana, who was very intent on eating her soup and refused to look at him.

Greta came in to clear the soup bowls and serve the salad. Conversation lagged as they ate. By the time they had finished the main course, Patty was chatting about some of her classmates. Briana found that she could meet Drake's look again without embarrassment, although she had to be careful not to lean back against her chair.

Drake wanted to linger over an after-dinner liqueur, but Briana refused to join him. "Is there something wrong?" he asked her quizzically. "You've been sitting there as stiff as a poker all through dinner."

"She's sunburned," Patty put in. "You ought to see her back, poor thing."

"Never mind my back," Briana said, getting slowly to her feet. "I know you two will excuse me. I really can't sit here any longer." She started to leave the room.

"Good heavens!" Drake exclaimed, and she halted, turning back again. "What happened to your legs?"

"Patty told you—I got a little too much sun."

"She wasn't kidding! How long were you out?"

"A couple of hours," Briana admitted with reluctance.

His look was one of surprise. "You should know better than that, even with your tan. Whatever possessed you to pull such a dumb stunt?"

Briana scowled at him. "Thanks a lot, Drake. I really needed that." She headed for the stairs, walking as quickly as she could without having her clothes chafe against her skin.

In her room she turned out the light with a heavy sigh. The soft cotton of her shirt rasped against her back as she raised it over her head. She undid her shorts, dropping them onto the floor. It was going to be an awkward night, she realized, as she stretched out on her stomach across the bed.

Her stay in Drake's house was proving to be a disaster. She hadn't been sleeping soundly, anyway, and now her sunburn added another distracting element. She had been tired to start with when she'd gone to the beach, and the sun had sapped even more of her energy. She felt leaden with weariness; in spite of her discomfort, she eventually drifted off to sleep.

WHEN SHE AWOKE sometime later, she lay still, staring into the darkness for long moments and trying to remember where she was. When she started to turn over, the tender skin on her back brought everything into focus. She groaned and flopped down on her stomach again. It was going to be an interminable night.

Something must have disturbed her, for she'd awakened abruptly. She listened, hearing the soft strumming sound of the electric bedside clock and the fainter hum of the air conditioner. Then she heard a movement near the bed and caught her breath.

"It's only me," said Drake. She felt his weight as he sat down beside her.

From her prone position she turned her head to peer around at him. She could barely make him out; he was only a slightly darker mass against the blackness of the room.

"What are you doing here?" She felt helpless and exposed in spite of the darkness and tugged at the sheet in a weak effort to cover herself. "I don't have any clothes on!"

"Lie still," he ordered. "I've brought some salve that will take the heat out of your sunburn."

She dropped her forehead against her arm and spoke against the sheet. "Patty already put lotion on it."

"This stuff is better." He touched her shoulder blade gently. "Dodie Gundersen makes it and sells it in her shop. It's an old family recipe and far more effective than commercial concoctions." His fingers began a slow circular movement on her back. "It may hurt a bit at first, but you'll feel much better in no time."

Briana trembled with a helpless rage that camouflaged her other emotions. "You've got nerve, coming into my room like this! Leave the salve, if you must, and I'll ask Patty to apply it in the morning."

"Be quiet." He smoothed more of the cooling salve onto her back, his fingers working their way down her spine slowly, fluidly. "You'll wake up the household. It might be rather embarrassing for you." She knew from the tone of his voice that he was smiling.

"More for you than for me, when I tell them you barged in here uninvited!" Sarcasm was the only defense she had against the insidious soothing of his fingers on her tender skin. His hand lingered now at the base of her spine.

"Straighten your arms," he said calmly. She obeyed, and his fingers massaged the salve into the back of one arm and then the other before he returned to her lower back. "Isn't that better?" he asked in a low neutral voice.

She had to admit that it was—much better. "Uh-huh," she murmured. Her eyelids drifted shut, and she gradually relaxed under the comforting hypnotic movement of his hands.

"How could you have slept for so long in the

sun?'' he inquired, his palm moving sensuously along the curve of her hip.

"I was tired," she mumbled sleepily.

"Still not sleeping well at night, eh?"

"Umm...."

"Does that feel good?"

"Umm...."

He chuckled. "Now for your legs." He shifted his weight and applied a dollop of salve at both ankles. He used both hands, one on each leg, and worked slowly upward. Briana drifted lazily on the edge of sleep. She felt so relaxed, as formless as liquid, and she wished the hands on her body would never stop what they were doing.

Until his hand slipped between her legs and feathered up her thigh. She moved restlessly. "I'm not sunburned there."

He laughed softly. "What about here?" His hand moved higher and slipped under her. "And here?" His touch became more intimate.

Fire rippled through Briana's body, forcing a soft moan from her lips. For endless agonizing moments Drake stroked her with gentle caresses until she felt breathless with excitement.

Then he bent over her, and his voice was low and thick as he nuzzled her ear. "You can turn on your side now."

It didn't occur to her to refuse. Within her, bands were loosening, barriers were crumbling. She had never felt so free of restraint in her life.

She rolled over, staring up into his shadowy face looming above her in the darkness.

"Is it too painful for you to lie like this?" Gently he rearranged the pillows so that she was propped between them and his own body.

She shook her head. "No, it isn't. The salve helps enormously. Thank you." What a ridiculous conversation they were having, she thought in bemusement.

He bent to brush his mouth over hers, teasing her lips until she ached with desire for more. With her free hand she touched the corded muscles in his neck and ran her fingers through his hair, feelings its smooth thickness against her palm.

"I've wanted this for so long," he whispered thickly against her mouth. "I've hardly been able to keep my hands off you these past few days, seeing you here, knowing every night that you were sleeping just down the hall. You're making me crazy, Briana. Crazy with wanting you."

His lips returned hungrily to hers, and his tongue began to probe her mouth. All the playfulness and teasing were gone now; his kiss was searing and intense. Briana could only cling to him, could only return the fervent pressure of his lips. There was no reality but Drake. It was he who had finally broken the barriers that had stood for so long, isolating her from men, from love.

His fingers were entangled in her hair, sliding sensuously through the long strands while his mouth played havoc with her face, her ears, her neck. His touch sent an electric response shuddering through her, ripping away the cautions she had imposed upon herself for so long. Desire flooded her, urgent sensations she had never experienced before. She pressed eagerly against the hand that cupped her breast. As his hand stroked her waist, then the curve of her hips, she arched her back, stretched languorously and shifted her thighs. "Drake," she murmured, her lips moist against his heated skin.

His breath was ragged when he pulled away to tug at his clothing. Then he sank down beside her again, gathering her closer with a desire that he held tautly reined, as if he couldn't believe in the reality of her eager response.

"Briana," he groaned, "say it's all right. Tell me you want me."

Her blood throbbed along her veins, and her hands ran restlessly over the smooth skin of his back. She was consumed by hunger for him, a hunger that she had always thought would be beyond her. She felt inebriated with wanting him, unable to think coherently, and she moaned with longing.

His mouth tasted the honey of her lips. "Say the words," he urged her. "I have to know it's all right."

"Please," she whispered hoarsely, "please, Drake...I want you."

He hesitated for a second longer, his mouth hovering above hers, his eyes dark and unreadable. "I won't hurt you, Briana," he promised fervently. "I'll never hurt you."

"I know," she breathed. "I know you won't."

"And remember that I'm Drake. No one else, my darling."

Then they were kissing and caressing each other in mutual desire, learning each other's bodies with hands and lips and tongues. Shivers of pleasure shook Briana, making her skin flush with longing. And when he entered her soft welcoming flesh, she moaned and arched to meet him. Never had she known such pleasure, such aching fulfillment. His sweat-moistened skin glided against hers with silken sweetness. Her arms held him closely, her fingers splayed against the small of his back, pressing him against her with an eagerness that threatened to explode.

Drake's breath came in gasps as he shifted above her, and they found the perfect rhythm with their mindless rapturous movements. Briana had never experienced such delicious sensation, such sublime closeness to another human being. For ecstatic moments her body's response shattered through her in waves that were almost too wonderful to bear. She trembled helplessly as the blissful feelings ran their course.

"Briana," Drake cried out as he reached the apex of his own pleasure. He tensed against her, holding her tightly as he shuddered once, then again. Slowly his body grew still, and he collapsed beside her, his labored breathing subsiding gradually.

Briana snuggled against his chest, running her palm languidly across the damp skin at his waist. Tears ran down her cheeks unnoticed. He wrapped his arms around her, molding her body against him. They lay like that for endless minutes.

"Thank you," she whispered finally.

Drake's mouth pressed against her forehead for a moment. "You took the words out of my mouth," he murmured, his lips moving against her skin.

"I never...it was never like this before...."

He touched a finger lightly to her lips, tracing the contours. "Haven't you been with anyone since your divorce?"

"No." Her reply was barely audible.

He sighed contentedly. "I'm glad. You're a beautiful, exciting woman, Briana, and I don't think I'll ever get enough of you. I thought I'd die, waiting for you."

She grew still, trying to fathom the meanings behind his words. Finally she said, "It was beautiful."

"It will be even better, honey, much better," he murmured drowsily.

She felt his muscles relaxing. "Drake...?"

"Hmm?"

"What happened...it doesn't mean it can be like this whenever you decide you want me. I have to think...about so many things."

"Shh. Not now. I only want to hold you." His hand slipped down to the curve of her hip and pulled her even closer against him. She lay quietly, content for the moment to lie within the hard circle of his arms and wonder at the awesome response of her own body, one that before tonight, before Drake, she had not known was possible. His arms around her relaxed, and his breathing became deep and even. She knew that he had drifted off to sleep. She smiled in the darkness, turning her face to press her cheek against the warm roughness of his chest. He was right. Tomorrow would be time enough to think about what had happened.

She closed her eyes and slept.

CHAPTER THIRTEEN

THE HAZY LIGHT of early morning washed the bedroom when Briana opened her eyes and yawned. She felt rested even though slightly disoriented. Contentment wrapped itself around her like a downy comforter. She closed her eyes and tried to slide back into the deep sleep that had held her all night. She hadn't slept so well in weeks.

She turned on her back and felt a slight soreness. Then in a flash the fragments of her consciousness came together, and she remembered what had happened the night before. She sat up, looking about wide-eyed. She was alone in the bed.

She lay back against the pillows, half relieved, half disappointed. She ran both hands through her tangled hair and let her head fall back, ignoring the faint tenderness she felt on her skin. As she stared at the high ceiling, she let her thoughts drift to Drake and to the moments they had shared. Last night seemed to have existed on another plane, another dimension. She had been carried away—carried out of herself—by passion, heedless of all else. But now the light of day had dawned, and she had to consider where her impetuousness had left her.

Was she really the same woman who had lain in this bed and responded to Drake's lovemaking with such abandon? Last night Drake had slipped past all her defenses and touched a soft vulnerable part of her that she usually kept well guarded. During the past four and a half years Briana had struggled through pain and self-doubt to a kind of unassailable serenity. If she lost that, all her weakness and inadequacy would be exposed. She had learned to depend on herself, to be in control of her own life and emotions, and slowly she had come to respect the woman who was Briana Ivensen.

It was a self-respect gained at tremendous cost. There had been times when she had had nothing but stubborn determination to sustain her. She had never meant to fall in love again, and she realized in this clear morning light that if she let herself, she could fall in love with Drake. But to love was to open oneself to being hurt, and that hurt could be deep and rending enough to destroy. Especially if he did not reciprocate in kind.

She was gripped by a chill of apprehension. Of all the men in the world, why did it have to be Drake Rutledge who moved her so? She couldn't shake off the suspicion that he had done what he had to subdue her, as he had Erik.

Is that what last night had been to him, a victory over another Ivensen? Did he want every last one of them at his mercy?

He had told her that day on the beach that he would have her, and he had—with her willing participation. Which was the only way Drake would want her, of course; taking her by superior force would be no real victory. Could she keep her self-respect and continue to work for him, an arrangement that made it impossible for her to avoid him? He would want her again; he had said so. Before last night she had been sure that she could resist his advances, but her treacherous body had other ideas. Now she knew she would want him again, too.

She sat up again, sliding her legs over the side of the bed. For a moment she sat there dejectedly, her chin supported by one hand. If only . . . if only he could separate her from her family! As if to mock her, the memory of Drake's words sounded in her head: "We'd found mother's body the evening before, and I'd been picturing her like that all night. . . . I felt I had to do something to avenge her." Drake had admitted he'd felt satisfaction in seeing her brother get himself deeper and deeper into trouble. Did he, this man who was now her lover, see the seduction of Frederik's daughter as a final bit of poetic justice?

Briana had a sudden urge to leave the house immediately. She wanted to run away from the situation just as she had run away from an impossible marriage more than four years ago. But it was only a momentary impulse, followed by the memory of her promise to Ruth and her feeling of responsibility for Patty.

Was she strong enough to stay here with Drake and resist the passion that had overtaken her last night? For a moment she listened to the slow thud of her heart and doubted her own strength. Then she came to her feet and headed for the bathroom and a shower. Somehow she would forget last night, she wouldn't allow it to happen again.

An hour later, when she entered the breakfast parlor, Patty greeted her with a smile.

Briana glanced at the girl's partially eaten breakfast and then at the clock on the wall. "It's later than I thought. Looks as if we all overslept this morning."

Greta bustled in with a glass of orange juice for her. "Except Mr. Drake. He left for work at the crack of dawn."

The housekeeper's statement released the tension in Briana. She was to have a reprieve before facing him. "I'd better take you to the ferry, Patty. I'll have my breakfast when I get back."

"No need," Patty told her. "We just heard on the radio that all the schools will be closed today. There's no water."

Several times a year most of the people on St.

Thomas were dependent on bottled water for a day or two. A burgeoning population coupled with the active tourist trade had put demands on the island's water supply that could not always be met. A desalination plant was being built with government funds, but for the time being, they had to get along on the rainwater that was caught in huge cisterns. Large hotels like the Grand Reef had their own desalination plants so that the guests didn't go without when the water was cut off.

While Briana sipped her juice, Greta asked, "Would you like a nice cheese omelet this morning, Miss Ivensen?"

"That would be fine, Greta," she responded, and the housekeeper left the room. "What do you say to going to Annaberg today instead of Wednesday?" she asked Patty. "We'll have the whole day instead of only the afternoon."

Patty had finished her own omelet and was placing her napkin beside her empty plate. "I'm really not in the mood, if you don't mind, Briana. I think I'll take advantage of my holiday to go back to bed for a while. But you go ahead."

Briana looked at her, surprised. "But I thought you wanted to write your composition about Annaberg."

The girl shrugged as she got to her feet. "Oh, I'll write about something else. You don't mind, do you?"

"No, of course not. It's your decision."

"And you won't mind going alone?"

Briana shook her head, wondering what had happened to Patty's seeming enthusiasm for the Annaberg trip only the evening before. Had she been pretending to be interested for Drake's sake?

"Then I'll see you later," Patty said. "I'll probably sleep until noon and then maybe go to the beach."

"If I get back in time, we can discuss your ideas for your composition."

"Don't hurry back on my account," Patty said airily. "I'll think of something to write about." She left the breakfast parlor, Briana heard her footsteps on the stairs.

She couldn't help feeling a little disappointed. She had been looking forward to taking Patty to Annaberg and telling her about St. John's old sugar plantations. She'd even hoped that she could impart some of her own enthusiasm to her pupil. She frowned slightly, still wondering what had brought on Patty's sudden turnabout. *It's her age,* she told herself finally. *Teenagers change their minds with the wind.*

After breakfast she dressed in comfortable cotton slacks and a pale blue sleeveless cotton shirt. She picked up her notebook and camera and, seeing that Drake had used Ruth's car to drive to the dock that morning, she got into the Pontiac and drove toward King's Road, the

island's major thoroughfare since the early eigh-
teenth century.

It was only a short drive to her destination.
Briana parked her car and got out, glad that she
had arrived ahead of most of the day's tourists.
She gathered up her handbag, notebook and
camera and walked toward the ruins, a large
area of crumbling stone buildings and walls,
white gray in the bright sunlight, with narrow
dirt paths winding among them. From her
studies she knew that Annaberg was one of
twenty-five active sugar-producing factories on
St. John in the 1700s. Molasses and rum had
also been produced here.

Looking around at the wooded rocky hills,
she realized what hard work had been required
of the laborers who had cleared and terraced the
hillsides, then fertilized the thin soil with ashes,
lime and dung under the hot Caribbean sun. It
had had to be watered, too, with fresh water, a
precious commodity on the island. Only slave
labor could have made farming St. John's steep
slopes financially possible. Freedom for the
Danish West Indian slaves in 1848 had gradually led to the disappearance of sugar, molasses
and rum production on the island. The ruins
Briana was visiting were from a time no living
person remembered.

She spent more than an hour wandering
among the factory ruins and taking pictures.
There were the slave quarters, small cabins of

wattle-and-daub construction; the slave-village site with an outdoor oven where the women had done much of their cooking. Archaeologists had not found the ruins of a great house, so it was assumed that the owners and overseers had lived some distance away.

Leaving the village site, she stopped to snap several shots of the windmill that had provided the energy to crush the cane. Beyond the windmill, with its circular stone base, were the remains of the horse mill, where mules, oxen and horses had provided power when the wind wasn't blowing.

Briana hesitated for long moments at a small chamber set into a corner of a stone wall. Because a chain and a pair of handcuffs had been found fastened to a post in the small room, historians guessed it had been used as a dungeon to house troublesome slaves. Standing there, imagining the hopeless existence of the Africans who had been forced into slavery in the islands, Briana understood why the slave rebellion in the 1700s had been inevitable. Any existence must have seemed preferable to this. And so the slaves had revolted, killing a number of whites and starting a guerilla warfare that had lasted for months. Eventually the French had sent the Danes some troops specially trained in jungle fighting. In time the slaves had been tracked down and captured, although some had preferred suicide to surrender.

Briana was in a pensive mood when she left Annaberg. Instead of turning back toward Drake's house, she followed the road that took her to the island's famous luxury resort at Caneel Bay. There she browsed in the hotel's gift shop before eating a leisurely lunch at a table that overlooked blue water and white sand. It was almost two o'clock when she got back to the house.

Feeling a little guilty about neglecting Patty all day, she went into the kitchen where Greta was baking pies. "Where's Patty?" she asked.

Greta closed the wide oven door and turned to smile at her. "So, you're back? I hope you didn't cut short your trip just to entertain Patty. She isn't here."

"Where is she?"

"She came back down soon after you left this morning. Said she couldn't sleep and had decided to go over to Charlotte Amalie for some shopping. She said she might drop in on a girl friend, too."

"Lissa?"

"Yes, that's the one."

"Did she say when she'd be back?"

"No, but I'm sure she'll be here for dinner. She knows Mr. Drake will be expecting her."

Briana went up to her bedroom, trying not to feel apprehensive about Patty's absence. She would have called Lissa's house if she knew the girl's number, just to put her mind at rest. But she couldn't even remember her last name. She freshened up, then went down to the kitchen for a glass of iced tea, which she carried out to the patio with a novel of Ruth's she'd found in the breakfast parlor. There was no reason to be worried about Patty, she told herself, but she hoped the girl returned before Drake got home.

UNFORTUNATELY THAT WASN'T THE CASE. She was still out on the patio reading an hour and a half later, when Drake appeared. He walked toward her, a frown knitting his tanned brow.

"Greta says Patty's been in Charlotte Amalie most of the day. Why didn't you go with her?"

Briana laid her book aside and looked up at him warily. "I went to Annaberg this morning. She decided to go back to bed since school was cancelled for today, rather than accompany me. When I got back, she was gone."

He looked worried as he said, "I wish you hadn't left her here alone."

"She wasn't *alone*, Drake."

"You know what I mean."

He was treating her like a paid companion. If last night had made any difference in his attitude toward her, it certainly didn't show in his face. "She was going to see a friend from school," Briana explained stiffly. "It's only natural for her to prefer being with people her own age."

"If I can't trust her, that's her fault," he snapped.

"Let her grow up!"

He eyed her levelly for a long moment, and she wondered what he was thinking. Did he imagine that after last night he could treat her any way he pleased, and she would stand for it? She got to her feet. "I'm going to my room to do some work on my dissertation."

He moved toward a chaise and, as she brushed past him, caught her arm, pulling her down with him so that she tumbled into his lap.

She tensed as she saw the dancing lights in his dark eyes. "Let me go."

His head dropped toward hers. "Don't worry. No one can see us."

Slowly, savoringly, he tasted her lips. Then he lifted his head to look into her eyes, at the same time running a lazy finger down the row of buttons on her shirt. "I thought about you all day."

"Did you?" she asked shakily and noticed that his eyes mirrored her own response.

"Oh, yes," he whispered. "Last night was so wonderful I couldn't think about anything but you today. I finally gave up trying to work and came home early."

A tremor ran through her, and she glanced away. "Don't, Drake. Please." She had succeeded in banishing him from her thoughts while she was at Annaberg. She had even managed to take an interest in the novel she had been reading. She'd been enjoying the lazy peace of the afternoon, the frosty glass of tea at her elbow, the occasional cry of a gull overhead and the lulling whisper of the waves. Now her calm was shattered by the emotion in his eyes, that deep dark glimmer that could so infuriatingly arouse an answering echo in her heart.

She felt his eyes on her for a long moment before he said, "All right." He was angry, obviously. He got up quickly, then his hands gripped her waist and set her on her feet. As he looked down at her, his dark eyes were opaque, the scar on his cheek a pale slash in stark contrast to the deep tan of his skin. "I'll see you at dinner," he said tightly.

Briana left him, her throat tight with dismay. She had tried ever since she had begun working for him to establish a comfortable relationship between them. What progress she had made had been wrecked by what had happened last night. The sexual awareness between them was much stronger than ever now, and she wondered if it was even possible for them to be in each other's company without clashing.

In her bedroom she closed the door and sat down at the desk where her papers were spread. She shuffled through them, trying to focus her thoughts on the dissertation. But after a while she gave up, lay down on the bed and stared at the ceiling, her mind full of Drake. Did he expect her to fall into his arms at the slightest opportunity now? He had been thinking about her all day, he'd said. Had those thoughts included seeing her as his mistress? As a willing partner who would be at his beck and call whenever he chose? Had he enjoyed imagining Margaret's indignation should she learn that Briana had taken him into her bed?

But Margaret must not learn of it. And it must not happen again. The faint exclamation that Briana uttered at this thought sounded hollow in the quiet room. Although she'd protested, she had responded strongly to Drake on the patio just now, to the feel of his strong arms wrapped around her, enclosing her in their heady warmth. When he kissed her, a deep throbbing had started in her blood. If he persisted in pursuing her as he was—kissing her, touching her—how long could she resist the yearnings of her own body? Now that her defenses had been breached, was it possible to set them up again, she wondered. Was it ever possible to go back?

Maybe she had made him angry enough on the patio for him to keep his distance, at least while she remained in the house. In any case she couldn't avoid him altogether. If she stayed in her room, he would know she was afraid to face him.

There was little point in trying to work in her present state of mind, so she went downstairs to find Greta in the kitchen.

"I just made a pot of coffee," the housekeeper greeted her. "Would you like a cup?"

"Please." Briana sat on a stool at the counter that separated the kitchen from the breakfast parlor. "Have you heard from Patty since she left?"

"Not a word. Mr. Drake was asking me that before he went to the study."

"Do you know Lissa's last name?"

Greta set Briana's coffee on the counter before her. "Patty's friend? No, I don't believe I ever heard her say." She gave Briana a sharp look. "Are you worried about her?"

"No, not exactly. I just feel I ought to keep track of her with Ruth gone." She was beginning to wonder, too, if Patty had meant to go to Charlotte Amalie all along, if she'd gone to her room after breakfast just to wait until Briana left the house. But she should stop imagining the worst. She was getting to be as bad as Drake. What harm could there be in Patty's spending the day in Charlotte Amalie? What if she *had* wanted to go alone? It didn't mean she was up to something that her mother and uncle would disapprove of.

Greta returned to chopping fresh vegetables for the dinner salad. "She'll be along," she said reassuringly.

In fact, it was only a short while later that they heard the front door opening. Greta glanced at Briana and smiled. "She's back. Didn't I tell you?"

"Where is everybody?" Patty ambled into the kitchen, squinting after being out in the brilliant sunlight. "Oh, here you are." Her pretty pink-and-white dress had become limp and wrinkled, and her dark hair was in disarray. She sat across from Briana at the counter. "Is there anything cold to drink, Greta? I'm pooped."

Briana eyed the small paper sack that Patty had sat down on the counter. "Was your shopping trip a success?"

The teenager wrinkled her nose and accepted a tall glass of iced lemonade from Greta. "Can you believe I've been trying on clothes all day, and I've come home with nothing but a couple of fashion magazines?"

"Did you try that new little shop in Palm Passage?"

Briana took a drink from her glass, then nodded. "I tried everywhere. I wanted to start getting a few things for college, but I wasn't sure what I wanted. I thought I'd know it when I saw it." She shrugged. "Maybe I ought to wait until I get to the mainland to buy my college clothes."

"There's plenty of time," Briana said. "It's probably a good idea to wait and see what the other girls are wearing before you buy too much."

Patty finished her lemonade. "Now you tell me," she teased. She slid off her stool. "I think I'll go to my room and get started on my English composition. I'll show you what I've done after dinner."

"Fine," Briana said, watching Patty's retreating figure and trying to ignore an irrational hunch that the girl had spent very little time that day shopping for clothes. More likely she'd been with the boy she'd mentioned earlier, the one who had been at Lissa's house the day they studied for their chemistry test.

"I'll go and see if Mr. Drake wants a cup of coffee," Greta said. "And I'll tell him Patty's home."

Briana didn't see Drake until dinner. When she did, she was almost relieved that Patty was the center of his attention.

"Will school be in session tomorrow?" he asked his niece when they were seated.

"I don't know. We should hear something on the news tonight on TV."

"If not," he went on, "and you decide to go out again, I want you to leave a number where you can be reached."

Patty thrust out her chin, and Briana realized suddenly that Drake did the same thing when he was angry. "Why don't you get us some walkie-talkies, Uncle Drake," the girl said, "then you can give me the third degree anytime you want."

"Don't be ridiculous," Drake said wryly. "I'm only asking you to let us know where you're going. What if we had an emergency and needed to get in touch with you?"

"That isn't why you want to know," Patty

retorted. "You—" She broke off abruptly. "Oh, never mind."

Drake watched her, a troubled frown knitting his forehead as she ate her salad. After a moment, however, he said to Briana, "I talked to Dodie Gundersen today. She said to tell you to drop by the shop if you want to talk to her, but that she doesn't know of any old papers or records in her family. I doubt that she's going to be much help to you."

"Thanks for speaking to her, anyway," Briana said. She met his glance, and this time he was the first to look away.

They were largely silent during the meal, each occupied with his own thoughts. When Patty excused herself, Briana did the same and followed the girl up the stairs.

"Don't be angry with your uncle," Briana said when they had reached the upstairs hall.

"He treats me like a child, and a stupid one at that!" Patty fumed. "I can't wait to get away from this place!" She opened her bedroom door and went inside, closing the door behind her.

Briana sighed and continued along the hall to her own room. She was able to work on her dissertation, fortunately, and kept at it until it was time for the evening news. Then she flipped on the television and watched until an announcement was made about the schools. They would be open the next day.

Turning off the set, she went into the bathroom to get ready for bed. Coming out a while later, dressed in her sheer white nightie, she stopped short. Drake was sitting in the chair beside the desk.

"What are you doing in here?" she gasped.

He laughed shortly and lifted his pipe. "Smoking."

"That isn't funny." She fumbled for her robe, which lay across the foot of the bed, and pulled it on. "I'd appreciate it if you'd knock before barging in here."

"I did. You must have had the water running and didn't hear me."

She faced him, the bed between them. "What do you want?"

With unhurried movements he laid his pipe on the desk, unfolded his length from the chair and came around the bed toward her. "You know the answer to that as well as I do," he said quietly.

Briana backed up against the bed until the mattress pressed against her legs. She couldn't speak as she looked into his eyes—eyes that held warm amusement, as well as some other emotion in their velvet depths. Suddenly her heart was thudding.

Their mouths met hungrily, clinging together as eagerly on her part as on his. His hands, which were gripping her shoulders, slid around her body and pulled her close. An explosion of heat filled Briana's veins. Her body melted against his, yielding, her hands clasping his broad shoulders almost desperately. She couldn't stop her telltale response.

The demanding urgency of his kiss deepened, and she began to tremble uncontrollably. Then, as he released her mouth to shower kisses along her neck, her head fell back, allowing him access. At the now familiar pressure of his body she moaned faintly. His hands caressed her, every touch reawakening the pleasures she'd felt the night before, and her throbbing heart betrayed her to him just as certainly as did the tips of her breasts thrusting against the sheer nylon of her gown, against his warm exploring palm.

Drake nuzzled her earlobe, muttering thickly, "Have you any idea how desirable you are?"

She didn't have to tell him that she found him desirable, too. But she had vowed not to let it happen again. She had meant to show him he couldn't make love to her upon demand. "I don't want this," she whispered hoarsely.

"Yes, you do," he said unsteadily. "You want it as much as I do." His hand reached up to caress her neck and stroke her cheek tenderly. "Don't pull away from me, Briana. I thought we got past all that last night."

"Last night," she said in a low voice, "was a mistake."

His finger touched her mouth, pressed gently against her bottom lip. "Last night was heaven, my darling." He caught her head in his hands and claimed her lips once more in a warm compelling kiss. Shaken by the exquisite persuasion of his mouth, her own lips parted in sweet surrender. Drake swung her up in his arms and carried her to the bed. As he looked down at her, his eyes filled with adoration. Her last resistance vanished, and she reached out for him, giving herself completely to the sweet pulsating hunger that claimed her.

CHAPTER FOURTEEN

Afterward, moonlight fell across the bed, bathing their naked bodies in a glow of enchantment. Drake's head lay on the pillow next to hers, his face relaxed and sated from their lovemaking. The scar on his cheek was just a blur in the soft light, and Briana lifted her hand to trace the jagged mark with the tips of her fingers.

"I'm sorry for the way this happened," she whispered.

"Do you find it repulsive?" There was an oddly vulnerable quality to his voice.

"No, I don't." To prove it, she leaned over and kissed his cheek. In response he tightened his grip on her breast for a moment and growled in her ear.

Briana laughed softly.

"I did for years," he went on. "Your father marked me for life, and now—" his hand slid slowly down the curve from her breast to her thigh, leaving a trembling warmth behind "—now I've marked his daughter. You will always carry my mark, Briana."

He cradled her against him again and shut his eyes, even though one thumb continued to stroke her skin. But for Briana the mood had been shattered by his words, which continued to echo in her ears. "I've marked his daughter." Did he mean to taunt her? To mock her for her weakness? His lips nuzzled her cheek, and she caught her breath, angry all at once with herself, with him. She had had no part in what had happened twenty years ago. Why must he continually remind her of it? She pressed her palms against his chest, her fingers spread out on his solid bulk.

"I carry no man's mark," she announced distantly.

Almost at once he lifted his head and caught her hands, pressing one palm and then the other against his lips. "What is this?" The words came out on a shaky laugh. "You aren't going to freeze up on me again, are you?" She stared up at him, resenting him, yet already wanting him once more. He smoothed her silken hair back from her forehead with unsteady fingers. "Do we really have to go through that again?" he murmured.

"Oh, Drake." Her confusion filled the two words.

"You're beautiful, Briana," he said and kissed her forehead, her eyes and finally her mouth, clinging as if he were starving for its sustenance. "Briana," he breathed again as his mouth traced a line of molten kisses along her jawline and down her neck. "I've never wanted anyone as much as I want you."

Briana worked her fingers into his hair while he bent to kiss her swollen breasts. Lying beneath him, she luxuriated again in the joy of his touch, unable to remember why only moments before she had wanted him to stop. He wanted her! For this moment that was enough. She was incapable of denying him, of refusing to respond....

A stab of self-awareness cut through the haze of pleasure she was feeling, and she caught her breath. She was in love with him! In love with Drake Rutledge, this wonderful passionate man. Why hadn't she realized it till now? She must have loved him for some time but had refused to admit it to herself, had been blind to the truth because of all the misunderstanding between them. Now, with the exquisite pleasure of his hands, of his lips on her flesh, there was no longer any possibility of denying it. She adored him.

Drake groaned and shifted his weight against her. "Please, not yet," she whispered shakily. "I want to see you. I want to touch you."

There was a sharp intake of his breath. In the moonlight she could see the dark intensity of his eyes. He laughed softly, rolled over on his back and stretched.

Her desire to prolong the sweet agony of their

foreplay obviously excited him. He reached out to touch her soft lips with his fingertips, and she lifted his hand to kiss each finger in turn. Then she raised herself on one elbow beside him, her senses dazzled by his masculine perfection. How wonderful it was to be here with the man she loved! Her fingers began to discover his body, her mouth tasting his skin exploringly. She was aware with a thrill of delight that his chest rose and fell unevenly. The feel of his flesh under her palm was warm and vibrant and incredibly exciting. "You're so beautiful," she breathed, running her hand down his ribs, down the jutting bone of his hip.

He groaned in his throat as her fingers curved to stroke and caress him. "God, Briana! How much do you think I can take?" he asked at last, reaching out and pulling her down on top of him. Her body's softness yielded to his male strength, molding itself against him. His hands slid down to guide her hips, and their bodies blended easily, silkenly. In the mutual rhythm they had found the night before, they flowed together—perfect. Glorious. Briana clung to him, whimpering softly as they rose to the heights of passion again, hovered there interminably, then plunged together into a sea of total fulfillment.

Afterward she lay in the cocoon of his warmth, her head on his shoulder, listening to the throbbing of his heart and his deep even breathing as he slept. She slipped one arm across his chest and snuggled closer, feeling her love for him coursing within her. The knowledge that Drake had never said he loved her came as a flash of pain that brought tears to her eyes. But the pain slipped away as she fell asleep.

WHEN SHE AWOKE, the moonlight had given way to bright sunlight, which flooded through the windows and fell upon the bed. She stirred sleepily and opened her eyes. Her arm was still flung across the bed, but now it clutched the rumpled sheet instead of Drake's chest. She lifted her head, and her glance fell on the bedside clock. Ten o'clock! How could she possibly have slept so late?

Grabbing clean underclothes from a bureau drawer, she hurried into the bathroom. The stinging shower spray quickly dissipated the last of the drugging sleep that clung to her, although it couldn't erase the languid satiated feeling in her body. *Why,* she asked herself ruefully, *does there always have to be a morning after?*

Drake.... How she had underestimated him! Or had she overestimated her own willpower; that was more to the point. Whatever it was, she had gone blithely ahead and agreed to stay with Patty while Ruth was gone, sure of her own powers of resistance. She might have been able to excuse herself somehow for the night before

last. But it had happened again last night, and
no matter how much she would have liked to,
she couldn't rationalize away what she now felt
for him, perhaps had always felt. Drake was the
man she had never thought she would find, he
was everything she'd ever dreamed of. She had
always felt safe in the dreaming because she was
sure that no such man existed for her. How
could she go on with her life alone after what
had happened, after what she now knew in her
heart of hearts?

Somehow she would find a way, she told herself grimly. Now more than ever. Drake Rutledge had a score to settle with all Ivensens, and
he had never intended to offer her any hint of
commitment. He would very likely grow tired of
her, once the novelty of having Frederik Ivensen's daughter in his bed had worn off. The
thought of Drake walking away from her was
the most dismal thought Briana had ever considered....

The only way for her to salvage a scrap of
pride from the affair was to be the one who ended it. Somewhere she had to find the strength to
do so. She had learned to love him; surely in
time she could learn to stop loving him! She had
got her life together after her disaster with
Ricardo after all.

She shut off the shower and stepped out on
the mat. As she toweled herself briskly, she
deliberately fanned her uncertainty into heated

determination. From the day Drake had walked
into the Ivensen house to ask when they would
be moving out, he had been persistently ma-
neuvering his way into her life. She had been
traveling a straight smooth course, content with
planning her career, certain of her future. Drake
had pushed and prodded until he had made her
question whether that future would be enough
for her. He had caused her to look beyond her
goal ani wonder if such a life would not be
bleak and unfulfilling without the added dimension of someone to share it with. He had made
her feel things she had never wanted to feel
again. Now she was filled with uncertainty and
doubt, and it was all his fault!

She dressed with angry movements, bitterly
determined to phone Ruth that very morning
and ask her to come home immediately. She had
already stayed longer than she had initially
planned.

As Briana descended the stairs, she was building a case for herself in her mind, reasons she
could give Ruth for needing to come back to
Charlotte Amalie. She was deep in thought
when she found Greta in the kitchen.

"'Morning, Miss Ivensen." The housekeeper
glanced at her, then back to the delicious-
smelling concoction she was stirring on the
range.

Did Greta know where Drake had spent the
past two nights, Briana wondered and felt her

cheeks grow warm. If she knew, the house-keeper was too discreet to allude to it. Her expression could not have been more placid. She couldn't know, Briana assured herself.

"I've overslept again," she said with the strength of her new determination in her voice. "Did Drake take Patty to the ferry this morning?"

"Oh, no," stated Greta cheerfully. "He was out of here long before that. Mrs. Heyward called at eight to say she was in Cruz Bay, so it worked out fine. I took Patty down and picked up her mother."

"Ruth's back?" She felt vastly relieved. Now she could go home without delay.

"Yes'm. She's out on the patio."

Briana poured herself a cup of coffee from the electric percolator and carried it outside with her. Ruth, who was sitting in one of the patio chairs gazing at the sea view, turned at the sound of her approach.

"Welcome back," Briana said. "You look wonderfully fresh and rested."

Indeed, Ruth's plump face seemed to have acquired a glow that hadn't been there before. "I had a wonderful time!" she replied. "I could have enjoyed staying another week, but I thought I'd imposed upon your kindness too long already. How did you get along here without me?"

"We managed."

Ruth laughed good-naturedly. "So it seems."

"Does Drake know you're back?"

"I phoned his office a while ago. Instead of carrying on about how much he missed me, he said I should have stayed another day or two. I got the feeling I'm not exactly indispensable around here." She laughed again. "By the way, Drake wanted me to tell you not to leave this afternoon until he gets home. He wants to talk to you about something."

Briana bit her bottom lip to keep from retorting. What Drake wanted was the least of her concerns at the moment. Who did he think he was, issuing orders right and left? If he really believed what he'd said last night, that he'd marked her somehow, he would soon find out differently. She intended to get the reins of her life firmly in her own hands again. She changed the subject, saying, "I'm glad you had such a nice time in St. Croix."

"Dorothy and her brother, Sam, wined and dined me until I felt like a celebrity. I didn't realize how much I needed a vacation. But I can't say I'm sorry to be home. Wining and dining can become very tiring after a while." She tilted her head and looked at Briana with open curiosity. "You look a little tired yourself. I'll bet you've been working half the night, every night, on your dissertation."

"I did make some progress on it."

"I admire your dedication. You're going to

be a fantastic teacher. Oh, I almost forgot, Patty left a rough draft of an English composition in the breakfast parlor for you to look at. She's going to make the final copy this afternoon.''

Briana had forgotten that it was Wednesday, with a tutoring session scheduled for that afternoon. ''I'll go over the composition and write down any suggestions I have,'' she said hastily. ''But I really don't think I can wait for Patty to come home. I must get back and see about grandmother. I've been checking on her by phone, but I'm not sure she would admit it if she weren't feeling well. I'd like to see for myself. I'm sure Patty can finish the composition without me.''

''Oh, don't worry about her. I can stand in for you if need be. The only thing is...well, Drake seemed adamant about wanting you to be here when he got home.''

''Drake is my employer,'' said Briana without thinking, ''not my lord and master.''

Ruth's brows rose quizzically. ''Briana, is anything wrong?''

''No. I can't wait here for Drake, that's all.'' She set her empty coffee cup aside and got to her feet.

''Thank you again for staying with Patty. I wouldn't have been able to relax and have so much fun if I hadn't known you were here.''

''I'm glad I could help. Now I'd better look

over Patty's composition, and then I'm going up to pack."

"I have a little something for you. I'll go to my room and get it."

"Oh, Ruth, you needn't have done that."

"It's only a small token of my appreciation. And I'll drive you to the dock when you're ready to go."

Ruth's gift turned out to be a flowing white caftan of the cool batik cotton made in the Caribbean. Bright hand-embroidered flowers formed a yoke and splashed down the front. "It's perfectly beautiful!" Briana exclaimed, touched by Ruth's thoughtfulness. She had to squelch the distress she felt at the thought that Drake would never see her in it.

SHE FINALLY GOT AWAY at noon, declining Ruth's offer of lunch before she departed. She didn't want to stay any longer than she had to. It would be just like Drake to decide to take the afternoon off and come home. She didn't feel up to sparring with him, particularly not in his sister's hearing.

Arriving at Red Hook dock, she got into her car, which felt like an oven after being parked in the sun for five days, and rolled down the windows. She drove as fast as she dared to create a breeze inside the car. After a few blocks she closed the windows and turned on the air conditioner.

At the house she found Erik lunching in the dining room. He leaned back in his chair and surveyed her with an amused expression. "Well, well, well. . . we thought you'd forgotten us."

"Hello, Erik," she responded absently as she passed through the dining room and entered the kitchen. Ida was having her lunch at the kitchen table. Her face lighted up at the sight of Briana.

"Lordy, am I happy to see you, Miss Briana."

"No happier than I am to be back, Nenie Ida. How are things here? How's grandmother?"

Ida shrugged her thin shoulders. "Oh, she feeling all right. She jes crochety because you been gone."

"Is she eating lunch in her apartment?"

"Yes'm. I don't mean to sound disrespectful, Miss Briana, but don't let that worry you. She jes poutin'. Been carryin' on about how nobody appreciates her. Everybody go off and forget all about her."

"I thought she must be feeling sorry for herself, even though I telephoned her every day. As you know, the past two days she wouldn't come to the phone."

"Those jes conscience calls, she say."

Briana sighed. "I'll try to calm her down after lunch. Could I get something to eat now?"

Ida got to her feet, wincing at the stiffness in her joints. "I thought you already had lunch. You go on in and sit down. I bring you something directly."

Erik was still at the table when she returned to the dining room. "Ida says grandmother's in one of her moods," she remarked.

"She's pretty upset with you, all right. You told her you'd be gone three days, four at the most."

"Ruth stayed away longer than she'd planned."

"So," said Erik, pouring himself more coffee. "Did you enjoy your stay in the home of the great mogul?"

She bridled at his contemptuous tone. "I wasn't there to enjoy myself," she snapped.

"Ah, yes, I forgot." His smile was mocking. "You were baby-sitting." He laughed outright. "If one can believe a seventeen-year-old girl needs looking after. But it's as good an excuse as any."

Ida arrived with her lunch. Briana glared at her brother and pressed her lips together until the black woman had returned to the kitchen. "I don't know what that snide remark is supposed to mean, but I don't appreciate your tone."

His eyes widened innocently. "You're mighty touchy today, little sister. I didn't mean to imply anything. I just find it laughable that Rutledge takes such a protective attitude toward his niece. He never struck me as the fatherly type."

He seemed sincere, so Briana relaxed and buttered a hot roll. "You never had occasion to see that side of him. If anything, he feels too responsible for Patty. It's probably good that she's going away to college.''

"To Connecticut?''

Briana glanced at him sharply. "How did you know that?''

"She mentioned it the day we had lunch in Palm Passage.'' He shook his head ruefully. "Don't look at me as if you suspect me of bugging Rutledge's telephone or something. Why are you so tense and defensive?''

She didn't recall that Patty's choice of college had been mentioned the day they had lunched with Erik, but there had been no other opportunity for him to have heard it. She really was on edge, she realized, and for once it wasn't Erik's fault. She gestured distractedly. "I'm sorry. I have a lot of things on my mind.''

He raised one blond brow. "Rutledge?''

"I was referring to my dissertation. I've a lot of work to do on it yet, and time is passing. I want to apply to the college for a position next fall, but I must have it finished first. I'd like to submit a copy of it with my employment application.''

Erik looked at her silently for a moment, a cunning gleam in his blue eyes. "Briana, I hope you aren't falling for him.''

She felt exposed under his knowing gaze and, to cover her uneasiness, occupied her hands with dishing up a bowl of fresh fruit and seasoning the baked fish Ida had brought her. Finally she said, "Falling for Drake is the last thing I intend." She hoped she sounded convincing enough to deflect Erik's suspicions. She couldn't make herself stop loving Drake overnight, but with time enough she would manage it. In the meantime she didn't want Erik or Margaret to know how she felt.

"Good," he said rather grimly. "Because if you do, you'll only end up getting hurt."

"Erik, if this is your way of showing brotherly concern, don't bother. I'm very capable of looking after myself."

"I hope so, because Drake Rutledge's number one concern is himself. It would suit his perverted sense of justice to make you fall in love with him. He might indulge in a casual affair, but in the end he'd drop you. And he'd enjoy watching you hurt when he did so."

Hot color crawled up Briana's neck and into her face. Was it obvious to everyone that she had already succumbed to Drake's powers of persuasion? But no, she told herself, Erik was only guessing. "You don't have much confidence in my judgment, do you? I'm as aware as you are of Drake's grudge against our family."

"Keep reminding yourself," he said as he pushed away from the table. "I'm glad you're back. Maybe grandmother will stop whining now. I'm going into town for a bit."

Briana murmured a response. She lingered

over lunch, putting off going to look in on Margaret. But finally it couldn't be postponed any longer. At her grandmother's apartment she knocked, then, without waiting for a response, she opened the door and went in.

Margaret was sitting at her secretary, writing in her journal. "Good afternoon, grandmother," Briana said as she dropped a light kiss on her pale lined cheek.

Margaret laid aside her pen and turned to gaze at her granddaughter. "Are you sure your employer can spare you for a few hours?" she inquired peevishly.

"Quite sure. I'm not due back there until Friday afternoon. How are you?"

"I'm very put out with you, Briana." Margaret pursed her lips in disapproval. "You assured me you would be gone only three days."

"Well, Ruth stayed on St. Croix longer than she originally planned. I'm sorry if you were inconvenienced in any way. I telephoned, and Ida said you didn't want to talk to me."

"Not on the phone," stated Margaret shortly. "I wanted you here where you belong."

"I'm here now." Briana smiled in an effort to coax her grandmother out of her disgruntled mood. "I thought you might like to go into town this afternoon or for a drive along the coast."

Margaret eyed her askance. "Now you're trying to ease your conscience again. You know I don't care for shopping or driving around aimlessly."

"It would do you good to get out."

"I'm perfectly content here in my own home," the old woman sniffed. "I wish I could say the same for my grandchildren. I've seen little more of Erik these past days than I have of you. I thought his impulsive trip to New York might have settled him down, but apparently it didn't. He stays away from the house all day and half the night. He hardly has time to stop in and say hello."

"You know he's seeing Jane Fitzcannon," Briana soothed. "He's probably looking for a job, too. I'm sure he doesn't mean to neglect you any more than I do."

"Actions," snapped Margaret, "speak louder than words."

Briana stifled her impatience and continued to speak reasonably. "If you're sure you don't want to get out of the house today, perhaps you wouldn't mind going over some of the von Scholten papers with me. There are a few notes that don't make much sense to me. I thought you might be able to clarify them." She would have preferred going to the study to work alone. But getting Margaret to talk about her ancestors was the only thing she could think of that might improve her frame of mind.

Margaret seemed to consider her request. Then she said grudgingly, "If I can help, I'm willing to tell you anything I can."

"Good. I'll go and get the papers, and I'll ask Ida to bring us some tea in about an hour."

As Briana went along the hall to the study, she sighed in frustration. Much of Margaret's ill humour was Erik's fault. She had counted on him spending some time with their grandmother while she was gone. Clearly he hadn't. Not that she was surprised by her brother's lack of interest in anyone besides himself. Even though she had suggested to Margaret that he'd been job hunting, she didn't believe it. Erik wouldn't take a job unless it was a last resort to keep the wolf from his door. More likely he'd been living it up with Jane Fitzcannon.

CHAPTER FIFTEEN

BY FRIDAY AFTERNOON, when Briana left the house to meet Patty and go back to St. John, Margaret's feathers were much less ruffled than they had been on Wednesday. Briana had spent a great deal of the intervening time with her grandmother, listening to her talk about the von Scholtens and the Ivensens and their various contributions to the islands. Incredible as it seemed, it was actually a relief to be going back to Drake's house. Of course, she intended to be back on St. Thomas before he arrived home from work that evening. After ignoring his instructions on Wednesday and leaving early, she had half expected him to telephone her, but he hadn't. She wasn't sure how to interpret his silence and decided it was useless to try. The less she thought about Drake, she told herself, the better off she would be.

Patty was in a distracted mood and had a difficult time keeping her attention on her history lesson. Briana stuck with it for an hour before she closed the textbook and eyed her student with exasperation. They were in the garden, seated beneath the African tulip tree. Red petals from the shedding blossoms carpeted the grass at their feet.

"Why are you so absentminded today?" she asked pointedly.

Patty looked only faintly embarrassed, and she couldn't suppress a bored groan. "I'm sick of history and English and chemistry, Briana. What good will it ever do me? What does it have to do with real life?"

"More than you realize," Briana said dryly. "After all, the best minds of many ages had a part in creating what you study in school. There must be a few useful things you can learn from them."

Patty wrinkled her nose in distaste. "How come the things people say are good for you are never any fun?"

Briana chuckled. "Maybe because one of the things that's good for you is to learn self-discipline. The regimen of a formal education is the best teacher of that, quite aside from the subject matter itself."

"Gosh, Briana, how can you be so serious all the time?"

"Life is serious," Briana responded lightly.

"It doesn't have to be—not all the time, anyway. Know what I'd like to be doing right now?"

Briana smiled and gave up any thought of continuing the tutoring session. "Tell me."

Patty gazed up at the tulip tree. "I'd like to be sitting at a table in one of those little sidewalk cafés in Paris. I'd be wearing a pink dress, something light and frilly, and a big floppy hat with pink flowers on it."

"Well, you've picked the right time," Briana told her. "April in Paris is lovely."

Patty turned an interested gaze on her. "You've been to Paris?"

"Several times—when I was living in Spain. I haven't been there in more than four years, although I doubt it's changed much."

"Have you seen New York and London, too?"

"Yes. Tell me, what brought on this sudden interest in the great cities of the world?"

"It isn't sudden! Oh, Briana, sometimes I'm afraid I'm going to grow old and die before I have a chance to do all the things I want to do!"

Briana's expression was amused. "Don't be so impatient, Patty. You have a whole lifetime ahead of you."

"Sometimes I feel as if I'm on hold, waiting for my life to start. Sometimes I don't think I'll ever get away from home."

"September's less than six months away. You're scheduled to take the entrance exams next week, and in the fall you'll be going to New England. Have you definitely decided in favor of that college in Connecticut?"

"What?" Patty's mind seemed to come back

from a more distant place than New England. "Oh, yes, I guess so. They have a big drama department, and it's close enough to go to New York for a weekend now and then."

The girl was clearly more interested in the excitement of bright lights than in college. Briana felt disappointed. Lately she'd been hoping that Patty's improved grades indicated a real interest in continuing her education. "Think of all the new friends you'll make on campus," she said, as if she hadn't noticed Patty's emphasis on weekends away from school.

"Umm," Patty mused absently. "It would be nice to have some close girl friends."

"Not to mention boyfriends," Briana teased. "Speaking of which, what happened to that boy at your school? You seemed quite taken with him."

Patty looked momentarily blank. "What boy?"

"The one who studied chemistry with you and Lissa. He taught you some new dance steps, didn't he?"

It was a moment before understanding dawned. "Oh, him." Patty shrugged. "He's okay. But he's so young."

"Isn't he your age?"

"Yes, but boys my age act as if they're about ten half the time."

"I see." Briana tried not to smile at Patty's bored tone. "Well, there will be a whole new crop of young men in Connecticut, and most of them older than you."

"Umm," Patty murmured again as if she were only half listening.

"Tell you what, let's call it quits for today. I don't think we're going to accomplish anything, anyway."

"Okay." Patty began gathering her books, and Briana left her to join Ruth on the patio.

She accepted a glass of iced tea as Ruth said, "I've been working in the flower garden all day, yesterday, too. You wouldn't believe how it got ahead of me in the few days I was gone."

Briana's gaze took in one of several meticulously groomed flower plots, this one bordering the patio. "I believe it. You keep this place looking like a professional nursery."

Ruth flushed with pleasure. "I enjoy it. But I only do the flowers; the gardener does the rest. There's nothing like digging in the dirt to get rid of depression and worry and anger...well, you name a negative emotion, and gardening will help to banish it. Speaking of anger, Drake was as cross as a bear when he arrived here Wednesday and found out you'd gone home."

"Maybe he ought to take up gardening," said Briana with a rather impatient gesture.

"He snapped at Patty and me all evening. Finally I got so irritated with him I told him to stop taking out his irritation at you on us. After that he went into the study and shut himself in for the night. I was afraid he would phone you and bawl you out. Did he?"

"No. I haven't heard from him."

Ruth sat forward in her chair. "I hope things weren't unpleasant for you here while I was gone. Lately I never know what to expect of Drake. How did he treat you?"

Briana shifted restlessly and sighed. "I don't know quite how to answer that. Part of the time he ignored me, and other times he was very congenial." Congenial, she thought. What a word to describe those intimate occasions with Drake. She laughed nervously. "Your brother isn't the easiest person to figure out."

"How do you feel about him?" Ruth persisted gently. "I've got the impression several times that you might be interested in him, romantically interested, I mean."

Briana found it difficult to meet Ruth's clear gaze. "I'm sure you've noticed, even if he is your brother, that Drake has a certain male appeal. He's also very forceful and dynamic and successful. There must be many women who are attracted to him."

"That doesn't really answer my question. Particularly since I returned from St. Croix, I've sensed you feel more than a casual attraction for him. The look on your face right now seems to confirm it. Am I reading the signs correctly?"

"Oh, darn it, Ruth, I don't know." Briana

began to play absently with a fold of her cotton skirt. "When he orders me around the way he did on Wednesday, I want to slap him. But then, when he's being charming, all he has to do is touch me and—" She broke off, appalled at her own words. She had never meant to admit the depth of her feelings for Drake to anyone. "Mostly he just makes me feel confused," she finished lamely.

"Love *is* confusing," Ruth said softly.

"Who said anything about love?" Briana protested with revealing fervency. But she was unable to meet Ruth's sympathetic gaze. She bent her head, concealing her eyes with the thick fringe of her dark lashes. A feeling of resignation overcame her, and after a moment she said, "Maybe I could fall in love with him if I let myself. But I won't! I don't want to fall in love with any man, and particularly not Drake. He...he'll never get over his resentment of my family or forget that I'm one of them. I'd be rather a glutton for punishment, wouldn't I, if I allowed myself to lose sight of that?"

"It sometimes happens," Ruth said, "that we fall in love in spite of our best intentions."

"Well, I haven't." Maybe, Briana thought, if she said it often enough, she would start to believe it herself.

"Drake has changed since he met you," Ruth went on. "I don't know what happened while I was gone, but whatever it was, it affected him greatly. He hardly hears me when I speak to him. You said that you feel something when he touches you. I suspect he feels something, too, or you wouldn't respond to him so strongly."

Briana hesitated a moment, then said, "Well, he may feel something, but it's nothing more than a physical attraction. That isn't enough for me. I made that mistake once, and I don't mean to do it again."

"But—"

"Please, Ruth," Briana interrupted wearily, "let's not talk about Drake anymore, all right?" She glanced at her wristwatch. "Besides, I'd better go now. I have some errands to do in Charlotte Amalie before I go home."

"And you don't want to run into Drake," Ruth added with a perceptive look.

"Did he tell you to keep me here until he arrived?"

Ruth chuckled. "Not exactly. He hinted that he might try to leave work early."

Briana got to her feet quickly. "Then I'll be off. Goodbye, Ruth. And I'd appreciate it if you wouldn't repeat this conversation to Drake."

"If you say so."

"Thank you." Briana smiled at the other woman. She was definitely starting to consider Ruth Heyward a friend, a feeling that had nothing to do with the fact that she was Drake's sister.

"Your confidence is safe with me," Ruth assured her. "See you next week."

Briana left, wondering what Ruth meant by "confidence" and suspecting that she had revealed even more to Ruth than she had thought.

IN CHARLOTTE AMALIE a half hour later, she stopped at the jeweler's to have a new safety chain put on her wristwatch, then ran into the grocer's to buy the bread and sugar Ida had asked her to pick up on her way home. She was leaving the grocer's when she met Jane Fitzcannon on the sidewalk.

"Briana! How nice to see you. It's been a long time."

Briana's gaze ran over the tall auburn-haired woman, noticing a brassy sort of hardness that hadn't been there the last time she'd seen Jane. It seemed obvious that Jane was living fast and free on the inheritance left by her grandparents. "It has been a long time, Jane. How have you been?"

"So-so." There was something brittle in Jane's manner. "We've some catching up to do. Let's go into the restaurant next door and have a drink."

"Well...I can't stay long." Jane had taken her arm and was urging her toward the restaurant.

Jane ordered a martini, and Briana asked for lemonade. "Now tell me," the other woman said, "what are you doing with yourself these days?"

"I'm keeping busy, finishing up the requirements for my doctorate degree and working part-time."

"Oh, yes, for Drake Rutledge. Erik told me." An avid glitter of curiosity appeared in Jane's hazel eyes. "Would you have believed when we were kids that he would come so far? Your brother said he's practically possessed when it comes to making money, and that he's a slave driver as an employer. Erik hated working for him. How do you do it?"

"Actually I don't see that much of Drake, but I've found him to be reasonable and fair when it comes to my job."

"Another country heard from," commented Jane, stirring her drink while she studied Briana. "Well, let's face it, Erik isn't exactly the nine-to-five type."

"Sooner or later," Briana said, "he's going to have to face facts. People without money have to work for a living."

"I think he's already arrived at that conclusion. He's been working on something, some kind of investment. At least that's what he told me the last time I saw him. All this dedication to business is making him boringly serious."

Briana shook her head, feeling bewildered. "I'm sorry, but I've no idea what you're talking about. Dedication to business? Erik? Are you sure you're talking about my brother?''

"Haven't you noticed how busy he's been lately?''

"Well, he's not home much. Grandmother has complained about it. Frankly I assumed he was gadding about with you.''

"If only that were true!'' Jane exclaimed. "I hardly ever see him these days.''

"Then where does he go? What's he been doing?''

She made a face. "He says he's working on a big financial deal. He's being maddeningly secretive about it. All I know is that it might mean a great deal of money for him.''

Briana felt a small chill of apprehension go up her backbone. Erik's big deals could not always stand the light of exposure. Upon his return from New York, he'd mentioned that he'd been gambling. If he got involved in that sort of thing too deeply, he might find himself in hock to a gambling syndicate. Those types wouldn't be likely to let him off as easily as Drake had done. "He hasn't breathed a word about this to me,'' she said worriedly.

Jane shook her head. "Well, you know he felt pretty sheepish about not finding a suitable position in New York and having to come back home. I guess he doesn't want to say anything this time until he's sure the investment, or whatever it is, is going to pay off.''

"You're probably right," Briana murmured, wishing she didn't feel so uneasy over Jane's revelation.

"I hope it doesn't take too long. Erik and I have such fun together. I miss having him around."

Why, thought Briana, *she really cares for him.* "I'll tell him that," she promised.

"Would you? Thanks, Briana. I've left word at your house twice for him to call me, but he hasn't."

"Ida may have forgotten to give him your messages. Well, I have to be going. It was nice seeing you again, Jane."

She left the other woman sitting in the restaurant, drinking a second martini. She had actually felt sorry for Jane. It appeared she cared more deeply for Erik than he did for her. Funny, not long ago she had been afraid that her brother might marry the woman. What, she asked herself anxiously, was her sly sibling up to now?

ERIK WASN'T AT HOME when she got there. She spent some time with her grandmother, and when he still didn't put in an appearance, they had an early dinner in Margaret's sitting room.

At seven-thirty that evening the front doorbell rang. Briana, sitting in the study with some of her papers spread out on the desk before her, went to answer it. She didn't want the noise to disturb Ida, who had gone to bed early with a headache.

No one ever dropped in on them unexpectedly. Perhaps Erik had forgotten his key, she decided as she released the lock and opened the door.

In the dusk beyond the yellow circle thrown by the entry light, she saw Drake's dark figure. Her hand gripped the edge of the half-open door, and she stood there facing him, wide-eyed in surprise. "What are you doing here?" she asked automatically.

Even in the shadows she could tell he wasn't smiling, and his eyes never left her face. "I want to talk to you."

"What? Couldn't you have phoned?"

"I didn't want to phone."

"Well, can't it wait until—"

"No," he interrupted imperiously, "it can't wait."

Her hand maintained its white-knuckled grip on the door. "We can't talk here."

He looked at her with eyes that were heavy lidded, their expression hidden from her. "Then come for a drive."

The note of demand in his voice sent a whisper of response along her spine. "This isn't a good time for me. I'm working."

"Either you come out here, or I'll come in. Which will it be?"

There was a moment of strained silence between them, and abruptly she was aware of his size, the reined power within him. He would force his way in if she refused. Her shoulders sagged. "I'll go and tell grandmother I have to go out for a while. Would you wait in your car, please?"

"I'll wait, but not long." He turned on his heel and walked back toward the drive.

She closed the door, thought momentarily of locking up and leaving him to stew outside, then discarded the notion as unwise. After giving Margaret a vague excuse about needing something from town, she joined Drake in the MG.

He was silent as he drove away from the house. Briana was determined not to be the one to start the conversation, so neither of them spoke until he had pulled off the road on a high promontory that overlooked the sea. He switched off the motor and turned toward her, his arm resting along the back of the seat.

"Why have you been avoiding me?"

The shadowy interior of the car, the faint odor of pipe tobacco and limey after-shave that clung to him, and the lulling lap of the waves against the shore below seemed to surround them with a cloak of intimacy. Briana couldn't stop the warm feeling that was flowing through her. She had missed him terribly.

"What makes you think I have been?" she countered.

Drake smiled cynically. "I've left word with

Ruth twice for you to wait for me at the house.
Both times you made a point of leaving early. I
believe you told Ruth something about my not
being your lord and master.''

''Well, you aren't! I don't have to do your bid-
ding except on my job. I resent the way you seem
to think I'll come running every time you crook
your finger, Drake. You have no claim on me!''

His fingers began to toy with a strand of her
hair. ''No?'' he asked suggestively.

''No!'' she repeated, the vehemence in her
voice totally at odds with the soft melting sensation she was experiencing.

''Then why do you tremble when I touch
you?''

She swallowed and moistened her lips. ''I . . . I
don't. You're mistaken.''

His hand on her hair grew still for a moment.
Then abruptly he got out of the car and strode
around to her side. Opening her door, he stated,
''I want some fresh air. Get out.''

''No, I—''

''Get out!''

She obeyed, and he took her arm, leading her
nearer to the edge of the cliff. The sea was
louder there; the waves crashing on the sand
below sounded frenzied. He sat down on the
grass, pulling her down beside him. She might
have resisted, but her legs felt suddenly too
weak to support her. No, she thought dazedly, it
can't happen again.

She felt the warmth of his hand on her shoulder, and her breath escaped her lungs in a soft sigh. She didn't resist when he pushed her gently down on her back, cradling her in his arms.

"You look beautiful in the moonlight," he said softly. "Your skin looks gilded. I wish I could see more of it—all of it."

She was shaking like a leaf, her senses craving the sensuous touch of his hand as he brushed back her hair and caressed her face and neck. The erotic response of her body to his words and touch was like an electric current coursing through her.

She lowered her eyelids. "Oh, Drake...."

He smiled softly, his teeth flashing white in the deep purple of the night. "Tell me what you're thinking, Briana."

Her breath trembled as she drew it in. "Drake—what happened between us at your house—it shouldn't have happened."

"Didn't you like it?" he inquired softly.

"You know I did, but we can't go on like this. There's no future in it."

Without a reply, his mouth came down on hers, nudging her lips apart in a deep yearning kiss of passion. A flame of response ignited her blood and threatened to engulf her. Only a small part of her wanted to fight against it. But this was the moment of truth. Somehow she knew that if she gave in to what she really wanted now, she would never be able to hold out against him again.

Yet when his mouth released her, she only sighed his name longingly. His hand slipped beneath the neckline of her blouse and found her breasts. She wasn't wearing a bra, and couldn't stop the pleasure she uttered. Drake moaned softly in answer, and his mouth searched for the sensitive spots that he had discovered during those passionate nights in his house.

Burying his face in her hair, he whispered against her ear, "Forget everything else and let me touch you. Let me worship your body with mine." He ran his hand possessively across her flesh, then slowly stroked the peak of one breast with erotic fingers. "Think about this moment, Briana. Our bodies are crying for more, and neither one of us wants to deny ourselves." He kissed the hollow of her throat, then returned to her mouth. His lips moved sensually, deliberately on hers, reviving everything.

A small groan of despair lodged in her throat. When he released her mouth, she said huskily, "I wish. . . ." But then she faltered.

His hand continued its relentless stroking of her breasts until she could think of nothing else. She wanted to be naked beside him, wanted his mouth and hands on her skin. She wanted him desperately—every cell, every secret part of her.

"What do you wish?" he asked huskily.

"I...I wish you were anyone but a Rutledge."

Drake's mouth was against her throat, but as she spoke, he lifted his head, and she felt him withdraw into himself. She pressed her shaking hand against her mouth, lest her desolate need shape itself into words and spill from her lips. When she had some control of herself, she said, "I can't deny I want you." She was amazed that she could sound so cool. "But I know later I'd feel disgusted with myself and ashamed, like the other times."

He rolled away from her onto his back and cursed softly. "You've no taste for the lower classes, is that what you mean?"

The cold anger in his words tore through Briana like a jagged shard of ice. She bit her lip. Let him think what he wanted. Anything was better than letting him know she was in love with him.

She sat up, pulling her blouse down over her feverish body. Maybe he would stay away from her now, and she could forget what it felt like when he made love to her.

After a moment he stood up and walked toward the car. She followed slowly, giving her heart time to slow down and her breathing to become even.

He drove quickly to her house, his hands gripping the steering wheel. When the car pulled to a stop, and she started to get out, he reached across her to keep her from opening the door.

"Tell me, Briana, didn't you like what you found out from my bank? Don't I have enough money for an Ivensen to lower herself to my level?"

"What?" she whispered, confused.

"Oh, yes, I know it was you," he said with deliberation. "Until tonight I wasn't sure."

"I don't know what you're talking about."

"Then I'll tell you. A woman called my bank a few days ago and tried to pass herself off as a broker. She said she had a client who was interested in investing in my corporation, but she needed to know my current financial status in order to advise her client. She was very convincing. The young teller's new on the job. He gave her quite a lot of information, including the size of the trust funds I've set up for Ruth and Patty, before he wondered if he should have checked with me before divulging anything."

"And you think it was me!" she blazed indignantly.

"I'm sure of it. The only thing that surprises me is that my very considerable assets aren't enough for you. How much do you think you're worth, Briana?"

Her anger erupted in a flash, and her hand came up to strike him. He caught her wrist and laughed unkindly.

"I hate you!" she ground out.

With his free hand, he opened the door beside

her and flung it wide. "Good night, Briana Ivensen." He emphasized her last name with a mocking inflection.

She scrambled out of the car, and he immediately drove off at high speed. She stood for a moment in the yard, trying to take in what had happened. How could he think that she would want to check on his financial status? His opinion of her was even lower than she had imagined.

It was several minutes before she went into the house. Erik was sitting in the front parlor reading a magazine.

"Hi," he greeted her, tossing the magazine aside. "Where have you been?"

"Out," she answered curtly.

"Ah. Must have been with Rutledge since you don't want to tell me." He grinned at her, and his eyes ran over the rumpled state of her clothing and hair. "Keep your little secrets if you want. I think I can guess what they are, anyway."

His knowing leer embarrassed and angered her. "Speaking of secrets," she retorted, "I ran into Jane Fitzcannon today. She told me you're investigating a big business deal of some kind. Odd you haven't mentioned anything about it to grandmother or me."

He gazed at her with a canny look, then shrugged. "I don't want to say anything prematurely. It's too soon to know if anything will come of it."

"Really?" Her tone was heavy with suspicion.

"Look, Briana. I failed at the Rutledge Corporation and again in New York. I don't want to get my hopes up this time. And I certainly don't want you and grandmother feeling sorry for me if this thing falls through. Do you blame me for keeping it to myself until I know something one way or the other?"

"No," she said reluctantly. "I only hope it doesn't have anything to do with gambling."

"It doesn't," he replied readily. "You can set your mind at rest on that score."

She tried to read in his eyes whether he was lying or not, but she couldn't. "I'm going to work in the study for a while. By the way, Jane is feeling neglected. She'd like you to call her." She left him without further conversation.

CHAPTER SIXTEEN

APRIL IN THE ISLANDS was brilliant and hot as usual. There was rain nearly every day for the first week, but it never lasted long, and the moisture it left behind was quickly burned off by the sun. After each shower everything looked refreshed, and the sun seemed to shine even more brightly than before. It was the kind of weather the travel brochures raved about.

The sidewalks of Charlotte Amalie were so crowded it seemed as if half the population of the mainland must have read those brochures and decided to flee from the northern states, where the weather was still cool and drizzly. But where did you flee to, Briana asked herself, when you already lived in the perfect setting? Not that she believed a change of scene would do anything to ward off the depression that had been closing in on her for days. It was a mood that had nothing to do with her physical surroundings.

She wondered ruefully if it were possible to have spring fever when the weather in the islands was temperate year round. If so, not only she but Patty seemed to be afflicted. The girl had spent a couple of days studying the book Briana had given her in preparation for her college entrance exams, but the rest of the time she seemed totally uninterested in her schoolwork. Briana had to prod her constantly to get her to turn in assignments on time. Her mind seemed to be absorbed by something else. And Briana had no idea what was distracting her, for Patty would not be drawn out.

"Mooning," Ruth called it. Finally she decided that Patty "had a virus or something," and she kept her home from school for two days. Patty's irritability quickly exhausted her mother's patience, however, and as a result she spent more time in Charlotte Amalie while she was on sick leave than she did at home.

"She's restless," Ruth explained to Briana. "I think she's impatient to be off to college. Drake doesn't like it, but I decided to let her roam for a few days and work off some of her pent-up energy."

After spending all one Saturday taking the entrance exams, Patty reported that she felt she had done reasonably well. Briana prayed that she was right. She doubted that Patty, in her present mood, would be very disappointed if she weren't.

Briana found herself anticipating her pupil's graduation from high school almost as much as Patty was. It would mean no more tutoring sessions. She might have to find another part-time job for the summer, but at least it wouldn't be in Drake's house.

Since that night three weeks before, when he had accused her of calling his bank, she hadn't seen him. It was evident that he was making it a point not to come home when he knew she would be there. They had switched roles, it seemed. Briana saw the irony of the situation, but didn't find it amusing. After the first week she couldn't help looking for him as she got off the ferry at Red Hook dock, but he was never there. He was making her pay for that night on the cliff, and for trying to check up on his financial status.

She still got angry when she thought about how unfair he had been in accusing her. Someone actually could have been thinking of investing in his corporation. Why did he insist on taking this suspicious view? How could he believe her capable of such deceit?

Briana combated her unhappiness as she always had in the past by burying herself in her work. During her years at university she had learned the trick of single-minded concentration on the task at hand. Consequently she was making good progress in writing her dissertation.

But she had lost a few pounds, and she wasn't sleeping well at all. She dreamed often of Drake, more than once waking up in a sweat to find herself reaching out for him. Her bed seemed desolate and uncomfortable to her restless body. By the end of the third week a deep sense of loss had descended on her.

Except for those two nights in Drake's arms, she had slept alone for almost five years and been grateful for it. It was ridiculous to feel now, as she lay awake in the early-morning hours, that a part of her had been cut away. It wasn't possible for a man to become a desperate need in such a short time. But even though her rational mind understood this, her aching heart and restless body knew it to be a lie.

Many of her sleepless nights were spent in recrimination. She had been a fool to let it happen. But the predawn hours had a way of ripping aside her self-delusions; and she knew that she would willingly do the same thing again. Drake had succeeded in demolishing her fears and forcing her to respond to him as a man. He had made her see that she was a normal woman after all, capable of arousing him to tenderness and warmth and fierce male passion—all the things she had hoped to find in her marriage and had not.

Yes, Drake had left his mark on her. That was an unalterable truth. God, how she missed him!

Yet she continued to rise at five o'clock every morning, make a pot of strong coffee and head straight for the study to lose herself once more in her dissertation. She was determined to exorcise Drake from her heart. As long as she kept her mind occupied, she could almost forget him for hours at a stretch. And so she worked very hard, rising early and falling into bed late at night. She left her desk only for meals and for Patty's tutoring sessions, and one afternoon for an interview with the head of the History Department at the college.

When she handed the professor a detailed outline of her dissertation along with her résumé, he seemed impressed. "We need researchers in this area," he said. "I'm especially intrigued by this projected chapter on St. Thomas's early sea trade. The subject's hardly been touched by anyone else. Where did you get your information?"

"From my grandmother's family papers."

He nodded respectfully. "I'm acquainted with Mrs. Ivensen, a great admirer of hers, in fact. I trust she's in good health."

"Reasonably good, given her age."

"How fortunate that she saved her family's records. So many people see no value in having them lying around and destroy them."

"I come from a family that rarely throws anything away," Briana told him. "You should see our attic."

He was studying her kindly. "I knew your father. You're not exactly what I expected his daughter to be. Don't misunderstand me. Frederik was a good kindhearted man, but he struck me as very much the aristocrat."

She smiled. "You're surprised that I'm pursuing a teaching career, aren't you?"

"How does your grandmother feel about it?"

"She doesn't understand me," Briana said frankly, "but I think my father would have if he'd lived."

"At the very least he'd be proud of you," the professor said. "I'd like to see your dissertation when you've finished it. Have you thought about seeking a publisher for it?"

"I'd love that, of course, if it's good enough. Perhaps you will be able to advise me once you've seen the manuscript."

"I'll look forward to it. You'll be interested in knowing that we do plan to expand the History Department. There will be two new openings next year. If your dissertation lives up to this outline and your grade-point average, I'd say you'll be one of the top contenders for a position here."

He took her on a tour of the campus and later invited her for tea in the private sitting room that adjoined his office. She felt greatly encouraged when she left him.

But even her interview didn't keep her spirits up for long. She wanted a teaching career as badly as she ever had, but now she knew it wouldn't be enough to fill the rest of her life.

She was reflecting upon this as she and Patty took the ferry to St. John one afternoon. She was rather amazed at how her ideas had changed in the last few months. Now she wanted a home of her own. She wanted children, Drake's children.

She shut off that line of thought swiftly. Instead she turned to Patty, who was staring out at the water, lost in one of her brooding moods. She'd had lunch with friends, meeting Briana afterward. At first glance Briana had known it would be a difficult day for tutoring.

"Your scores on the entrance exams ought to be arriving any day," Briana said.

"What?" Patty asked vaguely, not looking at her.

"Never mind. But get your daydreaming done. We've a lot of ground to cover this afternoon to prepare you for that literature test."

"I couldn't care less about any more tests," responded Patty grumpily.

"Why are you so irritable today?"

Patty didn't respond. She merely continued to stare out at the water. She was holding something in, Briana realized. But she wasn't able to find out what it was until they were alone on the patio, about to start reviewing for the literature test.

By then Patty had clearly kept quiet about what was bothering her for as long as she could. After glancing around to make sure Greta and Ruth weren't in earshot, she blurted out, "Did you know that Uncle Drake paid Abel to leave St. Thomas?"

Briana, who had convinced herself that Patty was never going to find out about that, was momentarily at a loss for words. She looked blankly at Patty's flushed angry face and tried to frame a diplomatic reply.

But Patty didn't wait for her to marshal her thoughts. "You did know, didn't you!" She looked as if Briana had struck her.

"Patty, let me try to explain—"

"Explain! How do you think you can explain my own uncle sneaking around behind my back like that?"

"Where did you hear this?"

Patty stared at her for a long moment, and Briana sensed she was fighting back tears. Finally she said, "Everyone in Charlotte Amalie knows everybody else's business. I can't believe you thought I wouldn't find out."

"Do you believe every rumor you hear?"

"Stop it!" Patty exclaimed, her face flushed with anger. "Stop treating me like a dim-witted kid!"

"Okay, Patty," said Briana, "I did know that Drake had an agreement with Abel Weldon."

"Mother did, too, I suppose."

"We both learned about it after the fact, and I guess we felt that what you didn't know couldn't hurt you."

"I thought I could trust you." Patty's brown eyes glittered with accusation. "You betrayed me, all of you!"

"Drake did it out of love for you," Briana said quietly.

"No, he didn't! He did it because he'll do anything to get his own way. He didn't care that I loved Abel. He didn't care how much I'd be hurt."

"Listen to me, Patty." Briana's voice was suddenly stern. "Drake believed you would be throwing your life away if you married that man. He wanted you to have a chance to gain some maturity before making such an important decision."

Patty merely glared at her.

"Tell the truth now, are you still sorry you didn't marry Abel?"

"Maybe not—but that's not the point. What makes Uncle Drake think he can make other people's decisions? He just shoves and pushes people until he gets what he wants."

"He only offered Abel money," Briana pointed out. "Abel didn't have to take it, but he was willing to let you go for a few thousand dollars. Do you think in that case that he truly loved you? Your Uncle Drake did you a favor. When you've had time to think about it, you'll know that's true."

Briana realized suddenly that knowing the cause of Abel Weldon's defection was hurting Patty more than the defection itself. "I want to make my own mistakes," the girl protested sullenly, "like everybody else."

"I wish that I'd had someone older and wiser running interference for me when I was younger," Briana said. "But then with hindsight it's always easy to say what should have happened. Drake may have been a little high-handed, but you've been spared a great deal of regret. Don't tell me you can't see that already."

"When Abel left, I thought my heart would break," said Patty stubbornly.

"But it didn't. Believe me, the pain you felt wasn't nearly as bad as you would have experienced in a disastrous marriage."

"Well...." It was a very reluctant admission to the possibility of truth in Briana's words. "I know now that I didn't love him as much as I thought I did. I never thought he would leave me for money! But that doesn't mean I've forgiven Uncle Drake."

"Will you do something for me?"

"What?"

"Don't say anything to Drake or your mother about this for a few days, until you've had time to think about it."

"I don't know what I'll do."

"It's finished. Let it be and try to learn something from it."

"Someday," Patty said ominously, "I'm going to show him he can't run my life."

She was still furious, that was clear. But Briana knew there was no point in trying to reason with her further at the moment. She began the tutoring session.

They were just winding up when Ruth called to them from the back door. "Patty, Briana!" She was waving a white envelope. "It's the exam scores!"

Ruth had torn open the envelope and was scanning the computer printout when they reached her. She looked up with a puzzled frown. "These numbers don't mean anything to me." She handed the sheet to Briana. "Is it good or bad?"

Briana, with Patty looking over her shoulder, read through the printout. "She's in the ninety-third percentile in language arts, in the eighties in social studies and math, and in the high seventies in science." She handed the sheet to Patty. "A very respectable average. Congratulations, Patty."

The girl was shaking her head uncomprehendingly over the figures. "Does this mean I'll be accepted at college?"

"I'd be willing to bet on it," Briana told her.

"Well!" Ruth beamed at her daughter. "Connecticut, here she comes!"

Patty glanced at her mother, and Briana knew from her expression that she was remembering what she considered to be her mother's betrayal. "I'm going to take this upstairs and study it."

Ruth watched her leave the kitchen. "I must say she doesn't act very excited about it. What's wrong with her?"

"It probably hasn't sunk in yet," Briana temporized.

"Drake will be happy, anyway. Do you have time for a cold drink before you leave?"

"No, thanks. I'd better get home."

Ruth smiled sympathetically. "How is the dissertation coming?"

"Very well," Briana said.

BUT LATER, when she was seated in the peaceful solitude of the Ivensen study, a fresh writing tablet in front of her, she couldn't seem to concentrate on history. When she found herself absentmindedly scribbling Drake's name in the margin, she crossed it out and laid her pen aside. Instead she picked up the typed sheets containing the inventory of the house's furnishings and stared at them for a moment.

She had been finished with the inventory for a week and could easily have handed it over to Ruth to give to Drake. She hadn't done so because she'd been hoping the inventory might give her an excuse to see Drake. She thought of Patty's exam scores again and realized they would give her another reason to contact him.

It gave her the courage to go to the hall telephone and dial the Grand Reef Hotel.

"I'll see if he can take your call," Drake's secretary said. "Who may I say is calling?"

Briana gave her name, then suffered several moments of despair, certain that Drake would refuse to speak to her. But he came on the line.

"Have you talked to Ruth this afternoon?" she asked, her heart pounding.

"No. I've been out of the office."

"Patty's exam scores came in the mail today. I knew you'd want to know. I'm sure she did well enough to get into that college in Connecticut."

"I never really doubted that she would, did you? She's worked hard under your tutelage."

There was a thick silence.

"I've finished the inventory," she said finally. "Shall I mail it to you at the hotel? Or would you like me to leave it with Ruth?"

He seemed to hesitate over his answer, then he said, "Neither. I'll pick you up for dinner, and you can give it to me personally."

It was more of an order than an invitation, but Briana was too happy at the prospect of seeing him to notice. "What time?"

He told her and rang off.

"ARE YOU HAVING DESSERT?" Drake's tone was cool, an inexplicable contrast to his burning gaze as it rested on her face. It had been like this all evening, and Briana's nerves were strung taut, almost to the breaking point. She wondered what she had expected, and realized that she had been hoping against hope that he would have forgiven her by now for that night on the cliff. She should have known better.

"No, I couldn't."

He got up and came around the table, pulling her chair back as she stood up. He didn't touch her.

She moved across the restaurant, the soft folds of her long white caftan brushing her legs with a quiet whisper. He was a step behind her, and she could feel his eyes boring into the back of her head. When they were in his car, she made a decision that she had been debating about all evening.

"I think you should know," she said, "that Patty heard a rumor that you'd paid Abel Weldon to leave St. Thomas. She confronted me with it, and I couldn't deny there had been some kind of agreement between you and Weldon."

He slid a narrow glance over her. "How did it get out? Have you mentioned it to anyone?"

"No," she replied curtly.

"I'm certain Ruth hasn't."

"Maybe Weldon told someone before he left."

"Probably. How did Patty take it?" he asked.

"She was extremely angry, but you can hardly blame her for that. I really think she's over Weldon now, but what infuriated her was what she calls your tendency to make other people's decisions."

"She'll get over it."

"I know—in time. I only hope she gives herself the time."

He turned to look at her sharply. "What do you mean?"

"She said something that sounded like a threat. Something about showing you you can't run other people's lives."

He was thoughtful for a moment. "What could she do? She doesn't know where Weldon is, so she can't contact him."

"Nothing, I suppose. She was probably just blowing off steam." She glanced out the window, for the first time noticing the road they were taking. "This isn't the route to my house. Where are we going?"

"To the hotel."

She heard the tension in his voice and a faint apprehension ran through her. "Why?"

He made a sound of cynical amusement. "Use your imagination, Briana."

"I'm not sure this is a good idea." Her voice was unsteady.

She saw his jaw tighten, and for a moment he regarded her silently. The desire in his eyes stirred a fever in her blood. "Why did you call me if you didn't have this in mind?"

Blast him! Was he right? Had she wanted to end the evening in his bed? Maybe subconsciously she had. But she was never going to get over him this way. She had been trying to convince herself all evening that she could live without him, that life would be bearable again once she'd launched her career. But now, looking at him, she felt the deep ache inside her throbbing more persistently than ever. She wanted to touch him, to feel his lips on hers, to press her body against his.

"Let's not pretend with each other," he began and stopped, his hands increasing their grip on the steering wheel. "You may despise the idea of who I am, but you didn't have to come to dinner with me tonight. You knew what I was really asking when I invited you, and you accepted. Briana I . . . I've missed you."

"Are you trying to make me feel sorry for you?" She meant it to sound unfeeling. It was the only defense she had against his humiliating hold over her.

"I don't want your pity." His chin was thrust forward as he turned the car into the hotel's private parking area. He turned off the engine, got out and came around to open her door.

Swiftly, before she knew his intent, he scooped her out of the car, swinging her up into his arms. His mouth took hers hungrily, and as they did so, her arms locked themselves around his neck. Her hands rubbed the hard muscles at the back of his neck, and she reveled in the feel of his warm skin under her palms. Any thought of her battered pride was swept away by the shock waves that jolted through her body because she was, at last, touching him again. Her mouth became as hungry as his, and she pressed against him, tasting him with her tongue and lips.

Drake broke the kiss reluctantly to stride toward a back entrance. Her body pressed against him, he carried her quickly up a narrow staircase, which opened into his private suite. The balcony curtains were pulled back, and moonlight flooded into the apartment.

He set her on her feet and almost at once ran his hands down her arms and over her hips. Then he reached for her hair, tugging at the pins that confined the blond strands in a chignon. His fingers threaded through the loose tresses, shaping themselves to her scalp in a warm caress and holding her head immobile so that his mouth had free access to her face and neck.

"That dress has been driving me crazy all evening," he told her. "Every time you moved, I could see the outline of your body, and I wanted to tear the thing apart and touch you." His voice was husky and thick as his teeth bit gently at her earlobe. "Did you buy it with the intention of driving me mad?"

She shivered as his tongue explored the inner curvature of her ear. "Ruth gave it to me," she whispered breathlessly.

"I must thank her sometime," he muttered as he pulled at the caftan, lifting the loose material up and over her head. He tossed it aside impatiently, and it settled on the dark carpeting, a pool of silvery white in the moonlight.

His fingers slid inside the cups of her bra, fumbling at the fastening and finally, releasing it. The lacy garment joined the caftan on the carpet, and he turned her so that the full globes of her breasts were gilded by the soft moonlight. For a moment his eyes devoured her, then his hands cradled her breasts, and he kissed her again, his tongue probing, urgent, and finding an eager response. He groaned and clutched her against him, burying his face in her hair, and she felt him struggling to control the desperate need that arose in him.

Briana trembled in his arms, lost to everything but her love, her desire. She was being consumed by her own need and could not begin to think of smashed pride or consequences, or anything at all but her hunger and Drake's. Her blood coursed along her veins, and she reached dazedly for his dinner jacket, pushing it off his shoulders and down his arms. Then her fingers fumbled with his tie and the buttons of his shirt until, an eternity later, it seemed, he stood naked from the waist up. Drake stripped off the rest of his clothing, his eyes never leaving her as she stepped out of her own lacy briefs.

Flesh met flesh. Clinging to each other, they sank onto the plush thickness of the carpet, and Briana felt the soft pile beneath her. Their hands and mouths roamed and caressed almost frenziedly as they rediscovered the wonders of each other's body. Briana was filled with a fever of desire, and she moaned with helpless longing. His strong hands came up to hold her head as he gazed deeply into her heavy-lidded eyes. He lay on top of her, his flesh warm and firm, pressing her down into the soft cushion of the carpet. She shuddered at the hard demand of his body and the response that was like molten fire in her loins.

But he didn't take her right away. Instead his hands trembled, and he confessed, "I've wanted you every minute since the last time we made love." One hand found her breast, and she gasped in pleasurable response. He laughed softly, thickly. "Have you wanted me, too, Briana? Tell me!"

She was completely open to him now. She felt as if every defense had been stripped away, every sensitive nerve exposed to the seductive heat of his body. They were floating together in an infinite sea of pleasure, and she could hear the relentless tide of their blood, feel the sensuous waves caressing them.

"Yes," she whispered, her eyes boldly telling him the truth.

He lifted himself slightly, poised above her. "Have you lain awake nights, wanting me?" he demanded, his voice unsteady.

"Yes." Her response was a moan this time.

"Yes," he gasped with satisfaction. "Oh, yes." And then his body plundered hers.

She arched against him as he moved within her, her hands sliding over the heated smoothness of his skin, moist now with perspiration.

She closed her eyes, flowing with the crescendo that was building inside her.

Drake's breath came in deep gasps as the rhythm of his lovemaking lifted Briana higher and higher in an explosion of sensation. She cried out with pleasure but a moment later wanted nothing so much as release from the torturous waves of rapture that swelled in her.

She was weeping by the time their passion reached its peak. And it was then, in the final moment, that she sighed, "I love you, Drake."

He cried out as he reached his own blissful peak, and then he collapsed against her, gathering her perspiring body to the dampness of his own, trembling with the aftermath of release.

"Briana, my darling, you are my own sweet love," he whispered as he cradled her in his strong arms, held her as if he would never let her go.

CHAPTER SEVENTEEN

IN TOTAL PEACE they lay together for endless minutes. Briana stroked the damp hair at the nape of Drake's neck, her body still, her mind floating free. Until it caught on those words she had uttered at the end, those words she hardly knew she'd said. She had told him that she loved him, and it was true, so painfully, utterly true. But he had not said the same words to her. He had not returned her vow of love. Something in her shriveled; the dreamlike spell was broken, and she shut her eyes tightly.

Drake raised himself on his elbow and kissed her breast. Then he gazed down at her with a languorous satisfied smile. "You belong to me, Briana!" He chuckled as he lay back on the rug and said, "I wonder what your grandmother would say if she knew?"

Briana slowly extricated her limbs from his and sat up. Suddenly she felt cold. Here she was aching for reassurance, and all he could do was revel in his mastery over her. Even in his most tender moments he never forgot that she was an Ivensen.

She reached for her clothes and began dressing. Drake watched her silently, his manner all at once withdrawn. "It's killing you, isn't it?" His tone was hard.

She slipped the caftan over her head, and it fell about her in soft swirls. "What is?"

"The fact that you want me, no matter how many times you tell yourself you don't." He laughed softly. "I'll bet your father is spinning in his grave."

She was standing now, pushing one foot and then the other into her high-heeled sandals. She bent to secure the ankle straps, then she straightened and faced him. He had moved away from her. His long lean frame was sprawled on the couch.

"You aren't handling this...attraction or sickness or whatever it is between us very well, either, Drake. Even when we're making love, a part of you despises me for who I am!"

"Is that what you think?" The words were low, angry.

"Yes."

His eyes watched her steadily, his face tight. Then without another word he got up and dressed quickly. Only when he was fully clothed again did he speak. "I'll take you home," he said curtly.

She walked past him and out into the lighted corridor. "I'm sorry I allowed you to bring me here tonight," she whispered, her voice unsteady. "We can't see each other again. I'll be tutoring Patty only a few more weeks. If you want to discuss her during that time, I'd prefer doing it by phone. All right?"

His jaw tightened. "No deals."

She stared at him for a moment, then followed him down the stairs and outside. She got out of the car at her house and went in without having exchanged another word with him.

IT WAS THE MOST SULTRY MAY Briana could remember. Patty's chafing at the restrictions of her schoolwork increased, and she was cross and irritable much of the time. Briana was restless herself. She longed for the arrival of June when her work with Patty would come to an end. She had found a half-time job in the college-registrar's office for the summer. It would see them through financially until she started teaching. She didn't even allow herself to entertain the possibility that she might not be hired by the History Department faculty. Nor did she think about what she would do if Drake refused to rent the house to her after she left his employ. Instead she concentrated on her dissertation and on preparing Patty for her final high-school exams.

One day in mid-May she was waiting for Patty at the school, as usual, but the girl didn't appear. Grumbling irritably to herself, she climbed out of her car and went inside. In the principal's office the secretary informed her that Patty had not been at school all day.

Thinking that Ruth had forgotten to phone and tell her, Briana used the school telephone to reach St. John. "Is Patty ill today?" she asked when Ruth came on the line.

"Not that I know of. Why?"

"I'm at the high school. Apparently she hasn't been here all day."

"Oh, no, not again!" Ruth sounded more exasperated than she customarily was when Patty behaved irresponsibly. "She left here at the usual time this morning. Where could she be?"

Briana sighed. "I have no idea."

"She's been sort of jumpy lately, and I haven't been able to get her to talk to me. I'm worried, Briana."

Ruth's anxiety was communicating itself to Briana. "She once mentioned a friend, Lissa something. Do you know her last name?"

"Lissa Grey."

"I'll see if Lissa is absent, too. If not, I'll drive down to the harbor and look around. I'll call you if I find out anything. If you do, phone me at the house later."

Lissa, it turned out, had been in school all morning. The secretary said that she usually went home for lunch, so Briana got her phone number from the school records. The girl claimed to know nothing about where Patty might have gone, however. As an afterthought, she said, "Maybe she's with her boyfriend."

"Is he a boy from school?"

"No, he's older, I think. Patty's real secretive

about him, but I know she's seeing someone."

Briana drove along the harbor road several times and questioned a few people who worked in nearby restaurants. She found out nothing of Patty's whereabouts. Finally she gave up and returned home, where Ida had a message for her. Ruth had called not five minutes before.

When Briana returned the call, the other woman was in a panic. "A few minutes ago I went into Patty's bedroom," she said. "She left a note on her pillow. Oh, Briana, I'm scared. I don't know what to do!"

"Have you called Drake?"

"I was about to when you phoned—" Her voice broke, and it was a moment before she had gained enough control of herself to speak again. "Part of her note doesn't make much sense to me. Listen, I'll read it to you:

'Mother, I'll never forgive you and Uncle Drake for going behind my back and sending Abel away. So I'm going away, too, with a wonderful man I've met. Erik loves me and promises to take me to all the places I've always wanted to see. Don't worry about me.

Patty.'"

Briana felt the blood leave her face. She leaned her forehead against the wall by the hall telephone and closed her eyes. Her fingers gripped the receiver at her ear convulsively. Erik! Patty couldn't mean her brother, Erik!

"How did she find out that Drake paid Abel to leave?" Ruth was saying, her voice shrill with concern. "And who is this Erik she speaks of? Where did she meet him? How many times has she seen him?"

"Ruth, try to calm down. Drake has to be told right away."

"He's going to have a fit."

"Do you want me to tell him?"

Ruth's relief was pathetically clear. "Would you? Oh, Briana, thank you."

"I'll go straight to the hotel. One of us will call you in a little while." She hung up.

She was shaking from head to toe as she went into the kitchen. "Ida, have you seen Erik today?" she asked.

The black woman was cleaning the old stove and glanced over her shoulder. "No'm. He left early this mornin'. Didn't even tell Mistress Ivensen where he goin'. She was askin' me about him a while ago."

Briana hadn't really thought Patty's Erik could be anyone other than her brother. They had been meeting secretly—somehow. It must have started that day when Erik took her and Patty to lunch. Patty had probably made up that story about learning new dance steps from a boy at school to throw Briana off. Had she even gone to Lissa's house that day, or had she been with Erik?

She left the house immediately and drove to the Grand Reef, trying to decide how to tell Drake what had happened. When she stood in his office, however, she forgot her cautiously worded explanation and just blurted out the truth.

He unfolded himself from behind his desk and got up slowly. Every muscle in his face seemed to tense up as he stared at her, and his jaw tightened. "How long have you known what was going on between Patty and Erik?" He spoke quietly with the deadly calm that comes from sudden barely controlled rage.

"What?" she cried. "How dare you ask me that!"

"Are you saying you haven't known all along?" His eyes never left her face.

"I never even suspected!"

"He's the one who told her about the payoff to Weldon, isn't he? You gave him that information. It couldn't have been anyone else."

She looked at him with eyes that were cold with anger. "I did not," she said contemptuously. "He...he must have guessed it. He suggested to me once that you probably paid Weldon, but I told him I didn't know." She had been operating on sheer adrenaline ever since her conversation with Ruth, and now her body seemed to sag with exhaustion. "I never knew what he was up to. Now...now a lot of things make sense."

He came around the desk and towered over her. "What things?" he demanded.

"Erik didn't care whether you had paid Weldon or not. But he wanted Patty to see it as cruel, as a betrayal, and he evidently convinced her. She's probably been meeting him for lunch. Those days when she skipped school or pretended to be ill so she could stay at home—she must have spent them with Erik."

"How the hell did they meet? He must have introduced himself in some restaurant where she was having lunch. She wouldn't have been afraid of him because he was your brother."

"Right after Erik came back from New York, he took Patty and me to lunch. I'm to blame for introducing them, but nothing more."

There was a moment of taut silence between them. "She's been going out after dark to walk on the beach almost every night for the past two weeks. Could they have been meeting then, too?"

"Erik has access to the Fitzcannons' boat," Briana said dully, certain that Drake's suspicion was true.

He took a step toward her and gripped her upper arms. His eyes were glittering as he looked down at her. "He's doing it to get back at me. If I ever find out you were involved in this, I'll make you very sorry, Briana."

A thrill of fear flashed through her. With an abrupt motion she wrenched herself free of his grasp. "Keep your hands off me! I told you I knew nothing about it." She hated him for even thinking she could betray his and Ruth's trust in her.

"Come with me," he said shortly. "We have to find them."

She didn't hesitate. As angry as she was with Drake for his attitude toward her, she was as worried as he was about Patty. And she was as certain, too, that this was Erik's means of revenge. He hated Drake for the success he had made of his life. He hated Drake for having once been his, Erik's, employer, and now Briana's. And he hated him most of all for having gained possession of the Ivensen house. Briana was sure her brother had somehow managed to convince himself that the blame for all of his troubles could be laid at Drake Rutledge's feet.

She was angry with herself for not suspecting Erik of something like this. That day when she had introduced him to Patty, he must have come to the school for that very purpose. Asking her to pick up a part for the lawn mower had only been an excuse.

They got into the MG and drove away from the hotel. "Where are we going?" she asked.

"We'll try the airport first. They're probably already off the island, but maybe we can find out where they've gone."

"I heard weeks ago that Erik was involved in some business deal. I thought he was gambling again. I worried about it, but he seemed to be taking more responsibility around the house." She spoke in a distracted tone, more to herself than to Drake. "I thought he was going to shape up. I guess I wanted to believe it."

"It's hard to think the worst of our relatives," he muttered, his eyes on the road. She wondered if that meant he now believed she had known nothing about Erik and Patty's clandestine meetings. But even if he had decided to believe her, that didn't alter the fact that his first reaction had been accusing and distrustful.

"The woman who phoned my bank," he went on after a moment. "Whoever it was, Erik must have put her up to it."

"It was probably Jane Fitzcannon," Briana decided. "Although I'm sure she had no idea what was behind Erik's interest in your financial status. She's in love with him."

"Poor fool."

"I know."

"The bank clerk mentioned Patty's trust fund. That must have been what precipitated this. Do you think he'd actually marry her to get his hands on that money?"

"I don't know. But if this hadn't happened, you'd have gone on thinking I was the one who phoned your bank."

He was silent for a brief moment. "I'm sorry about that. I don't think I ever really believed it."

Briana didn't respond. She sat forward in her seat as Drake brought the car to a stop in the airport parking lot. They hurried toward the terminal, Briana running to keep up with his long strides.

Drake made straight for one of the three ticket windows in the terminal. The second agent they questioned knew Drake slightly from having worked as a busboy at the Grand Reef a few years previously.

"We've had quite a lot of business this morning, Mr. Rutledge," the man said slowly, obviously wanting to be of help. "Two or three tour groups left today, and there were several young couples."

"These two would have been alone. The man's tall and blond, dresses well. My niece is seventeen—tall, too, with brown hair."

"Wait a minute." The agent's brow wrinkled as he tried to remember. "I do recall a young man and a girl. They might have been the two you describe. Got here early. The girl had brown hair, like you say—long and straight. And yes, I remember now—she was wearing something that looked like a uniform. It might have been a school uniform."

"That was my niece," Drake cut in. "Can you remember what their destination was?"

The agent bent to retrieve a folder full of papers from beneath the counter. "Not right offhand. Let me look through my records.

They'd be in this first batch." He shuffled through the papers, scanning them quickly. Briana shifted restlessly.

"I think—yes, I'm sure this is it. The one-way tickets to Miami. Their plane left at nine-forty-two." He named the airline and the scheduled time of arrival.

"When does the next flight leave for Miami?"

The agent consulted his schedule. "Not till tomorrow morning, Mr. Rutledge. Sorry."

Drake thanked the man, then glanced at Briana. "The company plane could be ready for takeoff in two hours."

"Are you going after them? Miami might not be their final destination. They could be almost anywhere by tomorrow."

He scowled darkly. "Let's have a cup of coffee and try to figure out what would be best."

After some discussion Drake decided to send the investigator he'd hired to watch Abel Weldon to Miami. "He'll know better than I do how to pick up their trail," he told Briana after he had phoned the investigator, and the man had agreed to leave on the corporation's private jet that afternoon. "I called Ruth, too," Drake added, "and told her what we've learned. She didn't know that the Erik involved was your brother."

"I couldn't bring myself to tell her," Briana said in a low voice.

"I called the police, too. I want all the help I can get," he said. "Now let's go have a talk with your grandmother."

He was already striding toward the exit door when Briana caught up with him. "Drake, please, you can't drop this in grandmother's lap without warning. She'll be confused—and hurt."

They had reached the MG. He looked at her over the hood of the car, his dark eyes adamant. "I'm far more concerned with finding Patty than with how Margaret Ivensen is going to take this! My niece has been abducted by your brother, and I'm going to find them if I have to turn all of St. Thomas and Miami upside down to do it!"

She realized that further reasoning would be useless, and she didn't try to talk to him as they drove to the house. In the entry hall, however, she faced him determinedly. "I want to have a few minutes alone with her first. She'll be in her sitting room. You can wait in the hall."

She found Margaret sitting in one of her Queen Anne chairs, sipping at a cup of tea and listening to a recording of Beethoven's *Fifth Symphony*. Briana shut the sitting-room door behind her.

Hearing the sound, Margaret glanced up. "Why, Briana, you're home early, aren't you? How nice."

Briana moved to the stereo player and turned

the sound off. "I have to talk to you, grandmother. It's important." She sat down on the
Victorian settee facing her.

Her grandmother must have detected the
urgency underlying her tone, for she frowned
and set her teacup down on the table. She leaned
forward in her chair. "You certainly sound
serious, dear. What is it?"

"Erik. He...well, you know that he's been
away from the house a lot lately."

"Indeed I do! I've made no secret of my feelings on the matter. I've told him that being a
part of a family carries with it certain responsibilities to—" She broke off, catching the anxiety in Briana's manner. "What's happened?"
she said in a tense voice. "Has there been an accident?"

"No, nothing like that." Briana brushed a
hand across her eyes. If only there was some
way to soften what she had to tell her grandmother. But there wasn't any kind way to put it.
"He's been spending time with Drake's niece,
Patty. Evidently they've been meeting for
lunch, and probably he's been taking the Fitzcannons' boat over to St. John after dark."

"But that's preposterous! She's merely a
child!" Margaret's faded blue eyes were in-
credulous. "You know he's become quite close
to Jane. Where did you get this ridiculous information, Briana? Surely you don't believe it!"

Briana drew a deep steadying breath. "It's

true, grandmother. Now he's talked Patty into running away with him. All we know is that they flew to Miami this morning.''

Margaret got up stiffly, twisting her hands together, and walked to a window. When she turned back, the look she gave Briana was one of distaste and disbelief. "There must be some mistake. How do you know this?"

"Patty left a note, and we—Drake and I—have been to the airport and questioned the agent who sold them their plane tickets. Drake's outside in the hall, grandmother. He wants to talk to you."

Margaret's restless movements had brought her to her secretary. She gripped the edge of the desk and lowered herself into the matching cherry-wood chair, facing the door. Her thin blue-veined hands were clasped in her lap, and they were trembling.

Briana opened the door and motioned for Drake to enter. He stood in the center of the room, looking large and out of place among Margaret's fragile mementos and antiques.

"I apologize for barging in on you like this, Mrs. Ivensen, but I thought you might be able to help me find my niece," he said softly.

"I've told Briana—there must be some mistake. I can't believe my grandson has run off with your niece."

"I know it must be hard for you," Drake said, "but it's quite true."

Margaret sat stiffly in her chair, eyeing Drake with some emotion Briana could not identify. "If your niece really was seeing Erik, why didn't you stop her? She's a minor, isn't she?"

"He didn't know it," Briana put in hastily. "None of us did until today. When I went to Patty's school to meet her, I found out she hadn't been there today. I called her mother, who told me Patty left for school this morning as usual. Then Ruth found a note in her bedroom. It seems Patty has been meeting Erik secretly for some time. The note said they were going away together."

"Did he say anything to you, drop any hints about what he might be planning?" Drake's impatience was clear.

The wrinkled skin on Margaret's high cheekbones was becoming flushed. "Certainly not! Nor do I believe that Erik has fallen in love with a seventeen-year-old girl!"

"Love has nothing to do with it!" Drake exploded.

"Drake, please." Briana's eyes pleaded with him to watch what he said. "We think Erik has done this out of spite against Drake," she told Margaret. "They never got along while he was working for the Rutledge Corporation, and they had a serious, er, disagreement before Erik left." She glanced at Drake only long enough to catch his heavily ironic expression. "Also," she rushed on, "Patty has a sizable trust fund, part of which will come to her when she's eighteen.''

As she listened to Briana's words, Margaret seemed to crumple in her chair. Then she buried her face in her hands. There was a long silence, and Briana put her arms around her thin shoulders protectively. ''Grandmother, I'm sorry we had to tell you like this, but we thought you might have a clue as to where they've gone.''

Margaret lifted her head and looked at Briana with stricken eyes. ''Must I pay for what I did the rest of my life?''

Briana exchanged a worried look with Drake. ''We've tired her. She doesn't know what she's saying.''

Drake was looking intently at Margaret. ''What did you do, Mrs. Ivensen?''

''I thought I knew what was best for my son, you must believe that.'' Her gaze, fixed on Briana, pleaded for understanding. Margaret drew a long sighing breath, then said, ''By the time I realized I was wrong, it was too late. Pearl was dead. He was so lonely after your mother died, Briana. Then Pearl came here to work, and I suppose she was lonely, too. They fell in love. Frederik told me he wanted to marry her.

''I...I refused to believe he knew his own mind, and while he was away from home, I fired Pearl. I told her Frederik would never marry her.'' She stiffened her spine and made herself look at Drake. Despite her aristocratic bearing her face was a mask of pain. ''I know it was wrong. When Frederik came home, I tried to convince him it would be best if he never saw Pearl again. All his life he'd tried to please me, so he agreed to think about it for a few days. But he was so withdrawn and unhappy that when we ran into Pearl in town, he didn't even see her. I, God forgive me, pretended not to, either.

"The next day he came to me to say he loved Pearl, and that he was going to marry her in spite of my objections. He. . .was leaving to go to your house, Drake, when you came here with that knife, screaming that he'd killed your mother."

Her voice had grown weak, and now it faded away. She stared straight ahead, her eyes clouded, as if she didn't really see them. Finally she went on, "But I did it. I'm responsible for Pearl's death, and for the fact that, although my son lived another ten years, they were not happy years for him." She looked directly at Drake then. "I only hope you will be able to forgive me someday."

She looked dreadfully pale and weak, as if the telling had utterly exhausted her. Drake cleared his throat. "Frederik tried to make amends," he said in a low voice. "He paid my hospital bill and gave my sister money that helped us through the time after mother's death. I think I've known for a long time that he loved mother, and that he was as heartbroken as Ruth and I when she died. But I wouldn't let go of the hatred. I wanted to blame someone.''

"You should have blamed me,'' said Margaret.

"I did,'' he told her. "I blamed you both.''

Briana was becoming alarmed by her grandmother's lack of color. She looked anxiously at Drake. "She's too tired to talk anymore now. I'll put her to bed. Please, Drake, wait for me in the parlor, okay?''

He went out without protest.

"Grandmother, why don't you lie down for a bit?'' she said gently, taking her thin arm and helping her to her feet. She led her into the adjoining bedroom, where Margaret lay down across the satin coverlet and closed her eyes. Briana poured a glass of water from a pitcher on the nightstand and got one of the tranquilizers the doctor had prescribed. Then she touched her elbow. "Here, take this.''

The old woman raised her head to swallow the pill, then lay back against her pillow again while Briana watched her anxiously.

"I don't suppose you could be mistaken about Erik,'' she said after several moments. Her voice sounded thin, frail.

"No,'' Briana answered regretfully.

"He's never seemed to care about anyone but himself,'' Margaret murmured after another pause. "I haven't wanted to believe it. I've told myself that he's young, that he'll be more responsible as he grows older. I'm to blame, you know. Frederik died such an unhappy man, and I carried the guilt for that around with me. After he died, I tried to put Erik in his place. It was almost as if I had been given a second chance. But I spoiled him. I protected him and worked things out somehow whenever he got into trouble. I could never bear to see him hurt, and so I took his responsibilities on my own shoulders. Eventually I saw that I was ruining him, but I couldn't seem to stop.'' She sounded pathetically beaten.

"Grandmother, don't be so hard on yourself. Erik is an adult. He's responsible for his own actions.''

Margaret sighed softly. "I'm tired, dear. I want to sleep now.''

Briana stayed with her until she was breathing deeply and evenly. Then she went into the parlor, where Drake was pacing restlessly across the faded carpet.

"How is she?'' he asked.

"I gave her a tranquilizer. She's sleeping.''

"Does she believe what we were telling her about Erik?''

"She believes it. Just now, before she went to sleep, she told me she was to blame for that, too, because she spoiled Erik.'' Briana shook her head distractedly. "She's felt so guilty over your mother's death and father's unhappiness all these years, and I never suspected.''

He looked uncertain. "I'm sorry if I upset her, but I had to know if she had any notion about where Erik might have taken Patty. Obviously she doesn't."

"No," Briana agreed. "And there's nothing to apologize for. Maybe it even helped her a little to say those things to you finally." She drew a heavy breath. "Have you had lunch? I haven't and I'm hungry."

"I had an omelet at noon, but I could eat again."

"I'll ask Ida to prepare something."

They ate in the dining room, talking quietly and listening all the while for the telephone to ring. Drake had left the number with Ruth, his pilot and his secretary as one place where he might be reached. Neither of them managed to eat much after all.

After they'd checked to make certain the corporation plane had left for Miami with the investigator on board, Briana looked in on her grandmother and found her sleeping soundly. She told Ida to keep an eye on her and wrote down the phone number of Drake's hotel suite in case she needed her later. Then she and Drake went to the hotel to await further word.

At five o'clock Ruth joined them. "I couldn't stay at the house alone any longer," she explained. Her face was pale and drawn, her eyes red from crying. She appeared to have aged ten years since Briana last saw her.

"Ruth, I'm so sorry for what's happened," Briana told her instantly. "You must believe I didn't have any inkling of what Erik was up to."

Ruth hugged her, patting her shoulder absently. "I know. Nobody's blaming you. Patty's the one I'd like to strangle. When I get my hands on that girl—if I do—" Her voice broke then, and she sobbed in Briana's arms.

Briana looked at Drake over Ruth's bent head. "Come and sit down, Ruth," he said, taking her from Briana's embrace and leading her to the couch. "Can I get you anything? Would you like a drink?"

Ruth wiped her eyes with the handkerchief he offered. "Maybe some coffee," she said, the words muffled in the handkerchief.

"I'll call room service," Briana offered.

They stayed there, the three of them, as darkness closed them in. Through the glass doors to the balcony, they could see the harbor lights coming on one by one. The hours seemed to drag interminably.

The investigator Drake had hired phoned when he landed in Miami. Arrangements were made for the man to contact Drake at the hotel every hour or two during the night to report what progress, if any, he had made.

After a late dinner in the suite Ruth finally fell asleep on the sofa, worn-out with worry. Briana went out to sit on the balcony, and moments later, Drake joined her, leaving one of the glass doors partially open so they could hear the phone if it rang.

They sat side by side in silence for a long time while Drake smoked his pipe. Then Briana said, "I never should have let Erik move back into the house."

"You really had no choice. You were protecting your grandmother. Erik would have told her that he'd lost the house if you'd refused to let him come back."

"I know," she said wearily. "But maybe I should have told her everything from the beginning."

"You made the right decision. I saw today how fragile she really is. I realized for the first time how much she's suffered for what happened twenty years ago—and now this thing with Erik. It's better if she doesn't know about the house."

She turned to peer at him in surprise. After a moment he said quietly, "I'm sorry for what I said to you this afternoon in the office. I didn't really think you were involved in Erik's scheme."

"But you weren't absolutely sure, were you? If you had been, you would never have said the things you did."

"I was angry."

"The things we say in anger are usually more truthful than what we say when we take time to think," she answered numbly.

"You haven't forgiven me."

Briana looked at him. His profile was accentuated by the soft light coming from the suite. He turned to meet her gaze, but his eyes were hooded, and she couldn't read their expression.

"Have I alienated you completely?" he asked with an air of gravity.

She shrugged. "Your accusation this afternoon was just another example of why our decision not to see each other again was the right one."

"It wasn't our decision, it was yours." There was a short pause, then he said, "Briana."

His quiet voice threatened to demolish her resolve. She pushed back her chair. "I think I'll try to get some rest. May I use the bed?"

He looked at her gravely and finally nodded.

She hesitated. "I don't think I'll be able to sleep, but in case I do—would you call me if you have any news?"

"Yes."

Still she hesitated. "You really should try to get a little rest, too."

He smiled at her. "I'll stay here. I'm all right."

She felt a glimmer of warmth easing around her heart. "Drake, I want to find them as much as you do."

"I know."

She left him then. In the bedroom she folded back the spread and, slipping off her shoes, lay down. She stared into the darkness for a long time, certain she wouldn't sleep. But somehow she did.

SHE WAS AWAKENED by the ringing of the telephone in the other room. She struggled out of sleep and sat up, disoriented. The sky outside the bedroom window had turned to a pale whitish gray. It was dawn; she had slept deeply for a few hours.

She stumbled into the living room. Drake was speaking into the receiver, and Ruth hovered at his elbow.

". . . Try to get hold of yourself," he was saying. "Stop crying. I can't understand you." He listened for a moment, then glanced toward the bedroom doorway where Briana stood. He motioned for her to come forward and then thrust the receiver into her hands. "I can't get any sense out of her. She was worse with Ruth. She keeps saying she wants to talk to you."

Briana took the phone. "Patty? Where are you?"

"Briana! Oh, thank goodness you're there. I can't. . . I couldn't tell Uncle Drake—oh, Briana, I'm so scared. I. . . I don't know what to do." Then she was weeping, the sound harsh and desolate coming across the line.

"Patty, listen to me. Try to stop crying. Tell me where you are."

Patty gulped down more sobs and finally

said, "In a hotel...in Miami. I'm calling from
the lobby. I...I couldn't stay in the room alone
any longer."

"Where's Erik?"

"He...he's gone."

"Gone! Where?"

"I don't know. Oh, Briana, he got so mad
I...I thought he was going to hit me."

"He didn't hurt you, did he, Patty? He didn't
harm you physically?"

"No. But when we got to Miami, he wanted
me to call Uncle Drake from the airport. He
wanted me to ask him for money and not tell
him where I was. I was supposed to tell him to
send it by wire and—I didn't understand it all—
except he wasn't going to take me to Paris if I
didn't call. But I didn't want to. By then—well,
I'd had time on the plane to think. I realized I'd
been stupid to run off like that. I wanted to hurt
Uncle Drake, but...I realized I was only hurting myself. I wanted to go back home."

"So you refused to call Drake?"

"Yes, and...and Erik was just awful—" She
had to stop for a moment to contain her weeping. "He...he said I was ugly and dumb, and
the only thing he ever liked about me was my
uncle's money. He...he never meant to marry
me at all. He never even meant to take me to all
those places, as he promised. He just wanted to
get as much money as he could out of Uncle
Drake before he sent me back home. We argued

all the way to the hotel, and finally he said if I wasn't going to be of any use to him, I could take care of myself—and he left. I...I don't even have enough money for taxi fare, and...I called the house, and Greta said you were all there, and...I didn't know what else to do. Briana, I'm scared!"

"You did exactly the right thing, honey. I want you to stay where you are, right there in the lobby. Drake has sent a man to Miami to look for you. He'll be calling us any minute. Drake will have him meet you there and bring you home. Here he is. You tell him where you are, and then you wait. Okay?"

Patty sniffled. "Okay. I guess I have to talk to him. He's going to kill me."

"I doubt that."

"I want to talk to mother, too, so I can tell her I'm all right."

Briana handed the phone to Drake. "She's all right."

He listened for a moment, then wrote down the address and phone number of the hotel. Then he handed the receiver to Ruth. When Ruth had finally hung up, crying softly with relief, they settled down to wait for the investigator's call.

CHAPTER EIGHTEEN

BRIANA STARED at the thick typed manuscript that lay on the desk before her. It was the complete first draft of her dissertation. Today she had planned to begin the revisions. She had allowed two weeks for that, after which she could type the final copy of her history of the Virgin Islands. But she had procrastinated all day, and now it was late afternoon, and she still hadn't started work.

Yesterday she had made her last trip to St. John to tutor Patty. The girl had been understandably subdued since her flight with Erik. But she was beginning to come out of it, to be her old self again. There was nothing left of her high-school year now except for the last three days of final exams. She didn't need help anymore, and so Briana's job there was finished.

Yesterday, after their last session, she and Patty had had a long talk, one that had left her feeling good about her pupil's future. Now that a little time had passed, Patty was taking her disillusionment with Erik better than Briana had expected, and she was eager to begin college.

She'd found a job clerking in a boutique in Charlotte Amalie for the summer, which would give her a much-yearned-for sense of independence and keep her occupied until autumn.

Erik had not returned to St. Thomas, and there was a warrant out for his arrest, charging him with the abduction of a minor. That night in the hotel suite, after Patty had called from Miami, Drake had told Briana that when Erik was found—and if he was convicted—he would probably spend some time in prison. Once the authorities had been brought into the case, it was out of Drake's hands.

Briana had tried to prepare Margaret for the possibility, for she felt certain it was only a matter of time until Erik was caught. Secretly she thought that a prison term might force her brother to take stock of his life at last. Margaret seemed to have come to terms with the situation, and surprisingly she didn't seem to blame Drake or anyone but Erik—and possibly herself.

Since Briana had finished tutoring Patty and wouldn't start her new job at the college for three weeks, it was the ideal time to finish her dissertation. Yet somehow she hadn't been able to keep her mind on it.

Sighing, she removed the first chapter from its folder and, picking up a blue pencil, settled back to read. She hadn't finished the first page when the hall telephone rang. Knowing that Ida was resting in her room, Briana laid the stack of pages on the desk and went to answer.

"Briana?" the instant she heard Drake's voice, she knew this was the reason she hadn't been able to concentrate on her work all day. She had been waiting, she supposed, for the other shoe to fall.

She hadn't seen Drake since that long anxious night she had spent with him and Ruth in his hotel suite, waiting for word of Patty. There had been no chance for a private conversation after that frantic phone call. And once they knew the investigator had found her and was bringing her home, Briana had left the hotel and driven back in the quiet early-morning hours to the house.

There was still the matter of the Ivensen house to be settled between them, and although she dreaded seeing Drake again, she wanted to know where she stood, if she would have to tell Margaret they must move to other quarters.

"Hello, Drake."

"We have some things to discuss."

"The house—yes, I know."

"I'm at the hotel. Can you be at my suite in a half hour?"

His tone sounded unemotional, businesslike, the voice of a stranger. She swallowed. "I'll be there."

She changed hurriedly into a summer crepe shirtwaist dress, applied a minimum of makeup and brushed her hair. She was standing at the door of Drake's suite with minutes to spare.

The man who opened the door and invited her in seemed different from the man who had spoken to her on the phone a half hour earlier. He was obviously tired. His gray trousers and white shirt were wrinkled, as if he might have worked through the night and all day without stopping. His dark eyes had the sheen of weariness, but there was also a familiar spark in them when they raked over her.

"You should always wear blue," he said. "It makes your eyes incredibly beautiful."

She had been prepared to settle the business of the house quickly, with perfect composure, and then say goodbye to him for the last time. If he agreed to let her rent the house, she could mail the rent checks to him at the hotel. There would be no reason for them ever to meet again.

Now she took in his weariness, the lines of fatigue around his mouth, and realized that some vital energy had gone out of him. She wanted nothing so much as to touch him, to smooth away the worry with her fingertips, to cradle his head against her breast.

"Thank you," she said, but her voice was not as cool as she tried to make it.

"Sit down." He walked toward the kitchen. "I've made fresh coffee. Or I could mix you a drink."

"Coffee will be fine." She sat on one end of

the couch and looked around her, remembering the recent night she had spent in this room, joined with Drake and Ruth in a common concern for a girl they all loved.

He came back with two mugs of coffee and, after handing her one of them, lowered himself with a sigh into the opposite corner of the couch. With one leg bent on the couch, he sat facing her. He lifted his coffee mug in both hands and gazed at her over the rim.

Briana stirred uneasily, realizing she didn't want coffee after all, and set her mug on the side table. She took a deep breath. "Now, about the house—"

"I didn't ask you here to talk about the house."

"But on the phone you said—"

"No, you assumed that was what I wanted to talk about. I let you assume it because it was the only way I could think of to get you here."

She saw the slow smoldering start of fire in his eyes and sucked in her breath. "I've found another job. I can pay rent. In fact, I insist upon it, if only you'll let us stay in the house."

He took a sip of coffee, then slowly set the mug aside. "Briana," he said gently, reaching a hand toward her, "I don't want to talk about the house. Not now."

Her heart seemed to lodge in her throat as he moved closer to her on the couch. His fingers touched her face lightly, carefully.

"Then why did you ask me here?" she asked.

"Because I couldn't stand another day without seeing you. Because there are so many things I want to say to you, and I don't know where to start. Because I have to know—"

His fingers were caressing her neck, sending the now familiar honeyed warmth sliding along her veins. She got to her feet and walked nervously to the balcony doors, having to put some distance between them. She stared out for a moment, then turned around as she realized he had come to stand behind her.

She took a step back, tensing. "Don't touch me, Drake. It isn't fair."

"Why isn't it fair? Briana, my Briana," he whispered, "don't be afraid of me."

"Don't call me that," she said weakly. "I don't belong to you, Drake."

"You still haven't forgiven me for suggesting you knew about Erik's relationship with Patty."

"It isn't only that," she answered, her eyes helpless and vulnerable. "You thought I was the one who phoned your bank."

"I apologized for that."

"You even told me once I was no different from the other Ivensens."

"I've been a fool. Can't you accept that and forgive me?" He reached toward her, and his hand gently stroked her arm from elbow to shoulder.

She couldn't resist the tone of pleading in his voice and the warm persuasion of his touch. Unprotestingly she let him enclose her body in his arms, and she rested her head against his shoulder.

"You feel so good like this," he whispered into her hair. "I've hardly slept the past week. I thought I could work hard enough and long enough to forget you. But late at night, when I fell into bed exhausted, my arms ached for you."

His hand stroked her back gently, and a tremor passed through her. "Drake—the way things are—I'm not going to bed with you again. Don't think you can persuade me."

"I won't try to persuade you, even though I'm dying for want of you."

"You won't?" she whispered, her face against the warm skin of his neck.

"Not until you want it as much as I do."

Her stomach plunged sickeningly. "That... that isn't the issue."

"Do you hate me so much?"

She swallowed convulsively. "Sometimes I do."

He was silent for a moment. "I know, love," he said at last. "I want to say some things to you now. Please listen to me, Briana. Don't say anything until I've finished. It's taken me a long time to get up enough courage to say it." His arms tightened around her, and she waited.

"For twenty years hatred for your family has been building up in me. Every time I thought of it, I felt like a helpless, abused fourteen-year-old boy again. After the accident with the knife, your father tried to tell me how sorry he was, how he wanted to help. I refused to listen to him, or to Ruth when she tried to talk to me about it. I even refused to have plastic surgery done on my face. I wanted to keep this scar so I could blame your father for it every time I looked in a mirror. I know it was irrational, but I felt I had to make somebody pay for my mother's death.

"When Erik applied for a position with the corporation, I saw it as an opportunity to get back at the Ivensens. I didn't know how, but I knew, with Erik working for me, I'd think of a way. When I learned he was embezzling funds, I deliberately let him go on until I had him where I wanted him. I wanted the Ivensen house for only one reason, the pleasure of evicting Erik and your grandmother. But when I came there that day and met you, for the first time I began to question my twenty-year pursuit of revenge."

She was quiet in the circle of his arms, hearing the even beating of his heart against her cheek. "And when I finally saw Margaret after all those years, I realized the woman I had built up in my mind into a monster was actually just a sick lonely old woman burdened with guilt and regrets. I can't put her out of her home. Somewhere along the way I lost the bitterness. You did that for me, Briana.''

She felt close to tears and bit her lip to keep them back. He lifted her chin to look into her eyes. ''The last time we were together, you said you loved me. Did you mean it?''

She looked wordlessly up at him, sure that he could read the answer in her eyes. ''Congratulations,'' she whispered. ''You've conquered another Ivensen.'' She turned her face away.

He took a deep breath, pressing her head against his shoulder again. ''Thank God! I've been torturing myself, wondering what I would do if you said no, wondering how I would possibly get over loving you. All I have to do now is make you trust me.''

All of a sudden the world had shifted, and where it had been gray, there appeared a blaze of hope. She had never thought to hear those words from him. He loved her! He had said he loved her! ''I want to trust you,'' she whispered.

''I know your ex-husband crushed something good and innocent in you, Briana, but I'll bring it to life again, I swear, if only you'll let me. I'll convince you that you can love me without fear of being hurt. I'll give you all the time you need, my darling.'' His hand stroked her hair.

She lifted her face to look at him wonderingly. He gave a helpless groan, and his mouth came down on hers. Her lips parted to accept his kiss, and the familiar heat began to course in her veins.

When he raised his mouth from hers, his eyes were deep with passion. "I love you," he said. Then he kissed her again more fiercely than before. Briana's arms came up to wind around his neck. Her hands wandered over the firm muscles beneath his shirt, and she held him tightly with all her strength.

"Drake," she breathed lovingly when his lips finally released hers for an instant.

He held her face in his hands and touched his warm lips to her brow and cheek. "I want you to be my wife, Briana. I want it more than anything. But you don't have to answer me now. I can give you time—all the time you need."

She closed her eyes, smiling as his mouth continued to trace the line of her cheek and jaw and throat, and she shuddered in response. She had never known what it was to be a woman until now. "Yes," she whispered finally, breathlessly.

He lifted his head, a question in his smoldering eyes. "Yes? You mean, yes, you'll marry me?"

"Yes, I love you. Yes, I'll marry you. And, yes, I want to stay here with you tonight."

He pressed her against him. "Are you sure?"

"Now I am. Before, I didn't think you loved me. I thought I was just another Ivensen to be conquered in your vendetta against my family."

"Maybe that was a part of it—only a very small part—in the beginning. But you turned the tables on me, Briana. You conquered my heart. Never doubt that, my sweet love."

"Oh, Drake, I never will."

He lifted her in his arms, and as he carried her into the bedroom, she could feel the hard strength of his powerful body. Then he laid her on the bed and with trembling fingers began to unbutton her dress.

She gave a sigh of yearning and moved languorously beneath his touch. "Drake, oh, Drake, it's been so long."

His eyes blazed down at her, and his hands, as they removed her clothing, trembled with emotion. "There aren't enough words to tell you how much I love you," he whispered thickly, "but I'll show you. I'll give you such pleasure. It will be better for you tonight than it has ever been."

"I'm not sure that's possible." Her low voice was shaking, but her heart was free at last, free of doubt and pain, and she offered it up to him without reservation.

His slow sensuous smile brought tears of joy to her eyes as he set out to immerse her, body and soul and heart, in loving ecstasy. "Yes, it is," he told her. "I'll prove it to you."

And he did.

Get this book FREE!

Mail to:

Harlequin Reader Service

In the U.S.
1440 South Priest Drive
Tempe, AZ 85281

In Canada
649 Ontario Street
Stratford, Ontario N5A 6W2

YES! I want to be one of the first to discover the new **Harlequin American Romances.** Send me FREE and without obligation *Twice in a Lifetime.* If you do not hear from me after I have examined my FREE book, please send me the 4 new **Harlequin American Romances** each month as soon as they come off the presses. I understand that I will be billed only $2.25 for each book (total $9.00). There are no shipping or handling charges. There is no minimum number of books that I have to purchase. In fact, I may cancel this arrangement at any time. *Twice in a Lifetime* is mine to keep as a FREE gift, even if I do not buy any additional books.

Name _____ (please print)

Address _____ Apt. no. _____

City _____ State/Prov. _____ Zip/Postal Code _____

Signature (If under 18, parent or guardian must sign.)

154-BPA-NACS